Henry S. Morais

Eminent Israelites of the Nineteenth Century

A series of biographical sketches

Henry S. Morais

Eminent Israelites of the Nineteenth Century
A series of biographical sketches

ISBN/EAN: 9783337029616

Printed in Europe, USA, Canada, Australia, Japan

Cover: Foto ©Raphael Reischuk / pixelio.de

More available books at **www.hansebooks.com**

EMINENT ISRAELITES

OF THE

NINETEENTH CENTURY.

A Series of Biographical Sketches.

BY

HENRY SAMUEL MORAIS.

PHILADELPHIA:
EDWARD STERN & CO.
1880.

PREFACE.

THE following pages form a work which is believed unique in the English language. Several productions of the same scope and nature, in foreign tongues, have emanated from very able pens. Their authors are assuredly entitled to gratitude, for having endeavored to instil into the hearts of Hebrews, a love for their religion and people, and, at the same time, to awaken a desire for the study of a rich and vast literature. Besides, such publications must tend, in a great degree, to uproot prejudice, and to call forth among non-Israelites, sentiments of respect for the ancient race. To lend a helping hand to this laudable undertaking, has been the author's cherished wish.

Considerable information, appearing in the volume here presented, was derived from a close inspection of cyclopædias and scattered biographical notices. The principal authorities, however, are persons whose knowledge of the lives and characters described is undoubted, and with whom an active correspondence has been conducted. The writer has clothed his sketches—seventy of which appeared *seriatim* in *The Jewish Record,* and have since been carefully revised—in a garb that he hopes will prove attractive, the length of each article being in accordance with the materials collected.

In the limits assigned to this series, it would be impossible to include as many names as can fully lay claim to attention; but it has been the author's constant aim and effort to offer clear and unvarnished records of all that are embraced in his design. This much by way of explanation, an extended preface being neither needful nor desirable.

Still, he who traces these lines must avail himself of the privilege to express his sincere acknowledgments to those who have aided this enterprise. He is particularly indebted to his honored father, the Rev. S. Morais, whose untiring assistance has greatly facilitated the task; to Dr. Abram S. Isaacs, the talented editor of *The Jewish Messenger;* to Simon A. Stern, Esq., of Philadelphia; to the Rev. Dr. Henry W. Schneeberger, of Baltimore, Md.; to the Rev. Dr. Henry Vidaver, of San Francisco, Cal.; to Dr. Mark Blumenthal, of New York; to James Picciotto, Esq., the distinguished Anglo-Jewish historian; also to the Jewish press for kind words of encouragement, and likewise to all who have shown their practical approval of his endeavors.

Without further remark, the author submits his work to the judgment of a discerning public.

CONTENTS.

EMINENT ISRAELITES

NINETEENTH CENTURY.

NATHAN MARCUS ADLER.

The lamented Dr. Hirschel could not have had a more worthy successor to the dignity of the Rabbinate than Dr. Nathan Marcus Adler. An uninterrupted period of thirty-five years has demonstrated to the British Jews of the *Ashkenaz* ritual the character and scholarship united in their ecclesiastical chief. Those who pressed his selection have not been balked in their expectations. The man of their choice, grown old in the execution of sacred duties, still enjoys the confidence and appreciation of an entire community.

The Rev. Dr. Nathan Marcus Adler was born at Hanover, Germany, in 1803. He received his theological education at the Universities of Göttingen, Erlangen, and Würzburg, respectively. Before arriving at manhood, he displayed abilities peculiarly adapted to the discharge of Rabbinical functions.

In 1829 Dr. Adler was appointed Chief Rabbi of Oldenburg, and so satisfactorily did he meet his official requirements that, in 1830, his jurisdiction was transferred to Hanover, and all its provinces. Dr. Adler, in ministering to his flock, used his talents and efforts to improve their religious state, urging upon all a strict adherence to the doctrines and precepts of Judaism. His fame travelled far beyond the Rhine, and reached England just when its Hebrew population stood in great need of a spiritual leader.

In 1844 an election took place for Chief Rabbi of the German Congregations. Other eminent scholars were among the candidates for the position; but Dr. Adler secured the majority of votes. He was inducted into office on July 9th, 1845.

Until very recently, the Rabbi has given unremitting attention to the demands of his station. He has preached in the principal Synagogue, and in the various houses of worship subject to his authority; has presided at the sittings of the *Beth Ha-Midrash*, and at meetings for religious purposes.

When, a few months ago, the Doctor desired to be relieved of active duties, by reason of advanced age, a very efficient assistant was already at hand in his son, Dr. Hermann Adler. This gentleman, who reckons among his teachers the renowned

Rapoport, and who, since 1864, has been ministerially connected with the Bayswater Synagogue, is favorably known for some learned writings. A spirited reply to Prof. Goldwin Smith's charge that Jews cannot be patriots, has specially commended the author to his brethren, and has given his essay a wide circulation in Europe and America.

It is fortunate that one so gifted, and so zealous for the honor of his people, should be chosen as aid to the Chief Rabbi. Still the opinions and decisions of Dr. Nathan Marcus Adler will continue to be asked, and they will be deemed authoritative. No act of which he disapproves will receive strength and validity.

Onerous occupations have not prevented the Chief Rabbi from penning excellent literary productions. In addition to " Sermons on the Jewish Faith," he has written several works in Hebrew, the principal of which is *Nethina La-Gér*, a commentary on the Targum of Onkelos, unfolding new ideas on the history of that famous Aramaic version of the Pentateuch.

Now that his mind is at rest from the constant pressure of ecclesiastical obligations, the venerable scholar may devote his leisure hours to pursuits which will prove acquisitions to Jewish literature, and shed further lustre on his name.

GRACE AGUILAR.

What is known needs no introduction. English-speaking Israelites must be acquainted with a writer who, from the very days of childhood, made time subservient to the cause of Judaism. The talented authoress, whose life—of too short duration—we are about to sketch, has built for herself a monument which all see, and ages will not destroy.

Grace Aguilar was born at Hackney, England, June 2d, 1816. She was the only daughter of Emanuel Aguilar, a descendant of a family of Jewish merchants who fled from Spain, on account of religious persecution, and found a refuge in England.

From her birth, Grace never enjoyed good health, a circumstance in direct contrast to the strength of her mind. She received instruction at home, and early exhibited a fondness for reading. The attention she devoted to her books was something extraordinary in a child. When only seven, she began to keep a diary.

The first composition from her pen, was a short drama, " Gustavus Vasa," written at the age of twelve years, but not published. This was soon followed by " The Magic Wreath," a collection of poems, issued anonymously. A profound student of the faith in which she had been born, and an ardent admirer of its principles, for which many had rushed exultingly to death, Miss Aguilar produced "The Vale of Cedars, or The Martyr," a romance of the Jews in Spain, and which some consider her best work. "The Spirit of Judaism," a volume intensely religious, and "Israel Defended," the latter being a translation from the French, appeared subsequently. Then came "The Days of Bruce," a story from Scottish history, in two volumes; "Jewish Faith," in which the moral beauties of Judaism are clearly set forth; "Women of Israel," an elaborate description of celebrated daughters of our race, in two volumes; "Home Scenes and Heart Studies"; "Home Influence"; "Josephine, or The Edict and Escape"; "The Mother's Recompense"; "Woman's Friendship"; and a short "History of the Jews in England." Miss Aguilar's works have been extensively read and admired, and of the many favorable criticisms we quote the following: "Grace Aguilar knew the female heart better than any writer of our day, and in every fiction from her pen we trace the same masterly analysis and development of the motives and feelings of woman's nature." This is the opinion of a non-Israelite.

It would, perhaps, be of interest to review at length some of the most important writings which won the subject of our sketch renown; but when abler persons have frequently commented thereon, we must remain silent. We could not add a tittle to what is so truthfully uttered by an author: "The ambition of Grace Aguilar was neither for wealth, reputation, nor distinction. The pure consciousness of raising the literary and religious character of the Jewish race, and of her own sex in particular, was at the same time her guiding motive and her reward."

Miss Aguilar was a lover of music, and she became a skilful performer on the piano and harp. Her singing was also admired.

Family troubles soon told upon the delicate frame. In 1835 her father, who had long been in failing health, breathed his last. Two brothers, tenderly endeared to her, were obliged to leave home, on account of their professions. The duty now devolved upon the single daughter, to minister to the comfort of her widowed mother, who had also been an invalid. This, together with the continued severe strain on her mental powers, broke down the already impaired constitution. She was advised by her physician to try the baths and mineral waters at Schwalbach, whither she repaired, but without success. After a prostrating illness of three weeks' duration, she expired at Frankfort-on-the-Main, on the 16th of September, 1847, when only thirty-one years of age. Her dying words were, "Though He slay me, yet will I trust in Him," plainly showing the deep religious feeling that always pervaded her heart and occupied her thoughts, even unto the end. She was interred in the Jewish cemetery at Frankfort.

The mother of Grace, Mrs. Sarah Aguilar, has written a memoir of her daughter's life, and prefaces to several of her works. She was instrumental in bringing the productions of her child to the attention of the American public.

All, regardless of creed, join in the encomiums bestowed upon one of the noblest women in Israel; a steadfast and effective laborer in the cause of education and progress.

BENJAMIN ARTOM.

By the side of Nieto and Meldola, Chief Rabbis of the Portuguese-Jewish community of Great Britain, may be placed Artom, their countryman and successor. Possibly, he may not have rivalled the first-named, in vastness of erudition, nor the second, in the knowledge of Talmudical and casuistical writers. But he surpassed both in one of the elements, considered, at the present time, most essential in the fulfilment of Rabbinical duties — preaching. Dr. Artom's sermons, marked by an unusual flow of eloquence, were delivered in a language which affords wide scope for oratorical powers—English. In the pulpit he showed the strength of his character, and the earnestness with which he meant to elevate Israel.

The Rev. Dr. Benjamin Artom was born at Asti, in Piedmont, Italy, in 1834. A relationship with Chevalier Isaac Artom—Private Secretary of the renowned statesman, Count Cavour, and Senator of Italy—has been claimed for the subject of our sketch. Having been left fatherless when a child, his maternal uncle supervised his training. A theological education was given him by Rabbi Mark Tedeschi. On completing his course of studies under that preceptor, he was awarded a diploma attesting his signal proficiency.

For a while, Dr. Artom officiated as minister of the congregation at Saluzzo. He then betook himself to Naples, and became the Rabbi of that city. In this capacity, his stirring addresses forcibly impressed his auditors.

It so happened that Miss Anna Maria Goldsmid, the well-known writer, while travelling through the peninsula, stopped at Naples. She had occasion to hear Dr. Artom lecture, and was so much delighted that she sought a personal introduction. On her return to London, Miss Goldsmid spoke of the learned Doctor in high terms. The well-bestowed encomium soon took a practical shape. Dr. Artom, who, in 1866, had journeyed from Italy to France was, on his arrival in Paris, apprised of the favorable reception he would likely meet in London. He proceeded thereto, and, by invitation, preached in the metropolis. Shortly after, he was chosen *Haham* of the Spanish and Portuguese Congregations of the United Kingdom, for life. This honorable post had been vacant since the death of the Rev. Dr. Raphael Meldola in 1828; questions on Jewish law being decided by an Ecclesiastical Board. Dr. Artom formally assumed his office on the 16th of December, 1866. He married a lady of the family of Sir Albert Sassoon, the merchant-prince of Bombay, Hindostan.

When first elected, the Rabbi could not venture to address his flock in English, and his discourses were, therefore, delivered in French. But in one year he mastered the vernacular, and then poured forth that impassioned eloquence which kindled every feature of the preacher's splendid *physique*. Dr. Artom introduced wholesome reforms in the schools of his community, and abolished several unnecessary offices in the Synagogue. In principles, the Doctor, though liberal, was strictly Orthodox. Through his instrumentality, the barrier that had long separated the Portuguese and German Jews, received its strongest blow. Dr. Artom enjoyed the friendship of both the Rev. Dr. N. M. Adler, Chief Rabbi of the *Ashkenazim*, and the Rev. Prof. D. W. Marks, head of the Reform Israelites of England.

Some of the *Haham's* sermons were published at the request of his congregation. The Rabbi wrote a number of prayers in Hebrew, sundry pieces of poetry in Italian, and contributed to different journals of the Continent.

The esteem which Dr. Artom secured, he was not permitted many years to experience in this nether world, though his healthy appearance seemed to indicate a long and useful career. While at Brighton, England, he was seized with a fatal disease, that brought a sudden termination to his existence, on January 6th, 1879, when only forty-five years of age. His remains were brought to London, and interred in the Mile End Cemetery, amidst the lamentations of those who had benefited by his ministrations, and evidences of the sorrow of the entire population of British Jews.

BERTHOLD AUERBACH.

Tales, full of extravagance, untrue to nature and offensive to good taste, are warping the minds of the young. The need of descriptions, borrowed from living surroundings, and imparting freshness and elasticity to the developing intellect, is universally felt. Berthold Auerbach has understood this, and has achieved great ends, alike as a novelist and miscellaneous writer.

Berthold Auerbach was born at Nordstetten, in the Black Forest of Würtemberg, Germany, February 28th, 1812. Evincing a preference for Jewish theology, he was sent to Hechingen, and afterwards to Carlsruhe, where he actively pursued his studies. In 1832 he completed his course at the Gymnasium of Stuttgardt. From that year until 1835, he attended the universities at Tübingen, Munich and Heidelberg. Shortly after, he abandoned Jewish theology, and sedulously applied himself to philosophy, history and literature.

His first work, "The Jewish Nation, and Its Recent Literature," appeared in 1836. It was followed the next year by a novel, "Poet and Merchant." Mr. Auerbach's sincere attachment to the doctrines of Spinoza, led him to publish a work on that philosopher's system in 1839, and a biography of the same author in 1841, accompanied by a translation of his complete writings. But Mr. Auerbach obtained great popularity in 1842 and 1843, when he issued "Educated Citizens; a Book for the Thinking Middle Classes," and "Village Tales from the Black Forest." Both of these productions were read with avidity, and were rendered into the English, Dutch and Swedish languages. One of his most finished poems, inserted in a novel entitled "The Professor's Wife," and brought forth in 1848, was subsequently dramatized. In 1845–6, he prepared and published an almanac, entitled " The Godfather," after the style of Dr. Franklin's " Poor Richard's Almanac," which was perused by all classes.

Mr. Auerbach has proved his strenuous advocacy of popular education in his many writings. Several novels and other compositions have emanated from his pen within the last decade. Notably, " The Villa on the Rhine," in three volumes, 1869, which met with extraordinary success, and was translated into English; " Ours Again," in 1871, affording a full account of the current opinions and different circumstances that marked the commencement of the war, then pending between France and Germany; " The Good Hour, or Evening Holiday;" " On the Heights;" and " Waldfried." The two last mentioned have been offered in an English garb, by Simon A. Stern, Esq., of Philadelphia. A new edition of Mr. Auerbach's complete works was published at Stuttgardt in 1871.

Of the notabilities whose intimate acquaintance Mr. Auerbach formed, may be named the late United States Minister to Germany, the Hon. Bayard Taylor, who won for himself an immortal name, by his scholarly attainments and multifarious literary labors.

The subject of this sketch was selected to deliver an oration at the grave of the lamented American, as the exponent of the deep grief which the people of Germany felt at the demise of one whom they had every reason to respect and love. It is needless to say that the tribute was worthy of the melancholy, but soul-stirring event.

Mr. Auerbach continues to enrich the literature of our day with important contributions, in the shape of new and interesting books which are always appreciated, and which tend to elevate their author in the opinion of the world.

LUDWIG BAMBERGER.

A reaction, strange and unaccountable, has taken place in lately liberalized Germany. The indomitable Chancellor, who planned the greatness of the Empire, knits his brows at any opposition. Jews, loyal to the *Vaterland*, mostly side with the Liberals. They approve of consolidation, but protest against centralization of power, and that, under the lead of a man elated by success. Hence, persons who made the walls of Parliament ring with their voices raised in the defence of the people, were left out at the last election. Bamberger was justly considered, next to Lasker, the most distinguished Jewish member of the Reichstag. The influence he wielded was brought to bear on all important questions.

Dr. Ludwig Bamberger was born at Mayence, Hesse-Darmstadt, July 22d, 1823. He studied in turn at Giessen, Heidelberg and Göttingen, and passed an examination in law at Mayence, where he took his last degree. The revolutionary movement of 1848, found in the patriotic Israelite an active participant. He gave assistance, besides, to those who were struggling for their rights, in Bavaria and in Baden. An attempt to coerce the authorities by force of arms into more lenient measures failed, and Dr. Bamberger was obliged to flee from the country. He travelled through Switzerland, England, Belgium and Holland. In 1853 he settled at Paris, and there became the manager of a banking-house.

Upon the establishment of the North-German Confederation, a political amnesty was proclaimed, which enabled Dr. Bamberger to return home. During his stay in foreign lands, the ideas he cherished had not altered. Fully aware of the necessity of an improved form of government, he at once decided to devote his abilities to securing a change for the better. His voice and pen soon told how staunch was his adherence to the cause espoused. Dr. Bamberger was chosen, in 1868, to represent Mayence, his birth-place, in the Customs Parliament, and, in 1871, Deputy to the German Reichstag.

Like his friend, Lasker, Dr. Bamberger at first supported Prince Bismarck's policy. But his liberal views prompted him, of late, to act in opposition to the Prime Minister, who endeavored to obtain the enforcement of acts hostile to freedom. To this is doubtless due the defeat he met at the Parliamentary election of 1879.

Dr. Bamberger's immense practical knowledge of economical affairs, gives his opinions a weight which does not at all depend upon the occupancy of a seat in the legislative hall. The Doctor is a polished speaker, endowed by nature with remarkable capatities.

Dr. Bamberger has acquired considerable of his fame as a journalist and political writer. In addition to articles inserted in various periodicals, he has published pamphlets on "The Labor Question," "The Bank and Coinage Question," and other subjects, evincing in all a thorough understanding of European politics, and the tact of a consistent reformer.

ELIAS BENAMOZEGH.

The Rabbinical profession in Italy is still represented by men who wield the pen with readiness and classical ability. In many instances, the pressure of official duties prevents a disclosure of that fact. But, not unfrequently, learned volumes prove that the country which gave birth to an Azariah De Rossi, is not destitute of men who have inherited his versatility. To cite a few cases in point, when

a large number rises before the mind, might seem
invidious. Yet, it may be said, without the least
reflection on others, that Mortara of Mantua, Levi
of Ferrara, Tedeschi of Trieste, Lattes of Venice,
and Benamozegh of Leghorn, are Rabbis who have
found time to contribute to the advancement of sacred literature. It is of the last-named, however,
that we purpose presenting some special characteristics. His wonderful activity has secured to him a
degree of prominence, which is not given to all to
attain.

Rabbi Prof. Elias Benamozegh, Chevalier of the
Crown of Italy, was born at Leghorn, in 1822.
His parents had emigrated from Fez, Morocco,
once so famous as the native place of grammarians
and theologians. Basnage, in his *Histoire des Juifs*,
makes mention of a certain Joshua Benamozegh who
was promoted to a high rank by the Emperor of
Morocco.

Elias had the misfortune of losing his father
when only four years old. But that lamentable circumstance did not involve the consequences often
attending it. Under the tuition of his maternal
uncle, Rabbi M. H. Curiat, the lad received Hé-
brew instruction of a peculiar nature. Cabbalism
formed an element which arrested the thought of
the young student. It gave a bent to his intellect,
that a perusal of any of his multifarious productions

cannot fail to show. When but a child, he would intelligently and fluently recite whole pages of the *Zohar*. His precocity became the subject of remark among the Jewish inhabitants of Leghorn, and some of the most literary sought his company. For the youth employed modern languages and general literature, as aids to his knowledge of Biblical and Rabbinical writings.

A desire to obtain a lucrative position led Benamozegh to a counting-house, where he remained for several years; but, clearly, commerce was not his mission. He relinquished it, to devote himself to the career in which he has gained celebrity. At the examination for the title of *Maskil*, preparatory to that of Rabbi, he acquitted himself in a manner that impressed the community most favorably. He afterward frequented the Franco institution, where men of learning daily congregated to cultivate the knowledge of the Talmud, and, at the same time, pursued by himself secular studies.

A Rabbi and an author, a philosopher and a publisher, the name of Elias Benamozegh has spread far and wide. But the feature which distinguishes him from his contemporaries, is the blending of Cabbalism, or as he terms it "Theosophy," with the dogmas, traditions, tenets and observances of Judaism. According to the views he entertains and expounds, what the supposititious work of Simeon

Ben Jochai, and the writings of the men of the school of Luria have imparted, form an essential in the Mosaic faith, deprived of which it cannot stand. There was a time in the life of the Leghorn Rabbi, when he felt disposed to cast aside this speculative science, on which the illustrious Prof. Adolphe Franck has built his theories. But it was a period of transition that gave away before a never-flagging advocacy of his Theosophy. The sacred books of the Orient, the Hellenistic Gnosticism, the emanations of Philo, and transcendental philosophy, exercised a mighty influence, and developed the Titan who fights the battles of Cabbalism, almost single-handed. Hebrew, French and Italian he makes subservient to his designs, and his language is terse and incisive.

Though an officiating Rabbi in the city of his birth, and Professor at the High School of Theology, Benamozegh does not allow his engagements to check the rapidity of his pen. He writes continuously, and contributes to a number of journals. Of his most noted books are (in Hebrew): *Emat Mafgiang*, a refutation of the anti-Cabbalistic work of Leon de Modena, entitled *Ari Nohem; Em La-mikra*, a commentary on the Pentateuch, with elucidations based on philosophical, critical, archæological and scientific researches; *Tangam Leschad*, a dialogue on Cabbalism, it being intended as a reply to a dia-

logue on the same subject by Prof. S. D. Luzzatto;
(in French): *Morale Juive et Morale Chrétienne*,
which won the prize offered by the *Alliance Israélite Universelle;* and (in Italian) *Teologia Dogmati-
ca e Apologetica*, on metaphysics, revealing a profound
acquaintance with the schools of Ancient and Modern Philosophy.

We might continue at great length, and name
pamphlets and volumes that Rabbi Benamozegh has
brought forth. But what has been said will support the assertion, that Jewish science can claim
him as an ardent and steadfast devotee.

SAMUEL CAHEN.

Literature has undergone a thorough revolution,
within a comparatively short period. Critical researches in all branches of learning disclose this remarkable fact. Hebrew lore has most sensibly felt
the effect of the change, for never before was it put
to such a test. The student will perceive that the
more he reads, the more striking is the diversity of
exposition between the commentators of the Middle Ages and those of our century. Some may
question the necessity of the many explanatory works,
especially on Holy Writ, which are constantly aug-
menting. But as each author invariably presents new
features, the reason becomes obvious. That Samuel

Cahen was a Hebraist of no mean calibre, as well as a journalist of great powers, the subjoined will show.

Samuel Cahen was born at Metz, France, August 4th, 1796. He spent his youth in Mayence, Hesse-Darmstadt, being destined to pursue a course of Rabbinical studies. His eagerness for knowledge was soon observed. He devoted much attention to modern languages and literature, and his excellent acquaintance therewith evidenced a steadiness of purpose in cultivating innate faculties.

After completing his education, Cahen was engaged as a private tutor in Germany. In 1822 he went to Paris, and assumed the directorship of the Jewish consistorial school of that city, holding the position for a number of years. Identified altogether with Jewish matters, he deemed it of special importance for his fellow-believers in France to have an organ to represent their views, and also to give publicity to the numerous works that gradually swell the size of Hebrew literature. Impressed with that opinion, M. Cahen brought out, in 1840, his fortnightly periodical, known throughout Europe as the *Archives Israélites*. As its editor he gained a wide-spread reputation, and the magazine, so ably directed, took a prominent station among Jewish publications. Teeming with instructive articles, it also contained light compositions pleasing to the generality of readers. The circulation increased, and to this day the peri-

odical flourishes and retains its influence under M.
Isidore Cahen, son of its founder. The *Archives* has
warmly espoused the objects of that noble organization, the *Alliance Israélite Universelle*, and has boldly
spoken in behalf of oppressed Hebrews in the East.

In addition to lectures, and various writings on
the Hebrew language and history, M. Cahen issued
several works. A translation of the Bible into French,
with the Hebrew on opposite pages, and critical notes
and dissertations by himself and others, may be ac-
counted his principal labor. The entire edition, consisting of eighteen volumes, appeared in 1851. Despite adverse criticism, it must be admitted that the
undertaking was heavy and difficult, and that it
was performed with diligence and wisdom.

M. Cahen died at Paris, France, January 8th, 1862.
His chief literary product, of which we have just
spoken, not less than his journalistic efforts, will,
doubtless, serve to commend him to all who can
rightly appreciate the services of a well-spent life.

JACOB DA SILVA SOLIS COHEN.

The assertion that Elisha, who cured the poison-
ous taste of the pottage of wild gourds, and that
Isaiah, who healed the diseased King of Judah by
the application of a fig-plaster, were adepts in medical science, might sound extravagant, if not hereti-
cal. Not so the statement that Jews have, in

all ages, excelled as physicians. Unbiased historians have set forth, as the result of their own investigations, a vast array of men among the descendants of the Prophets, who may divide honors with Hippocrates. It may be still further averred that, in the Middle Ages, the lives of monarchs were entrusted into the hands of those who had first studied the laws of hygiene, as recorded by Moses. That no deterioration on that score can be detected, a cursory glance at the list of the medical faculty of any city will suffice to prove. Philadelphia gives an enviable standing to a practitioner whose skill in the treatment of an important specialty is as great, as his adherence to the ancestral belief is unquestioned.

Jacob Da Silva Solis Cohen, M. D., was born in the city of New York, on the 28th of February, 1838. His parents having settled in Philadelphia, the boy obtained preparatory instruction in its public schools. He completed his studies at the Central High School, graduating from that institution, as *Bachelor of Arts*, in February, 1855. The next year the youth attended lectures at the Jefferson Medical College, and from 1859–60 at the Medical Department of the University of Pennsylvania, where he received his degree of M. D.

For a time, Dr. Cohen resided in Memphis, Tennessee, and again in Philadelphia, and in New York.

But finally, in 1866, he chose Philadelphia as his permanent home, and there he has since steadily followed the profession for which he had been designed by natural qualifications.

Without abandoning general practice, Dr. Cohen took up the diseases of the throat and chest. He attained so much success in this specialty that it led to his being selected as lecturer on laryngoscopy and diseases of the throat and chest, in the Jefferson Medical College, a position he still fills with credit. His services in the branch to which he mostly devotes his attention are eagerly sought after, and the opinion he expresses on matters appertaining thereto is regarded as an undisputed authority.

On the outbreak of the Civil War, Dr. Cohen became assistant surgeon of the Twenty-sixth Pennsylvania Regiment, the first mustered into the service of the Government. He was subsequently appointed acting assistant surgeon in the United States Navy, and detailed to the steamer Florida, in which vessel he accompanied Commodore Dupont's expedition to Port Royal. The Doctor remained in the South Atlantic blockading squadron until January, 1864, when he resigned. At the request of the medical authorities, he afterwards tended the wounded in the army hospitals at Philadelphia.

Of the numerous organizations with which Dr. Cohen is connected, there may be named the Philadelphia College of Physicians, to which he is also Mütter lecturer; the Northern Medical Association of Philadelphia, of which he has been Vice-President and President; the Philadelphia County Medical Society; the Pathological Society; the Pennsylvania State Medical Society; the American Medical Association; the Franklin Institute; and the Philadelphia Academy of Natural Sciences. He has occupied a post in the Philadelphia Hospital; also on the staff of the Northern Dispensary, and of the Jewish Hospital, both of Philadelphia. He is now attending physician to the German Hospital, and to the Jefferson Medical College Hospital.

Dr. Cohen has published some valuable works on medicine, which evidence thorough searching and abilities of a high order. Among them are "A Treatise on Inhalation;" "Diseases of the Throat," a labor which has particularly met with universal approval; "Croup in its Relations to Tracheotomy;" several minor monographs, and a number of papers inserted in leading medical journals, and Transactions of medical societies. The Doctor has likewise done good work as one of the translators of Ziemssen's Cyclopædia.

The past, serving as a criterion, predicts a future of uninterrupted usefulness.

ALBERT COHN.

Only three years have passed away, since the lamented scholar and philanthropist, Albert Cohn, was laid to rest in the silent grave. But though decades may glide by, the memory of the virtues which this far-famed Hebrew possessed will not be effaced. For as numerous as the admirers of his excellencies, are the evidences of his enlarged benevolence.

Albert Cohn was born at Presburg, Hungary, on the 14th of September, 1814. At the age of twelve he went to Vienna, where, for two years, he pursued his studies. The medical profession was intended for his future vocation, but he early showed a decided aversion to it, and a desire for philology and philosophy. He obtained instruction in theology, archæology, and several Oriental languages, and, with but the aid of a dictionary, he mastered the Arabic and Syriac. Young Cohn's talents attracted the notice of Prof. Wernich, of the Protestant Seminary, a distinguished Orientalist, who took a great interest in the Jewish youth, and often assisted him with good counsel. At the instance of the aforenamed, Cohn was appointed to teach Hebrew in the Seminary. He held the position for two years, to the satisfaction of both pupils and professors.

It must be borne in mind that, even at this late

period, Jews were excluded from the learned professions, in several countries of Europe. It became clear to Albert Cohn that the avenues to promotion would be closed against him, if he remained in Austria, and he was advised to go to Paris. He accordingly left Vienna in June, 1836, provided with letters of recommendation from noted celebrities. Reaching Frankfort-on-the-Main, he was favored with an introduction to the Rothschilds, who treated him very courteously. At Paris, he again applied himself to study, and spent much of his time in the public libraries. Before long, he had become familiar with the German, French, English, Spanish, Italian, Hebrew and Arabic languages. Cohn studied Persian under the well-known scholar, Sylvestre de Sacy, and, whenever at leisure, he bestowed his attention on works of theology. Private tuition afforded him the means of support.

In 1838 the Rothschilds invited Albert Cohn to accompany them on a tour through Italy. He accepted the invitation, and visited several cities of interest to Israelites, specially Leghorn, where he was presented with a copy of a Samaritan letter, addressed to the Jewish community of that city. Pope Gregory XVI. gave him permission to etablish an industrial school in Rome. The sight of the Ghetto —the place wherein Hebrews were compelled to live amid suffering and misery—made a painful and last-

ing impression upon M. Cohn. Happily, he lived to
see that horrid quarter torn down by the arm of
freedom, and his brethren released from the oppression of ages. His knowledge of Oriental languages
led the scholar frequently to confer with that wonderful linguist, Cardinal Mezzofante. The year 1839
found M. Cohn at Naples. From thence he travelled
through Switzerland and Austria, visited Presburg,
his native city, and returned to Paris, after an absence
of twelve months. From that period he remained .
closely associated with the Rothschilds, and dedicated
his life to the service of mankind. At religious meetings he imparted instruction to the Jewish pupils of
the schools. In charitable and in educational societies his influence was sensibly felt. With the name
of Rothschild as his standard, all obstacles were overcome. The mere mention of the many organizations
of various natures, which M. Cohn either established
or gave his valuable aid to, would unduly extend the
limits of a single sketch. Suffice it to say, that all
had an aim which emanated from the noblest source
of philanthropy.

Albert Cohn was looked upon as a great bene-
factor, who made learning and wealth the servants
of righteousness. Chosen as orator on important occasions, his ability as such won him un-
stinted praise. In Synagogues and at colleges, his
eloquence flowed naturally, and at the funerals of

Prof. Munk, and of the Barons Solomon and James de Rothschild, his remarks were reverentially listened to. As a member of the *Alliance Israélite Universelle*, he did much to further its progress. He was one of a deputation that waited upon the Shah of Persia, on July 12th, 1873, to present to his Majesty an appeal on behalf of the Jews of Persia. M. Cohn devoted a large portion of his life to ameliorate the condition of his fellow-believers in the East. Acting conjointly with Sir Moses Montefiore, Sir Anthony de Rothschild, Dr. Ludwig Philippson and others, he obtained a recognition of the rights of Israelites in Turkey. His efficient assistance was given towards bettering the condition of the down-trodden Hebrews of Palestine, and he himself journeyed to Jerusalem, in 1854, to seek out the cause of their distress. He found the Jewish community there sadly in need of educational as well as other institutions, the lack of which had contributed to its deplorable state. He set to work, and before leaving the Holy Land he had the pleasure of seeing a hospital erected, and schools founded. In his projects he was, of course, materially aided by the Rothschilds, through whom the Emperor of Austria lent his royal influence.

M. Cohn's linguistic attainments proved of great advantage to him in his travels, and on his way to and from the East he stopped at several cities to ascertain the condition of Israelitish inhabitants. At Constantinople, he was successful in establishing schools for Jewish children. On arriving at Vienna the Emperor received him with high favor, and gave him the assurance of his protection to the Hebrews of the Orient. He celebrated his return to Paris by a donation of sixty thousand francs to different institutions of benevolence. Shortly after he went to London, to consult with the Chief Rabbi, Dr. N. M. Adler; Sir Moses Montefiore, Baron Lionel N. de Rothschild and Sir David Salomons, about the most advisable course to be followed for the elevation of Palestinian Jews.

In 1856 Albert Cohn again visited Jerusalem, effecting, as on the former occasion, much good. In many cities of the East where Jews resided, he succeeded in establishing schools, and asylums for the homeless, for the sick, and for the poor. In 1860 he exerted himself to allay the tribulations of persecuted Christians in Syria, for whom liberal subscriptions were given by Jews. Hebrews were ready to shed their blood for the cause of religious toleration. M. Cohn made two more journeys to the Holy Land, in 1864 and 1869, and noted with pleasure the advancement of his Eastern brethren, chiefly due to his personal endeavors. The indefatigable Hebrew never tired, and, availing himself of the protection of the French Government, he improved the moral status of his co-religionists in Algeria, and in other portions of the Barbary States.

Notwithstanding these manifold labors, Albert Cohn cultivated literature and science, and he was ever ready to pecuniarily assist authors, in the publication of useful works. He wrote learned articles for the *Archives Israélites* and other periodicals, and brought forth his "Jewish Letters," descriptive of his travels, besides minor productions. He was strongly attached to Prof. Munk, and proved to the latter a friend in need. In recognition of his unwearied endeavors, the French Government, in 1867, created him a Chevalier of the Legion of Honor. His restless activity during the last Franco-German war, and the excitement of those stirring times, served to weaken his constitution. But not until the spring of 1876 did a disease, that soon developed into alarming proportions, force him to retire from customary pursuits. Still his interest in the welfare of the societies with which he had been closely identified, was manifested to the last.

On the 17th of March, 1877, when not sixty-three years old, Albert Cohn was summoned to the realms of bliss, there to receive an eternal reward.

ISAAC ADOLPHE CREMIEUX.

The saying of the Biblical moralist, that "a hoary head is a crown of glory," has been beautifully illustrated in one whose personal history is interwoven with the annals of his country. That man, who wore the precious diadem which age put on, first opened his eyes to the light of day to see France revolutionize a political system, effete and insupportably burdensome. Every breath he drew was amidst surroundings inspiring love of freedom, and detestation of tyranny. Under such influences the child grew to become what the whole world knew him to be—an honor to the human race, the boast of his people.

Isaac Adolphe Crémieux was born at Nimes, April 30th, 1796. He early adopted the law as a profession, and was admitted to the Bar in 1817. Eloquence and thorough legal knowledge soon brought him to public notice. He removed to Paris, and there was engaged as counsel for the defence in the celebrated case of Guernon-Ranville, a minister of Charles X., charged with having been one of the authors of the ordinances issued in July, 1830. He afterwards defended Raspail, Marrast, and other republicans, prosecuted by the government.

M. Crémieux accompanied Sir Moses Montefiore

to the East in 1840, and became instrumental in alleviating the sufferings of his brethren.   In 1842 he was chosen a member of the Chamber of Deputies, for the Left.   He encouraged the Revolution of 1848, and advised Louis Philippe to quit France. Under the provisional government he held the important office of Minister of Justice, but soon resigned, to act as counsel for Louis Blanc, in his defence against the government.

While a member of the Assembly, M. Crémieux voted for Louis Napoleon as President of France. Soon, however, consistently with the liberal views entertained, he changed side, and opposed the usurper's policy.   When Napoleon, forswearing himself, mounted the throne, Crémieux, together with Thiers and a host of patriots who resisted the the outrageous suppression of freedom, was imprisoned. But the course of events soon compelled the *parvenu* to liberate the advocates of equality.

M. Crémieux continued antagonistic to the arbitrary measures of Napoleon III.   After the surrender of the latter at Sedan he again became Minister of Justice, and was subsequently one of the members of the delegation at Tours and Bordeaux.   He resigned February 10th, 1871.   The payment of the war-debt to Germany was strongly urged by him, his own donation to the fund being one hundred thousand francs.   The city of Algiers recognized Crémieux's worth, by electing him to the National Assembly in 1873, while the land of his birth titled him a life-Senator.

The French statesman ever lent effective help towards improving the condition of his fellow-believers of the Orient. When the *Alliance Israélite Universelle* was organized he became its President, and filled the position to the ever-increasing success of the objects cherished by the association.

The International Jewish Conference, convened at Paris in June, 1878, and, graced by leading men in Israel from near and far, exalted itself when it placed the venerable Crémieux in the Presidential chair. His greeting was an outburst of fiery eloquence. It electrified the august assemblage. As he depicted the unity of the Hebrew race, the martyrdom of the past, and the glories of the future, the thundering applause which the words elicited told of the speaker's powers, and of the philanthropist's undying compassion for the oppressed.

The voice that moved multitudes is now hushed in death. On the 1st of February, 1880, Crémieux experienced a sorrow, the intensity of which may have occasioned the loss that France and Israel now bemoan. His consort, distinguished for social, not less than for domestic virtues, she who had shared his toils and spurred him on to deeds of greatness, passed away. On the 10th of February Crémieux was no more.

ARTHUR LUMLEY DAVIDS.

Not unfrequently has the Jewish community been called upon to mourn the loss of faithful members who devoted long and useful lives solely to benefit their race. But how much greater the sorrow, when individuals of surprising attainments are stricken down in the bloom of youth.

Arthur Lumley Davids was born in England, in 1811. Little is recorded of his early days, save of his intense application to reading. He had made considerable progress in the study of the law, but, as he possessed a competence, he did not adopt the legal profession.

At the age of fifteen, Davids began the preparation of a work of vast magnitude, a " Biblical Encyclopædia ;" while, at the same time, he kept actively engaged in acquiring the knowledge of the Turkish and other foreign languages. Wishing to help a movement for the withdrawal of Jewish disabilities, he contributed several learned articles to *The Times* upon that subject.

A short time elapsed ere the Hebrews of Great Britain were made aware that there existed in their midst a young man who exercised his extensive abilities to elevate society; and Davids at once became the cynosure of all eyes. But marks of approval for what had been already accomplished, did not at all abate his energies. On December 23d, 1830, when only nineteen years old, he delivered a lecture on the "Philosophy of the Jews," before the Society for the Cultivation of Hebrew Literature. To say it was a great effort, would but faintly represent facts.

The fame of Davids soon spread abroad, and his reputation increased by the appearance of *A Grammar of the Turkish Language, with a Preliminary Discourse on the Language and Literature of the Turkish Nation, etc.* The *London Literary Gazette*, an acknowledged authority in those days, spoke of it in the following terms: "We are informed that the author of this volume has not yet completed his twenty-first year; and if we were disposed to think very highly indeed of the learning and research which it displays, even had they marked the labor of grey hairs, how much more must we prize and estimate them, when we learn that the extraordinary effort proceeds from the verge of boyhood."

The Sultan of Turkey, Mahmoud II., to whom the aforenamed production was dedicated, expressed his high approbation thereof; and, at the death of the author, sent the bereaved mother a splendid diamond ring, accompanied by a letter of condolence on the irreparable loss sustained.

Merely a few of the good and sterling qualities

adorning the character of Arthur Lumley Davids have been here enumerated. Short, but brilliant, was the career which closed on the 19th of July, 1832,—a model that every youth should strive to copy.

LELIO DELLA TORRE.

The great Zunz stated in one of his writings that sacred oratory is unknown among the Hebrews of the Italian peninsula; that Cabbalistic subtleties form the most important part of the sermons delivered in the Synagogues. The profound critic obviously labored under a misapprehension. While he so asserted, Rabbi Aaron Lattes—to cite but one instance, —at Venice, preached in choice words and faultless rhetoric. But the sweeping charge hurt the feelings of a man who had directed his energies to the elevation of the art of public speaking, and who sanguinely anticipated happy results. The belief that he could bring these to pass, won his election to a responsible position. He was to train Talmudic scholars, by rule and by practice, to preach acceptably before large audiences.

Prof. Lelio Della Torre was born at Cuneo, Italy, on January 11th, 1805. Left fatherless when only two years old, the child found shelter at the home of his grandparents. After a time, his maternal uncle, the venerated Rabbi and admired preacher,

S. G. Treves, took the boy in charge. It was entirely to him that the nephew owed his advancement. For the kind relative generously offered the lad support and education. In touching language, Della Torre has repeatedly acknowledged his indebtedness. But nature had largely provided for the reception of a fruitful tuition.

In his eighteenth year, the youth was chosen to teach Hebrew and Biblical exegesis at a college in Turin. Over a hundred students attended that institute, and there, for six consecutive years, a numerous class listened to elucidations of the construction and meaning of Holy Writ. During one half of that period, the young preceptor performed likewise the duties of assistant Rabbi.

In 1829 Padua, famous in the annals of secular literature, became also a high seat of sacred lore. The Austrian Government—then ruling Lombardy and Venice—encouraged and subsidized a college, and many among the faithful contributed to the maintenance thereof. Della Torre now saw bearded men bend to receive what flowed from his richly-stored intellect. His influence raised the standard of Talmudical, studies, for logic and system dislodged hair-splitting sophistry or Pilpulism. Persons who had pored over volumes of the *Gemara* and found the task irksome, travelled far to learn afresh what is demanded of those who wish to exercise the Rabbinate, suitably to the needs of the present age.

In an erudite discourse, delivered soon after the opening of the institute, the Professor explained how theology, based on the books of tradition, can be made a science attractive to the minds of the thoughtful. He promised to accomplish, in the department assigned to him, what his already distinguished colleague, Samuel David Luzzatto, would do in Scriptural hermeneutics. That declaration was carried out to the end, as proved by the testimony of many disciples now officiating in various cities throughout Italy and in foreign lands.

Like the Sages of old, Prof. Della Torre communicated his teachings orally. None of his illustrations found their way into the press. He has, however, bequeathed to posterity writings which evidence great linguistic acquirements, a ready pen and a polished style. We will mention some, published both prior to and after his death.

A volume of sermons, with a preface, in which the author pleads for pulpit instruction, and for the dissemination of good lectures based on solid Jewish grounds, was issued at Padua. This work became the starting-point in the course which the Professor seemed delighted to pursue. Homiletics found in him a staunch devotee, and he inspired his pupils with love for that important branch of literature. In addition to many addresses, orations and panegyrics, there appeared " Thoughts on the Sections of the Pentateuch for the Sabbath," comprising forty-nine lectures, which may serve as a pattern to students. There was also published an Italian rendition of the Book of Psalms, with explanatory headings. A volume of notes to this production, through various mishaps, did not come out till a number of years later, and then only incomplete. An Italian translation of the liturgy, and an essay, "Woman Among the Hebrews," emanated from the same source. A selection of Hebrew poems, entitled *Tal Yalduth*, was subsequently given to the public. It contains effusions suggested by circumstances which happened in the author's early life, besides rhythmical versions of Latin, Italian, and German compositions, and a valuable introduction.

Della Torre showed his admiration for Moses Mendelssohn, Isaac Noah Mannheimer and Grace Aguilar, by inditing separate sketches of the lives and deeds of those illustrious members of the Hebrew race. The ease with which he employed foreign languages made his learned articles a *desideratum* in periodicals issued in France and Germany. His contributions, if put together, would form a book of considerable size.

Closely watching every movement in the religious community of his Italian brethren, the Professor made himself heard, through different journals, in his native land, on subjects relating to the Synagogue and the ritual.

An existence of sixty-six years closed at Padua, Italy, on July 9th, 1871.

The sons of Prof. Della Torre, who have turned aside from engrossing occupations to bring to light much that their father left unpublished, assert that a number of Hebrew manuscripts, principally on casuistical questions, are among the paternal relics. Let us hope that they may not be lost in the ravages of time. Should they have gone to Pesth, whose Rabbinical college possesses the superb library of the Italian literator, men like Prof. Dr. David Kaufmann will know how to turn writings so valuable to good account.

JOSEPH DERENBOURG.

The life of a Hebrew who has searched deep and brought forth what has given his co-religionists just cause for glory, should be descanted upon. Deprived of the satisfaction of following a strong inclination, we hope that the little about to be said will serve to create an idea—however faint—of the acquisitions of a singularly-gifted intellect.

Prof. Joseph Derenbourg was born at Mayence, in Hesse-Darmstadt, Germany, in 1811. He received preliminary instruction in his native city. When sufficiently advanced to enter a University, he repaired to Giessen; but it was at Bonn that he completed his studies. The scholar's mental powers had now developed to a wide extent.

M. Derenbourg spent a number of years at Amsterdam, Holland. There he became known by his literary endeavors. These comprised a number of essays exhibiting deep penetration and the grasp of a thorough critic. Arriving in France, he associated himself with Munk and Albert Cohn, those two great and good Israelites who aimed with singleness of purpose at the improvement of their people.

Derenbourg demonstrated how beneficially he could employ his talents, by founding an educational institute for boys, and by contributing numerous articles to French, German and Dutch magazines; among these were the *Orientalia*, the *Asiatic Journal*, Jost's *Annals*, and one of Geiger's publications. Our author also took a prominent part in collating the Catalogue of Hebrew Manuscripts in the Imperial Library.

The French Government has, on several occasions, recognized M. Derenbourg's services. With other co-religionists, he shares the distinction of wearing the decoration of the Legion of Honor. For two years this eminent Israelite has filled the chair of Rabbinical Hebrew, in a school established and maintained by the public. As a reward to the earnest worker the Academy of Inscriptions and Belles Lettres inscribed his name on the roll of its members.

The productions of M. Derenbourg are chiefly on subjects connected with the history and literature of the East, and they are authoritative on the questions treated. Notes on the Last Passover of Jesus; and on the Ancient Hebrew Grammar—1841, were followed by an edition of Lokman, with a French translation—1850; the second edition of the *séances* of Harriri, conjointly with M. Reinaud—1852; "History and Geography of Palestine"—1867; "Notes on Epigraphy"—1868-'69; " Hebrew Grammar "—1875; etc., etc. A revised edition of several minor writings of Jona ibn Ganach is now being prepared, and it will, in all likelihood, appear in a short time.

Though nearing an age which calls for repose, Joseph Derenbourg does not depart from his original resolve. He will continue in the same goodly path, until he reaches the terminus of life's journey.

DAVID AARON DE SOLA.

Holland, where the famous Menasseh Ben Israel was reared, has considerably lengthened the list of Jewish literators with the names of her children. There Saul Levi Morteira wrote; there Solomon De Oliveira and David Franco Mendes issued their poetical effusions; and from the midst thereof proceeded some who held honored positions abroad, both as ministers and authors. The career of Mr. De Sola affords a striking example.

The Rev. David Aaron De Sola was a descendant of an ancient family who had emigrated from Spain, on the expulsion of the Jews by Ferdinand and Isabella, in 1492, and settled in The Netherlands. He was born at Amsterdam, on the 26th of December, 1796. The desire of his relations had been to train him for the medical profession, but he exhibited a preference for Hebrew theology. When rather young—eleven years old—he gained admission into the Jewish Seminary of his native city. He remained there nine years, during which time he was promoted to the highest scholarship.

In 1818 the Portuguese Congregation of London decided to elect a second *Hazan* or minister —the Rev. Isaac Almosnino being the first—and Mr. De Sola became a candidate for the office. He arrived in England on the 9th of July of the same year, and was duly chosen on the 12th of August following.

Notwithstanding the arduous duties attending the ministry, Mr. De Sola actively engaged in literary pursuits. The work he first published, " The Blessings," with an introductory Essay on Thanksgiving, originated with Sir Moses Montefiore, to whom he acknowledged himself deeply indebted. The book was designed to convey religious information, regarding the various precepts, etc. Mr. De Sola began to preach in March, 1831, and his occasional English sermons—then quite a novelty

in the Portuguese Synagogue—created a very favorable impression.   The Society for the Cultivation
of the Hebrew Language and Literature numbered
him among its ardent laborers.   Before it, he delivered a course of lectures on " Sacred Biography
as Connected with Hebrew Literature."

One of the most important tasks of Mr. De
Sola was a rendition into English of the complete
Portuguese Jewish Prayers,—a decided improvement
on the versions of A. Alexander (London, 1771),
and David Levi (London, 1791).   In conjunction
with the Rev. Dr. M. J. Raphall, he presented an
English translation of eighteen treatises of the
" Mishna;" and began the publication of an edition of the Bible, with the same gentleman and
Mr. I. L. Lindenthal.   Owing to the removal of
Dr. Raphall to Birmingham, the enterprise was
abandoned after the Book of Genesis had appeared.
On the death of the Rev. Mr. Almosnino, in 1843,
Mr. De Sola was appointed senior-minister, which
position he occupied during the remainder of his
life, his colleague being the Rev. David Piza.   He
evinced a lively interest in the establishment of an
Association for the promotion of Jewish Literature,
and lent his aid in the the issue of several of Miss
Aguilar's works.   Mrs. Charlotte Montefiore and
Miss Miriam Mendes Belisario likewise secured
his able assistance, when preparing their various
productions.

Mr. De Sola brought forth, in 1855, a biography of the celebrated Italian scholar, Isaac Samuel Reggio, in the Dutch language, and which has since received an English translation from the late Rev. Jacob J. Peres. In addition to a number of miscellaneous writings and contributions to the press, he published " The Ancient Melodies of the Spanish and Portuguese Jews," an important work, in connection with Mr. Emanuel Aguilar, a musician of note and a brother of the gifted authoress. Appended to this was " An Historical Essay on the Poets, Poetry and Melodies of the Sephardic Liturgy."

Mr. De Sola left behind him a mass of literary correspondence with some of the master minds of the Jewish people, whose confidence he enjoyed. He expired on the 29th of October, 1860, lamented by all who had valued his friendship and profited by his knowledge.

ABRAHAM DE SOLA.

At a time when the Jewish inhabitants of America needed able expounders of the religion of the Hebrew Bible and traditions—persons whose characters could impart dignity to the ancestral worship—a young man arrived on this continent. He was peculiarly fitted, by training and early associations, for the sacred undertaking, which had led him far away from home. In the school and at the Synagogue, he had learnt that the history of the chosen race must be presented in an attractive, but not meretricious, garb; that the service of God's people must be solemn, but not strained. Thus furnished with the means for giving a healthy impetus to what he wished to preserve, the new comer set himself to work. What follows will show how the community benefited by the endeavors of this public servant.

The Rev. Prof. Abraham De Sola, LL.D., was born at London, England, on the 18th of September, 1825. His father, the Rev. David Aaron De Sola, enjoyed a high reputation as a divine and scholar. Young De Sola received a careful education, under paternal supervision. After having finished his academical studies, he took to Hebrew, Literature and Theology. Diligence and perseverance soon produced the results which always attend them. Before reaching manhood, Mr. De Sola was urged by many who recognized his worth to apply for a ministerial office in his native city. But a wider sphere of action had been opened for him in the New World. In 1847 he responded to a call from the Portuguese Hebrew Congregation, of Montreal, Canada.

There began Dr. De Sola's steadfast labors. In

the first year of his residence at Montreal, he lectured before the Mercantile Library Association, on the " History of the Jews of England," and that his efforts were duly appreciated is evidenced by his having been requested to address the same society, as well as the Mechanics' Institute, every succeeding winter during which a course of lectures was given. The Doctor was chosen President of the Natural History Society, of Montreal, a position he still retains. Before that organization, he has delivered very interesting lectures on Jewish history, and on the zoology, cosmogony, and botany of the Scriptures; displaying in all a rare scholarship, and a thorough acquaintance with the subjects.

In a short space of time Dr. De Sola's talents had brought him out so prominently, that in 1848 he was appointed Professor of Hebrew and Semitic Literature in M'Gill College. The duties attached to that honorable office he has discharged with commendable zeal. So · popular he became in the said institution that the degree of *Doctor of Laws* was conferred on him, and he was selected to address the graduates, on behalf of the Faculty, at one of the commencements,—a token of distinction accorded only to preceptors of marked abilities.

Prof. De Sola has labored for the welfare of his brethren as a minister, but more particularly as a writer.   Many articles from his pen have graced the columns of the secular and the Jewish press, and the drift thereof has been the exaltation of the religion of Israel, and the exposing to view of the grand literature of our people.   The author's style is clear and choice, and his logical arguments leave a deep impression.   Of the Professor's writings we may mention " Notes on the Jews of Persia," "Commentary on Samuel Hannagid's Introduction to the Talmud," " Peritsol's Cosmography," " Life of Shabethai Tsevi," " History of the Jews of Poland," " History of the Jews of France;" and also, in conjunction with the late Rev. Jacques J. Lyons, of New York, "The Jewish Calendar."

Dr. De Sola, who was in close literary relations with the Rev. Isaac Leeser, purchased from the latter's executors the plates of all his works, and reissued several of these, principally the forms of prayer, according to both the Spanish and Portuguese, and the German rituals.   But recently the Doctor has published, in six volumes, a revised translation of the liturgy exclusively in use among the *Sephardim*, a labor undertaken at the instance of the late Rev. Dr. Benjamin Artom, Chief Rabbi of the Spanish and Portuguese Congregations of the British Empire, and dedicated to Sir Moses Montefiore and to the memory of his lamented consort, Lady Judith.

In addition to all this, Dr. De Sola has constantly identified himself with educational, charitable and literary associations, alike of his fellow-believers and of Christians, who hold him in high regard. On the 9th of January, 1872, Prof. De Sola was granted the privilege of opening the United States House of Representatives with prayer, he being the first foreign clergyman to invoke the Divine blessing within the halls of Congress. His outpourings elicited favorable comments, by reason of their broad and humanitarian character, free from the least tincture of sectarianism.

Several voyages to Europe have tended to increase Prof. DeSola's popularity in the Old World, and, at the same time, proved a benefit to his health, and a restorative to his mental powers; as desired by all who hope to see him long engaged in the service of his brethren.

EMANUEL OSCAR MENAHEM DEUTSCH.

It has been truly said that there is no intellectual movement for the advancement of the masses, in which Israelites do not figure conspicuously. The correctness of this assertion can be ascertained by glancing at the careers of numbers of Hebrews who devoted their best energies to the accomplishment of a sole object, viz.: the general diffusion of

knowledge. Thus Jews and Gentiles are largely in-
indebted to the literary research of Dr. Emanuel
Oscar Menahem Deutsch for the revelation of important facts regarding a work which will outlive posterity—the Talmud.

Dr. Deutsch was born at Neisse, in the province
of Silesia, Prussia, on the 28th of October, 1829.
When but six years old, he attended the gymnasium of his birth-place, and continued there some
time. The boy's uncle, David Deutsch, of Mislowitz,
desired to be entrusted with his nephew's education,
and in compliance with the wish expressed, Emanuel
remained under the charge of that relative until
his thirteenth year. The lad was subjected to a
rather stern discipline, being obliged to rise daily
at five o'clock, having but half an hour for recreation, as the rest of the time had to be entirely
spent in hard study. This continued strain, though
it laid the foundation of an accurate scholarship,
proved a severe blow to the health of the student
in after years. On returning home, young Deutsch
again proceeded to the gymnasium, where he was en-
rolled in the highest class. At the age of sixteen
he went to the Berlin University, where theology
and the Talmud mainly occupied his thoughts.

Deutsch supported himself by teaching, and he
wrote several stories and poems for magazines. It
was not long before he completely mastered the
English language and its literature.

In 1855 Dr. Deutsch was appointed assistant in the library of the British Museum, which position afforded him the opportunity to largely exercise his talents. He contributed numerous papers to *Chambers' Encyclopædia*, essays to Kitto's and Smith's Bible Dictionaries, and articles to different journals. His principal aim, however, was a treatise on the Talmud—the ideal of his childhood. This took a practical form in October, 1867, when his article on the above-named work appeared in the London *Quarterly Review*. The great merit of the production at once established his fame, and within twelve months it was translated into French, German Russian, Swedish, Dutch, and Danish.

Dr. Deutsch having conceived a strong affection for the East, was granted leave of absence for ten weeks. He left England on the 7th of March, 1869, and visited, among other places, Palestine, remaining awhile in Jerusalem. Profound emotions seized his heart, when he stood by the ruins of the ancient Temple (called " The Wailing-Place of the Jews "), the spot where the faithful, on each eve of the Sabbath, bemoan the loss of the Hebrew nationality. The rapidity and fatigue of Dr. Deutsch's journey to the Orient, seriously impaired his constitution. He reached England on the 10th of May, submitted a valuable report of his travels to the trustees of the British Museum, and delivered a number of lectures, chiefly on Phœnicia. In October, 1869, his article on "Islam," was published in the *Quarterly Review*.

Overwork, together with ill-health and the death of attached friends, caused much depression of spirits, and the old longing for the East revived with greater force. Towards the close of 1872, Dr. Deutsch obtained six months' vacation, and set out for Italy and Egypt. But his physical powers were now entirely exhausted, and the severity of the winter helped to weaken his already broken-down frame. He reached Cairo on the 30th of March, 1873, and was thence removed to Alexandria. All efforts to restore him became of no avail, and on the 12th of May following he breathed his last. He was interred in the Jewish Cemetery of Alexandria, where a granite stone marks the grave of this lamented author.

Dr. Deutsch added to his remarkable knowledge of European languages, and of Hebrew, a thorough acquaintance with the Sanscrit, Chaldaic, Aramaic and Phœnician tongues. Of his connection with the British Museum, he thus speaks: "For nigh twenty years, it was my privilege to dwell in the very midst of that pantheon called the British Museum, the treasures whereof, be they Egyptian, Homeric, palimpsest, or Babylonian cuneiforms, the mutilated glories of the Parthenon, or the Etruscan mysterious grotesqueness, were all at my beck and call, all days, all hours."

A large accumulation of manuscripts was found after Dr. Deutsch's death, containing parts of the Talmud, copied or translated, beginning in a child's hand-writing, and reaching down to a comparatively late period. His *Literary Remains*, consisting of nineteen papers on such subjects as "The Talmud" and "Islam," before mentioned; "Semitic Culture," "Egypt, Ancient and Modern," "Semitic Languages," "The Targums," "The Samaritan Pentateuch," and "Arabic Poetry," edited by Lady Strangford, appeared in 1874.

A void, not easily filled, was created in the world of letters, when he, that surpassed many of his coevals in the accomplishment of extraordinary designs, was summoned from the sphere of his activity.

ISAAC D'ISRAELI.

Few of England's prose-writers have acquired as much distinction as Isaac D'Israeli. The fact may be attributed to the wide interest which his writings command, and likewise to their characteristic elegance and purity of style. Mr. D'Israeli, though never professing a strict adherence to Jewish observances, always considered it an especial pride to be numbered among the descendants of

Abraham ; nor did his religious convictions waver.

Isaac D'Israeli was born at Enfield, in May, 1766. He belonged to a Hebrew family that had been driven from Spain by the Inquisition, and had settled at Venice. His father, Benjamin D'Israeli, removed to England in 1748, at the age of eighteen, and there became a prominent merchant, amassing, in a short time, a considerable fortune. Isaac, when a small child, displayed a precocity which promised a brilliant future. His time was entirely occupied with books, and he evinced a decided aversion to worldly pursuits, which action his parents by no means sustained. In order to change the bent of the boy's mind, his father sent him to school at Amsterdam, where he remained four or five years. Bayle, Voltaire, and Rousseau were his favorite studies. Before returning to England, he wrote a long poem against commerce, which was submitted to Dr. Samuel Johnson, but the death of the latter prevented its examination.

Mr. D'Israeli intended to place his son in a commercial house at Bordeaux, but the opposition with which he met, induced the father to give up his purpose, and the youth was allowed to follow his own disposition. He travelled in France, and spent some months in Paris, in the society of men devoted to literary pursuits, which formed the delight of young D'Israeli.

Coming home in 1788, he published an anonymous poem, "On the Abuse of Satire," after the manner of Pope. It was intended as an attack on "Peter Pindar" (Dr. John Wolcot) and the favor it obtained laid the corner-stone of Mr. D'Israeli's literary fame. Much speculation was indulged in as to its authorship, and such were the merits of the poetic effusion, that several popular writers received the credit, ere the name of its real author leaked out.

Mr. D'Israeli's mind was now wholly engrossed in the preparation of the work by which he is best known. The first volume of the "Curiosities of Literature," appeared in 1791; the second in 1793; and the third, which completed the series, in 1817. "Miscellanies, or Literary Recreations," in 1796; "Calamities of Authors," in 1812; and "Quarrels of Authors," in 1814, fully sustained the writer's high reputation. It would take many pages to enumerate the various productions of a pen so fertile. Suffice the mention of "Despotism, or the Fall of the Jesuits," a novel (2 vols.); ".Vaurien, or Sketches of the Times," a philosophical novel (2 vols.); apologetic of the "Character of James I.;" "The Literary Character," an essay; and "Commentary on the Life and Reign of Charles I." The work last mentioned gained for Mr. D'Israeli the title of D. C. L., from the University of Oxford, in acknowledgment of his abilities as an historian.

In July, 1820, he contributed an article to the London *Quarterly Review*, in defence of Pope. It created quite a sensation, there being at that period a spirited controversy as to the merits and demerits of the English poet. A proof of the esteem for Mr. D'Israeli as a man of letters, is a remark of Lord Byron, who alluded to him as "that most entertaining and searching writer."

It is fitting now to refer to several momentous incidents in the life of Mr. D'Israeli, which had an important bearing on his career, and exercised much influence in the rearing of his family. Benjamin D'Israeli, the father of Isaac, on arriving in England, joined the Portuguese Synagogue. Though not a strict conformant to the tenets of his religion, he, nevertheless, contributed a yearly sum to the support of the congregation. His son, Isaac, married Maria Basevi, sister of George Basevi, the architect, all being members of the Portuguese Synagogue. Mr. Isaac D'Israeli seldom attended worship, but paid regularly his *finta* or tax of £10 per annum. On October 3d, 1813, he was elected *Parnass* or Warden of the Bevis Marks Synagogue, which position he declined with thanks; at the same time expressing his readiness to continue giving his mite, without assuming any active part. No notice was taken of his action, and, pursuant to the rules, he was fined £40. This drew from him an interesting letter, which plainly shows the injustice against which he strongly protested.* The determination of the elders of the Synagogue was not shaken by this communication, and he was informed, "that, in accordance with the present laws, it is not possible to grant him the exemptions he desires."

When Mr. D'Israeli received his annual account in March, 1814, he refused to pay the fine for his non-acceptance of office, though he showed his willingness to discharge the usual tax. The unpleasant circumstance occasioned several summonses to meetings of the congregation, which elicited further correspondence. In March, 1817, the matter terminated, in Mr. D'Israeli withdrawing from the Synagogue; his brother-in-law, Mr. Basevi, also severing his connection. How the Jewish community was injuriously affected by what has just been narrated, we shall proceed to demonstrate.

The sons of Mr. D'Israeli,—Benjamin, Ralph, and James,—all born prior to the dispute mentioned, were admitted into the Abrahamic covenant, and the daughter, Sarah, was bred in her parents' faith. But the Right Hon. Benjamin *Disraeli* (who has so altered his surname) became affiliated to the Church of England, through the influence of a Christian friend,—the poet, Samuel Rogers.

---

*See Picciotto's "Sketches of Anglo-Jewish History," p. 297.

The history of the present Premier of Great Britain is as familiar as a household word, and late events have amply testified to his controlling power in European affairs.

The Earl of Beaconsfield has published a complete edition of his father's writings, and prefaced it with an introduction, in the course of which this passage occurs: "He was a complete literary character, a man who really passed his life in his library,"—a graphic description of him whose life has been sketched.

Isaac D'Israeli's estrangement from a people whose very appellation his predecessors had chosen as a distinctive family name, must needs be lamented; but his attachment to the principles of the ancestral faith is proven in his excellent work, entitled "Genius of Judaism." Mr. D'Israeli died on the 19th of January, 1848, having approached the ripe age of eighty-two years, bequeathing to the world the fruits of his long literary labors.

DAVID EINHORN.

THE extreme wing of Reform in Judaism has prominent leaders in America. But one lately removed from among the living, displayed a skill that caused many to confide in his generalship. Ardent, fearless, uncompromising, his word, always uttered with intense earnestness, sounded like a command that dared not be disobeyed. From the very outset, he directed his steps in a path which he deemed progressive. With unabated vigor he entered the lists against the opponents of his views, and struggled for a victorious issue. But we must not anticipate the narrative of Dr. Einhorn's history. Let that tell of the iron will exhibited throughout a checkered life.

The Rev. Dr. David Einhorn was born at Dispeck, in Bavaria, Germany, on November 10th, 1809. Enjoying the advantage which not all students possess—that of having a home supplied with comforts—he could gratify a natural love for books. His extraordinary talents early developed under careful tuition.

In his ninth year, Einhorn gained admission into the Rabbinical High School at Fürth, then in charge of the widely-known Rabbi Wolf Hamburger. It was a great pleasure for the instructor to count among his pupils, a lad so apt that he could learn almost intuitively. Observing the quickness with which young Einhorn settled the sharp disputations raised in the Talmud, to the astonishment of the whole class, the unsophisticated Rabbi formed, perchance, hopes which were not to be realized. He may have imagined that he had discovered in that *Bachur*, a successor who would shine brilliantly as a champion

of the old school. The title of Rabbi is not gen-
·erally conferred on beardless youths, but Einhorn
obtained it when only sixteen years of age.

The same eagerness the young man had felt for
the pursuit of religious studies, he experienced when
cultivating branches of secular learning. At the University of Würzburg, and subsequently at that of
München, he fathomed the depths of philosophy,
while his mind was disciplined by Mathematics, and
exalted by the classics. At the end of four years he
quitted college, as *Doctor of Philosophy*, amid the
congratulations of his preceptors.

Then began the real battle of life. Schelling
had displaced what Hamburger fancied he had firmly set in. Einhorn warmly espoused the cause of
radical Reform. But in those days the promises
of success to a minister who turned aside from
Orthodoxy were anything but encouraging. Our
preacher, notwithstanding his eloquence, met with
refusals when in quest of a position. After hot discussions, and even legal proceedings had been re-
sorted to, Einhorn finally found a Rabbinical office
in the town of Hopstadten. While officiating there,
he attended the second conference of Reform Rabbis
at Frankfort-on-the-Main in 1845, and made his
mark by incisive arguments and scholastic learning.

A little later, Dr. Einhorn succeeded Dr. Samuel
Holdheim, as Chief Rabbi of the Grand Duchy of

Mecklenburg-Schwerin. A warm friendship sprung up between the two congenial spirits, but Einhorn, more than once, arose to combat the opinion of that foe of the Talmud, who sought to support his extreme views by quoting the very work he wished to demolish. The Doctor was also led to oppose the theory of Prof. Delitsch, the very scholarly Christian, who maintained that a male child of Jewish parents cannot be considered an Israelite, unless he is admitted into the covenant of Abraham.

Dr. Einhorn was destined to encounter a still stronger antagonism at Pesth. He had been called and welcomed there as Rabbi in 1851, and those who shared his convictions listened admiringly to his sermons. But a storm was raised by the Conservative party. Availing themselves of the reaction in politics, throughout Europe, the adversaries of Reform, represented the Synagogue of the emphatic preacher as a nursery of revolutionary doctrines. The Austrian Government therefore ordered the Temple to be closed, despite Einhorn's protestations and entreaties. About this period appeared "Principles of Mosaism," in which the author endeavors to prove that the statutes of the Pentateuch are not unchangeable; that, while the truths enunciated therein must remain and rule Israel everywhere, the ceremonial code may be modified and altered, or even abrogated, agreeably to times and circumstances.

In 1855 Dr. Einhorn responded to an invitation from the *Har Sinai* Congregation of Baltimore, to become its spiritual guide. America and its institutions had always possessed a charm for the liberal German. During his incumbency as pastor in the afore-named city, he published his prayer-book, '*Olath Tamid*, which was received with much favor by many Reform Temples. There he also issued a monthly magazine, called *Sinai*, in the interest of radical Reform. But at the outbreak of the Civil War, in 1861, the editor scourged with his pen and tongue the defenders of Negro-slavery. Such boldness in a place decidedly Southern in its proclivities, rendered his stay dangerous. It is even reported that the Doctor's life had been threatened, and consequently he sought Philadelphia as a refuge, where he soon became Rabbi of the Congregation *Keneseth Israel*. In that city he brought out *Ner Tamid*, a catechism which has been adopted by schools conducted in accordance with the principles he advocated.

In 1866 Dr. Einhorn repaired to New York, where a larger scope was offered to his efforts in the *Adath Jeshurun* Congregation. This influential body united, in 1874, with the old *Anshe Chesed* Congregation, and formed the present *Beth-El*. Dr. Einhorn continued his ministration till within a short period of his demise.

The controlling idea of the man manifested itself in his forcible and eloquent addresses, and in his general demeanor. At a convention held in Philadelphia, in 1869, he urged the acceptance of rules aiming to abolish Jewish divorce regulations, the Leviratical law, and other observances.

In the summer of 1879 Dr. Einhorn resolved to retire from office. On Sabbath, July 12th, of that year, he delivered his farewell sermon, in which he reviewed his career. In the course of his remarks, he exhorted his flock to cling to the principles he had strenuously maintained, and to stand by his successor and son-in-law, the Rev. Dr. Kaufmann Kohler, "who," the speaker remarked, "though young in years, is rich in theological lore."

David Einhorn did not long survive to enjoy the earthly rest which he had sought. On November 2d, 1879, he departed for " the undiscovered country, from whose bourn no traveller returns."

A collection of the inedited writings of Dr. Einhorn might be a valuable addition to American Jewish literature.

HERSCHELL FILIPOWSKI.*

THE writings of the first Hebrew Grammarians and Lexicographers lay buried for ages in oblivion.

---

* Mr. Denizen H. Filipowski has furnished useful information towards the preparation of this sketch of his father's life.

At different periods in this century the endeavors
of men like Dukes, Blumenfeld, and Goldberg, unearthed what proved of value. But that which was
brought forth served only to excite a keen wish
for seeing more. To gratify that laudable desire an
organization, known as the Hebrew Antiquarian Society, engaged the capacities of a learned Israelite
—Herschell Filipowski. He ransacked libraries, and
availing himself of the light which his predecessors
—principally Prof. Luzzatto—had furnished, drew out
a volume of primary importance in the history of
Biblical exegesis. It was the work of no less a
writer than Menahem Ben Saruk. Mr. Filipowski
arranged it in a complete form, and made it still
more interesting by his abridged English version,
and by the narrative of a stirring episode in the
life of the Spanish author. The scholar of our day
who labored so acceptably is the subject of the
remarks here appended.

Herschell Filipowski was born in Poland, in
1817. He gave early promise of attaining an eminent
position. When only fifteen, he published "An
Almanac for One Hundred Years," both in the
Polish and Russian tongues. In 1840 he went to
England, and received the appointment of Teacher
of Hebrew and Oriental Languages in the Jews'
College, Finsbury Square. Subsequently, he became
connected with the Colonial and Standard Life Offices

of Edinburgh, remaining in that city a number of years. It was during his residence in the capital of Scotland, that Mr. Filipowski issued some excellent works.

Our author brought out, in 1849, a production that secured his fame among Actuaries, namely, that on Anti-Logarithms. This was followed, in 1854, by a condensed translation of "The First Hebrew and Chaldaic Lexicon to the Old Testament," indited in the tenth century by Menahem Ben Saruk, to which allusion has already been made; in 1857, by a rendition into English, from the Latin, of "Napier's Canon of Logarithms"; and, in 1864 and 1866, by an edition, in two volumes, of "Baily's Doctrine of Life Annuities and Assurances." *The Actuarial Magazine*, a monthly, devoted to tables of different kinds, was edited by Mr. Filipowski for a short time. An extensive knowledge of typography proved of great service in the publication of his works. The industrious laborer invented a font of Hebrew type, with points attached to each letter, from which a Hebrew and English Prayer-book was printed in 1862.

Mr. Filipowski made another journalistic attempt in 1867, when *The Hebrew National* appeared. In a short existence of six months, it presented articles from the pens of many well-known scholars, besides the contributions of its talented editor. But its dis-

continuance did not - put an end to the unceasing
exertions of Mr. Filipowski. He published a number of productions in Hebrew and Chaldaic, and
shortly before his death, which occurred on the 12th
of July, 1872, he had completed a "Hebrew and
Roman Almanac," from the year 1 A. C. E. to
perpetuity. This book exhibits a vast amount of
learning and tact, as a mere glance will reveal. The
date of any event, together with other instructive
matter, can be found therein, thus making the
volume almost indispensable.

Mr. Filipowski's linguistic powers may be judged
from the assertion that he was conversant with
Polish, Russian, Latin, Hebrew, Arabic, Spanish,
French, English, German and Chinese. But believing that great advantages in the relations of mankind would be derived from a universal language,
he urged its adoption in his various writings. The
idea, certainly utopian, evinces, nevertheless, a spirit
of benevolence and broad humanitarianism.

ACHILLE FOULD.

Modern governments have not failed to notice
the tact and skill characteristic of the Jew. High
offices of trust have therefore been confided to members of the ancient race, and the integrity and
sagacity displayed in the discharge thereof, en-

sured a share of respect, proportionate to the responsibilities of the positions. Before our vision stands a Hebrew who was justly recognized as a leading financier and statesman. For the most intricate questions, relative to the stability of a government, were unravelled and settled by his keen discernment.

Achille Fould was born at Paris, France, November 17th, 1800. He early associated with his father in the banking business, which he afterwards managed alone. Besides receiving a very careful and varied education, he travelled for self-improvement through portions of Europe and the East. A lover of the beautiful, he spent some time in Italy, and visited the Eastern coasts of the Mediterranean, to develop his knowledge of the fine arts.

M. Fould entered political life in 1842, as a member of the Chamber of Deputies for the department of Tarbes. In that body he became a conspicuous figure from his thorough acquaintance with economical and financial matters. He secured a reelection in 1846, and two years later sat in the Constituent Assembly. He acquiesced in the Revolution of 1848, and his ideas on finance exercised a decided weight on the then Provisional Government.

Under the presidency of Louis Napoleon, M. Fould was four times Minister of Finance. He took

a leading part in the movements to reform commerce. His disagreements with the president, however, led him twice to retire from office, but he
was each time re-appointed. Strongly opposed to
free trade, and firm in his conservative tendencies,
he hailed the establishment of the new Empire.
On the 25th of January, 1852, in consequence of
the decree confiscating the property of the Orleans
family, M. Fould relinquished the ministry of finance,
but he was, on the same day, made Senator, and,
soon after, he rejoined the Government, as Minister
of State, and of the Imperial Household. In that
capacity, he directed the Paris Exhibition of 1855.
The events of November, 1860, urged him once
more to resign, but he was recalled to the ministry
of finance, in November of the following year. On
the promulgation of the order of the 19th of January, 1867, making changes in the administration of
affairs, he retired from office, and did not thereafter accept any position.

While in the Cabinet, M. Fould reduced the
floating debt, which the Mexican war had increased,
by the negotiation of a loan of three hundred millions of francs. Whatever his political proclivities
may have been, none will deny that he discharged
his duties with zeal and fidelity.

M. Fould was created a Commander of the Legion of Honor in 1852, and an honorary member

of the Academy of Fine Arts, in 1857. During his public career, he issued several pamphlets on finance, of which may be mentioned *Pas d' Assignats*, and *Opinion de M. A. Fould sur les Assignats*, both against the use of paper money. He died at Tarbes, France, October 5th, 1867.

The various monetary schemes and other public measures introduced by M. Fould have been attended with the happiest results, both in contributing to the prosperity of his native country, and in extending his fame as a financier of exceptional ability.

ADOLPHE FRANCK.

Philosophy, in its literal definition, is coeval with human thought. The mind has always gone in search of wisdom. But the introduction of the term in its multifarious applications is due to the Greeks. To attempt to define at present the meaning which that word conveys, would be to engage in a description of all that is known and knowable of the heavens above, and of the earth beneath. There was, indeed, a period, in which the world regarded one single individual as having compassed all, and having given, not merely an outline of the learning implied by *philosophy*, but a full and unquestionable delineation. Aristotle enjoyed the reputation of being the very quintessence of wisdom. Any branch of science, treated in a manner at variance with that of the Stagirite, had perforce to be declared faulty. But the sceptre of even that monarch of knowledge passed into the hands of others, who, in their turn, wielded it with more or less pretension. What then is philosophy; or which branch thereof can lay claim to perfection? The question grows more perplexing every day. Its solution will long remain problematic.

Herein is presented the record of an eclectic philosopher, who, nothwithstanding the mystical nature of some of the subjects discussed, writes with elegance and perspicuity.

Prof. Adolphe Franck, was born at Liocourt, in the department of Meurthe, France, October 9th, 1809. At Nancy and Toulouse he pursued studies with signal success. Determined to become an instructor, possessed, in every way, of the necessary qualifications, he held fast to his industrious habits, and at the examination in 1832, he obtained the highest average in philosophy, over many competitors. This achievement added strength to his will.

Franck taught for a while in provincial towns. But such abilities as he commanded, could not be cramped. They must be allowed free scope. The man's writings soon made him famous.

In 1840 M. Franck was called to Paris, as Professor of Philosophy at Charlemagne College. Alive to the importance of the position, he applied himself to deeper studies, and with so much diligence, that it occasioned a severe illness, which forced a withdrawal from active duties in 1843, and a demand for relaxation in sunny Italy. Prior to this untoward event, M. Franck had been appointed to a high office in the Royal Library. He devoted his leisure hours to meditation and authorship. Several literary productions tended to his being chosen a member of the Academy of Moral and Political Sciences, in 1844. Restored to health, he returned home, and undertook, in conjuction with others, the publication of " The Dictionary of Philosophical Sciences," in six volumes—1844-'52, an erudite and valuable work, in which many excellent articles emanate from the subject of this sketch.

Having taught social science with success, M. Franck was requested by M. Barthélemy, in 1849, to substitute him as Saint Hilaire Professor of Greek and Latin Philosophy in the College of France. This post he occupied until 1852. In 1854 he was selected to fill the Chair of International Law in the same institution, though he did not receive the degree of *Professor* until 1856. He still adorns that station, and the inestimable services rendered, have met with the entire appreciation of his associates, and the community at large. The capacities of M. Franck must have been obviously manifest, since he could, in the midst of an assemblage of *literati*, earn so decisive a triumph.

M. Franck's earnest endeavors as a teacher, and his frequent publications, illustrate his activity. The Professor is identified with the eclectic school of philosophy. His doctrines cannot, therefore, strictly claim originality, but they are advanced in a clear diction, as the results of conscientious meditations, and they evince sincerity in the expression of opinions long entertained. In addition to the articles furnished the *Journal des Débats*, and the Annals of the Academy of Sciences, and essays on Thomas Moore, Bodin, Machiavelli, and other noted personages, the following works have proceeded from his pen: " A Sketch of the History of Logic "—1838; " The Cabbala, or Religious Philosophy of the Hebrews "— 1843, a production in which the author's tendencies are distinctly shown, and which has been translated into German by the celebrated scholar, Dr. Adolph Jellinek of Vienna; " Communism Judged by History "—1849, wherein the ideas set forth by visionaries meet a vigorous opposition; " Philosophy of Penal Laws "—1864; " Philosophy of Ecclesiastical Laws "—1864; " Mystic Philosophy in France towards the Close of the Eighteenth Century "—1866; etc., etc.

For two decades, Prof. Franck has been a member of the Superior Council of Public Instruction.

As Vice-President of the Israelitish Consistory at Paris, he displayed much interest in the workings of that body, but resigned his position in 1873. The decoration of the Legion of Honor was conferred on the Professor in 1869.

The noble son of France is still concerned in the welfare of his brethren. What inures to their spiritual benefit, can never cease to excite the sympathy of him whose labors have so eminently contributed to raise their social standing.

ZACHARIAS FRANKEL.

A difficult task would it be, to portray the characteristics of a man whose depth of intellect and immense practical knowledge, placed him on a level with the most renowned scholars of his day. But notwithstanding this fact, to remain altogether silent, might justly be deemed an unpardonable omission. Our inability to rise equal to the subject must secure the indulgence of the public, in the little that will be related of the literary merits and personal traits of an honored Israelite.

Dr. Zacharias Frankel was born at Prague, in Bohemia, Austria, on the 1st of October, 1801, of a family noted for piety and erudition. He early showed a strong desire for mental culture, and, when but a lad, his training in Jewish lore gained him the reputation of a Talmudist. Young Frankel's attention, however, was not given solely to the Talmud. He frequented the Gymnasium, where classical literature occupied his time and thoughts. At the University of Pesth, he principally studied mathematics, thus completing the course, and in 1831 he received the degree of *Doctor of Philosophy*.

In 1832 Dr. Frankel was chosen District-Rabbi of Leitmeritz, in Bohemia, where he first introduced preaching in the German language; and, in 1836, Chief Rabbi of Dresden and Leipsic. His active labors now began. The Jews of Dresden, besides suffering from political disabilities, stood greatly in need of enlightenment in their own faith. Frankel not only became their spiritual guide, but he publicly defended their cause, and with so much vigor, that he obtained for them their rights as citizens. His work, " The Jewish Oath from a Theological and Historical Standpoint," published in 1840, wherein he calls upon the authorities to judge equitably, and not from ill-formed opinions, at the same time making an earnest appeal for freedom, had an important effect in the accomplishment of the noble purpose. Another production, entitled: " The Mosaic-Talmudic Law of Evidence," brought forth in 1846, strongly rebukes and condemns the practice of declaring it illegal for a Jew to be witness in a case, or take an oath in court.

It will thus be seen that Frankel's first efforts were used to procure full equality for his co-religionists. Having won this victory, he turned to the moral and religious condition of the Jews of Dresden. He found that the want of educational institutions, was the main cause of their unsettled state. But Frankel, never tiring, soon roused his fellow-believers to a sense of their duty. Ere long, a Synagogue was erected, and dedicated to God's worship, in the presence of many who had formerly shown their hostility to Judaism, but whose opinions, through the benign influence of Zacharias Frankel, had undergone a decided change. The valuable assistance rendered to Frankel, by his friend Dr. Bernhard Beer, must not be overlooked, for it greatly encouraged the former, in the carrying out of his schemes.

Dr. Frankel's labors in the field of Jewish theology and literature, have principally built up his world-wide fame. Profound thoughts and a complete mastery of the subject, are revealed in every one of his writings. Thus, for example, his work on the Septuagint, in which he traces the origin, development and character of Jewish law, evinces patient research, and wonderful acquaintance with ancient and modern literature. This production earned for him an enviable reputation in learned circles. In 1844 Frankel started, conjointly with others, the *Magazine for the*

Religious Interests of Judaism, which, though it lasted but three years, contained articles of great merit, from the pens of acknowledged scholars. In 1852 the *Monatschrift* first appeared, and continued under Dr. Frankel's management until 1868, when Prof. Dr. H. Graetz, the great historian, assumed the editorship. In the second year of the *Monatschrift*, Dr. Frankel issued a call for the establishment of a Jewish College. This led to his appointment in 1854 as Director of the Theological Seminary at Breslau, in Silesia, Prussia, an institution erected through the munificence of Jonas Fraenckel.

All agreed as to the excellence of the choice, and that the public voice confirmed it, may be shown by the fact that, in a short time, Frankel had endeared himself both to professors and students. It would fill many pages to speak of his activity at the Breslau Seminary; how he raised the standard and usefulness of that seat of learning, until it became as famous as its Director. But we may still name a few of the important works, written during this period. Dr. Frankel brought forth "The Palestinian and Alexandrian Bible Criticism," in 1859, and "Mosaic-Talmudic Marriage Laws," in 1860. There also appeared his "Introduction to the Mishna," written in Hebrew, and a "Sketch of the History of the Literature of Post-Talmudic Decisions." But his most extensive labor was accomplished in his old age, viz.: "Introduction to the Jerusalem Talmud," in Hebrew, published in 1870; followed, in 1874, by the first part of said Talmud with exhaustive commentaries. The introduction to the second part was finished the day prior to Frankel's death. For obvious reasons, no attempt has been made here to give a notice of these remarkable writings.

Dr. Frankel, liberal in his views, held firmly to historical Judaism. He battled, however, against bigots, as well as radicals, for he accepted the tenets without superstition, and without new notions engrafted thereon. Nevertheless, Frankel was looked upon with reverential esteem by all parties, and the teachings of the Sage were reflected in the ardor of his students.

On the 13th of February, 1875, the earthly pilgrimage of Zacharias Frankel suddenly ended. He went to rest on the Sabbath, a proper day for the righteous to be translated to the land of spirits. Of all those representatives of Israel's glory who have departed from this sublunary scene within the last quarter of a century, we do not think there has been one more lamented than Zacharias Frankel, whose vast acquirements and many virtues have reserved for him a golden page in the history of his people.

LUDWIG AUGUST FRANKL.

"What comes from the heart goes to the heart," is a trite adage. In any language which man may choose for expressing his thoughts, he will sway multitudes, when the utterances of his lips bear the impress of earnestness. But if the speaker or writer can clothe his words in the golden garb of poetry, that is, if he can borrow from nature illustrations which give his feelings a life-like aspect, the effect will be electrical. For a sympathetic current is thus opened that reaches and stirs the very soul. Truly, such emotional language may dispense with the accompaniment of rhythm; flowing verses cannot lend it vigor. Yet, an inexplicable leaning to a metrical form seems innate in man. For, like song, it possesses a softening influence.

Hebrews of Teutonic nations, whose achievements in literature in the present age have few parallels in history, can also boast of their poets who know how to embalm their sublime ideas in sweet rhymes. Among those who have excelled, Ludwig August Frankl may worthily be mentioned.

Herr Frankl was born at Chrast, in Bohemia, Austria, on the 3d of February, 1810. Thirsting for knowledge, he travelled to Italy and pursued medical studies. On the completion of his course, in 1837, he received a diploma, bearing testimony to high qualifications. The newly-recognized physician did not, however, exclusively confine himself to the practice of his profession. A yearning for journalism led him to seize the pen, which he could so gracefully wield.

Frankl rendered valuable services as Secretary and Archivist of the Hebrew community in Vienna. His cultured and richly-endowed mind was daily dispensing of its resources. How fitting that he who had shown intense love for the beautiful, should be chosen Professor of Æsthetics in the city of his residence. But in the East, whose historic associations possess a magnetic influence, Frankl devised plans for the elevation of the lowly. Beholding the state of abjection into which his fellow-believers of the Holy Land had sunk, through untoward circumstances, he opened a school in Jerusalem. The pitiful condition of those Hebrews, owing to misgovernment and internal dissensions, is graphically depicted in his *Nach Jerusalem*, which appeared in 1858. Another work on the Hebrews of the Orient, entitled *Aus Ægypten*, was published in 1860.

Of Frankl's productions, his short poem, *Die Universität*, deserves special attention. It came out in 1848, immediately after the abolition of the censorship in Austria, and so eager was the desire to read it, that, within a short period, five hundred thousand copies were sold. *Zur Geschichte der Juden in Wien,* on the history of the Jews in Vienna, in two volumes, was issued in 1847-'53. An anonymous writing, *Magyarenkönig*, in 1850, made Frankl very popular with the Hungarians, whose defence he undertook; but the Austrian authorities in Pesth, destroyed the edition. *Ahnenbilder* and *Libanon*, two later works, include poems, descriptive of the author's impressions of the East. *Helden und Liederbuch*, (Hero and Song-Book) contains short pieces.

Frankl's epic poems, *Cristoforo Colombo, Don Juan d'Austria*, and *Der Primator*, confessedly deserve to take a stand among the finest of that class. They mirror forth the spirit of a poet. Grandeur of conception, and elegance of diction, are · discernible throughout.

Herr Frankl has translated into German, several of the lofty creations of Moore and Byron; and also some Servian ballads, under the title of *Gusle*.

The compatriots of Ludwig August Frankl have paid homage to a prolific writer. The volumes, with which his versatility increased the size of modern literature, have found a place, in different versions, in private and public libraries. But every one who has formed an acquaintance with the German language, should seek the original to obtain the instruction and recreation which Frankl's works readily offer.

JULIUS FÜRST.

A dire dispersion has not impaired Israel's mental vigor. Under the most distressing circumstances the intellect has asserted its supremacy. But the growth and expansion of knowledge have been singularly noticeable during the present age. A matchless band of scholars have enlarged the Temple of Fame within late years. We survey the spot, and find Julius Fürst occupying a lofty seat. Thus are we led to relate the following incidents.

Dr. Julius Fürst was born at Zerkowo, in the province of Posen, Prussian Poland, on the 12th of May, 1805. Designed for a Rabbi, he studied the Bible and Talmud with energy and zeal, so that when very young, he had gained an extensive acquaintance with the language of the Scriptures, and with the writings of the Sages. At fifteen, he entered the Berlin gymnasium, whence he passed to the University in 1825. But pecuniary troubles forced him to return home, long before the completion of his studies. To satisfy pressing wants, he accepted the position of teacher in the Jewish school of his native city. But the bigotry of the *Hassidim* and the intolerance of the ultra-Rabbinists made the young man disgusted with his surroundings.

In 1827 Fürst went to Breslau, where he resumed his collegiate course, and pursued theology and Oriental philology.   He removed to Halle in 1839, and listened to the erudite elucidations of Gesenius, Wegscheider, and Tholuck.   Taking up his residence at Leipsic, he gave private instruction until 1839, when his talents were requited by an appointment as lecturer in the University.

A wide field was now open to our scholar, and he made practical use of his learning, by sowing broadcast the seeds of knowledge.   So faithfully did he discharge his duties, giving sure evidences of vast attainments, that his election as a professor followed in 1869.   He filled this post until his death.

Dr. Fürst, while laboring for a livelihood, brought forth his different productions.   These have eminently contributed to enhance Hebrew literature, and they are invaluable to a student, by reason of the variety of essential topics treated.   A passing allusion will have to suffice.   The first part of *Lehrgebäude der Aramäischen Idiome*, on the Aramaic idioms, a work which remained incomplete, appeared in 1835.   From 1837 to 1840, Fürst was engaged upon his *Concordantiæ*, an excellent edition of Buxtorf's Hebrew and Chaldee Concordance, with valuable appendices, in the preparation of which he was greatly assisted by Delitsch.   In 1851 he issued *Hebräisches u. Chaldäisches Handwörterbuch*, (Hebrew and Chaldaic Dictionary) which has been translated into English by Dr. Samuel Davidson.

This work possesses much merit, and the method adopted respecting the roots of words, is generally accepted by scholars. It is a needed addition to Bibliography. *Geschichte des Karäerthums*, (History of the Karaites) came out in 1865; and *Geschichte der Biblischen Literatur und des Jüdisch-Hellenischen Schriftthums*, (History of Biblical Literature, and of Jewish Hellenistic Writings), begun in 1867, was finished in 1870. Dr. Fürst also edited a valuable *Bibliotheca Judaica*, from 1849 to 1863, and he was the author of several other works of minor importance. From 1840 to 1851, he conducted *Der Orient*, a journal devoted to the language, literature, history and antiquities of the Jews.

The entire literary career of Dr. Fürst was a triumph to learning. Not only as a Hebraist, but as an Orientalist and a master of abstruse sciences, the subject of our sketch can worthily be numbered with the Munks, the Renans, the Opperts, and the Lenormants.

The earthly labors of Julius Fürst terminated on the 9th of February, 1873, at Leipsic, in Saxony, Germany.

The above account, though brief, will, it is hoped, fulfil a purpose; that of urging the reader to search into the rich literature of modern Hebrews. Then will he be truly convinced of the debt of gratitude owed to Dr. Fürst, and of the fittingness of holding his memory in profound reverence.

ABRAHAM GEIGER.

Great among the greatest, for originality of thought and masterly ability in treating a variety of subjects, is Abraham Geiger. An imperishable evidence of the depth of his understanding and versatility of his powers, he has left in works upon which scholars will long ponder, not only for the broad knowledge they disclose of Hebrew literature, but also for the insight into Semitic languages that the author affords the student. The many incidents which attended the career of Dr. Geiger, would suffice to justify a notice, though our endeavors will be mainly directed to offer a faint representation of the literary productions which serve as eternal testimonies of his worth.

Dr. Abraham Geiger was born at Frankfort-on-the-Main, on the 24th day of May, 1810. Bible and Talmud formed his chief studies in early life. Afterwards, he attended a Gymnasium, whence he proceeded to the University of Heidelberg, and completed his course at the University of Bonn. At the latter institution, he gained distinction by his essay, " What has Mohammed borrowed from Judaism ?", which was awarded the philosophical prize, and deemed worthy of being published,—as it was in 1833—under the auspices of the Faculty. In this critical dissertation, a thorough searching mind manifests itself.

In 1832 Dr. Geiger received a Rabbinical call from Wiesbaden, which he accepted, and became Rabbi successively at Breslau, in 1838, at his native city, in 1863, and at Berlin, in 1869.

From his very entrance into maturity, Dr. Geiger identified himself with the party designing to reform the Jewish Synagogue, the ritual, and laws and customs. With the history of that movement we have no immediate concern, but it must here be stated, that, although Dr. Geiger favored it and gave it a fresh impetus, he did not sanction an entire divorce from the traditions of the past. He did not cross the boundary beyond which Nihilism rules. The doctrines he propounded brought him, however, as large a share of adherents as of opponents. Maintaining the stand he took with dignity, strengthened in it, no doubt, by his mode of interpreting the written and oral law, he nevertheless refused to become preacher of the Reform Congregation at Berlin, that body having advanced a step farther than what he deemed advisable or practicable.

Dr. Geiger did not attempt to foist his opinions on the community. Rather than act singly, he urged a uniformity, based on the decision of an ecclesiastical court. Accordingly, his influence brought about a convention of Rabbis at Brunswick, in 1844; a second followed at Frankfort, in 1847; and a third at Breslau, some time after. At the conference held

at the last-named city he presided, and the results
of the deliberations led to the adoption of the system now in vogue in many places of Jewish worship.

Frequently was Dr. Geiger obliged to use both
pen and pulpit to shield his views from bitter
attacks. This circumstance, coupled with the fact
that the functions of a Rabbi are onerous, might
have exempted the Doctor from accomplishing aught
else.   Must one not wonder then at the immensity
of his literary labors ?   The subjoined account has
much significance, as a sign of human indefatigability.

From 1835 to 1847 Dr. Geiger edited his *Magazine for Jewish Theology*, one of the ablest expon-
ents of learning, among all publications of that nature throughout Europe.   Suspended awhile, it was
taken up again in 1861, and it continued to appear
until 1874.

But we wish to refer briefly to some of the
Rabbi's multifarious works.   Besides numerous articles on Rabbinical literature, contributed to Hebrew
periodicals, and other writings for papers, circulated
in the vernacular tongue, he adorned the Journal of
the German Oriental Society, with those learned
delineations of his pen, which specially present to
view Syriac lexicography and Samaritan literature.
Concerning his capacity in the latter subject, Dr.
Adolph Neubauer remarks, " he was, doubtless, the
highest living authority."   Great, indeed, must have

been the merits of the man, whose labors so eminent a scholar illimitably prizes. His acknowledged abilities as a Talmudist, won him the respect and friendship of *savants*.

Monographs on Maimonides, on the exegetical school of the Rabbis in the north of France, and on other Jewish celebrities of the Middle Ages, on Elias del Medigo and Leon de Modena, were issued at different periods. His work on the Karaite "Isaac Troki, the Apologist of Judaism, at the close of the Sixteenth Century," was published in 1853. In a "Translation of the Divan of the Castilians of Abul Hassan Jehudah Halevy," with a commentary and a biographical notice, and in "Solomon ibn Gabirol," Geiger evinced his poetic genius and talent as an interpreter of some of the grand effusions of those noted Jewish bards of Spain. His production, in two volumes, on the defence of the Israelites against the attacks of Christians in the Mediæval times, wherein he brings to light a vast deal of the rich literature of those days, is deserving of a perusal by all who value the efforts of our heroes of the past. "A Manual of the Dialect of the Mishna" teems with erudite observations, and it is a necessary companion in the study of the writings of the Sages. "Judaism and its History," a course of lectures of a highly-instructive character, was presented in an English garb, by the late Dr. Maurice Mayer. But

Geiger's *chef d'œuvre* is *Urschrift*, the product of
twenty years' labor, it being a critical investigation
of the Bible, which came out in 1857. The ideas held
forth were adversely commented on by the learned
of the opposite school. The author was, for some
time, compelled to face a raging storm. While the
work is confessedly the best from the pen of that
writer, it is said to advance more radical opinions
than had been anticipated. Dr. Neubauer observes:
"The chief merit of Geiger's researches in regard to
this branch of study, is his powerful analysis of obscure Talmudical passages." This assertion cannot
be illustrated by quotations, but the above account
may convey a fair idea of the activity of a man, who,
to repeat ourself, we must say, was great among the
greatest.

Dr. Geiger died at Berlin, Prussia, on the 25th
of October, 1874.

A new edition of his works, together with his
life and letters, has just been issued by his son, Dr.
Ludwig Geiger, whose acumen and skill as a writer
are well-known, and justly appreciated in literary
circles.

GOLDSMID.

Prior to the rise of the Goldsmid family, the influence of the German-Jewish community in England
was confined in narrow bounds. The Portuguese

Jews, being the first settlers in Great Britain, after the revocation of the inhuman edict of banishment, proclaimed and enforced by Edward I., soon rose to high standing, and the power they wielded in religious affairs became a recognized fact. The German Hebrews did not establish themselves in sufficient numbers, even to erect a place of worship, until the reign of William III; and, for many years, few could be found in their ranks, qualified to act as representatives, and set forth their claims.

———

AARON GOLDSMID, a Dutch merchant, came with his family to England in 1765, and there took up a permanent residence. The lively interest evinced in matters pertaining to his faith, brought Mr. Goldsmid into prominence. He had four sons, the eldest of whom, George, was admitted a partner with his father, in the firm of Aaron Goldsmid & Son. Asher, the second son, joined Mr. Mocatta, and established the co-partnership of Mocatta & Goldsmid, who became bullion-brokers to the Bank of England. The two other sons, Benjamin and Abraham, began business as brokers, and the former made a trip through different parts of Europe, seeking into the condition of his fellow-believers, and distributing of his means, with munificence, to the needy. Aaron Goldsmid died some time after Benjamin's return, and his death was attended with circumstances of a very peculiar nature, which we forbear mentioning, lest we transcend our limits.*

BENJAMIN AND ABRAHAM GOLDSMID, gradually enhanced the reputation of their banking-house, until at length it became one of the principal firms in the British Kingdom, business being conducted on an extensive scale. Benjamin Goldsmid wedded a lady with a dowry of £100,000, which, of course, materially added to the credit of the house. Large sums of money continually passed through the hands of the Goldsmids, and their transactions amounted annually to millions. Within a short period, they occupied the first place in the Stock Exchange. Both brothers displayed actual genius in their monetary schemes. When a severe crisis occurred in the Money Market, in 1793, by which some of the oldest houses fell to pieces, the firm of Goldsmid lost but £50.

Both Benjamin and Abraham lived in grand style, but were as much noted for their charity and beneficence, which flowed in abundance to the poor of every denomination. They founded and supported asylums and other institutions, and commanded the

*See Picciotto's "Sketches of Anglo-Jewish History," pp. 245–248.

respect of all classes. Some pecuniary embarrassments, however, occasioned depression of spirit. Benjamin Goldsmid, while laboring under a fit of despondency, took his own life, on the 15th of April, 1808, at the age of fifty-five, and his brother, Abraham, died from a similiar cause; on the 28th of September, 1810. There was no special reason, at the time, for Benjamin to act in this wise, but Abraham, who had met with serious losses, on account of the reduction in the price of stocks, was called upon to negotiate Exchequer Bills, to the amount of £500,000, placed in his hands by the East India Company. The payment had been fixed for Friday, of the date last mentioned. Unprepared for the exigency, his honesty of character made him shrink from facing, what he considered, a sure disgrace. And yet, it is said, that, on that very Friday morning, a relative hastened to his home, with the good news that the funds for the East India Company were ready. Too late: Abraham Goldsmid had committed the fatal deed.

These two painful occurrences had, at their different periods, considerable effect on the Market, and the press abounded with eulogies of the deceased, whose kind-heartedness thousands were made to enjoy.

We have spoken thus briefly of the early members of the Goldsmid family, in order to reserve space for those who lived in this eventful century. Their indefatigable labors claim attention. Before proceeding, however, we must acknowledge, in justice to those already named, that to them belongs the merit of having opened a wide field for their successors. But it was left to Sir I. L. Goldsmid, and his noble son, Sir F. H. Goldsmid, to revive the glories of their house, and shed additional lustre on the name they bore.

SIR ISAAC LYON GOLDSMID, BART., son of Mr. Asher Goldsmid, and nephew of Benjamin and Abraham Goldsmid, was born at London, England, in 1778. He gained an education at a school in Finsbury Square. An ardent student, he became a fluent Latin scholar and a fair mathematician. He also cultivated Jewish theology, philosophy and political science.

Mr. Goldsmid entered as a partner in the firm of Mocatta & Goldsmid, to which we have alluded before. Though at first not successful in his financial undertakings, he eventually raised the standard of the business, and amassed a large fortune. Mr. Goldsmid lent his valuable assistance to the promotion of industrial projects, and co-operated in improving the moral and educational condition of the masses. He took an active part in the founding of colleges and other educational institutions. His philanthropy was as far-reaching as that of his uncles, and he dispensed with an open hand to the unfortunate.

The operations of the house grew fast, and loans were advanced to Portugal, Brazil and Turkey. Mr. Goldsmid received visits from political exiles, among them Prince Louis Napoleon, afterward Napoleon III., though the English banker never gave his support to the French Emperor. Mr. Goldsmid was created a Baronet of the United Kingdom, and shortly after, a Knight of the Tower and Sword of Portugal. Subsequently the King of the last-mentioned country, conferred on him the title of Baron da Palmeira, with a small estate. He accepted these honors, more from a desire to uphold his people than for their real worth.

Sir I. L. Goldsmid's labors for the recognition of Jewish rights in Great Britain were untiring. He worked arduously as a member of the Board of Deputies, and employed his influence, his time and wealth, to serve his co-religionists in every possible way. Happily, he lived to witness the consummation of what many years' unceasing perseverance had wrought. Mr. Goldsmid retired from business when sixty years old, and made a tour through France, Italy and Germany, for the benefit of his health. Returning to England, his activity was restless till within a few years of his demise, which took place in 1859, at a very old age. During his whole life, Mr. Goldsmid remained a strict conformant to Jewish observances, and his death deprived the Hebrews of an earnest advocate, and England of an upright citizen, who had contributed a large share to promote the interests of her inhabitants.

———

SIR FRANCIS HENRY GOLDSMID, BART., M. P., second son of Sir Isaac Lyon Goldsmid, was born at London, England, on May 1st, 1808. After receiving careful instruction, he was called to the Bar in Hilary term 1833, being the first Jew who ever obtained that distinction in Great Britain. Mr. Goldsmid practiced for a short time in the Court of Chancery, but gradually relinquished his connection with legal matters. This action created general regret, for Mr. Goldsmid's forensic career had been exceedingly brilliant, and had he continued, he might have soon become one of the brightest ornaments of the profession. At all events, he paved the way for others of his own race, who have since attained the highest position at the Bar.

Mr. Goldsmid won an enviable name during the agitation for the removal of Jewish disabilities. He wrote several able pamphlets in behalf of the cause. One, entitled "Remarks on the Civil Disabilities of the Jews," was published in 1830, and another, "Reply to the Argument Against the Enfranchisement of the Jews," in 1848.

Among the numerous offices filled by Sir Francis

Goldsmid were those of a Bencher of Lincoln's Inn, a Deputy-Lieutenant of Berkshire, a Justice of the Peace for Berkshire and Gloucestershire, a Fellow of the Royal Geographical Society and a Vice-President of the Anglo-Jewish Association. In 1860 he was elected to Parliament from Reading, which constituency he worthily represented to his death, and never lost an opportunity to defend the rights of his brethren. Sir Francis succeeded to all his father's titles, among them that of the Baron of the Kingdom of Portugal.

The subject of this sketch devoted a large portion of his life to succor the afflicted and the poverty-stricken of all creeds. He contributed to sustain societies and corporations of various natures. His staunch adherence to the prescriptions of Judaism is another testimony of the nobility of his character. Sir Francis died, the victim of a lamentable railroad accident, on May 2d, 1878, thus closing a career, signalized by the practice of rare virtues.

It may be noticed that the different members of the Goldsmid family, morally bear a strong resemblance to those of the Rothschild. In one instance like the other, individual exertions raised comparative obscurity to high eminence; and in

both, princely liberality to relieve suffering humanity, and further the world's progress, gained a renown which has spread far and wide.

HIRSCH GRAETZ.*

A few months ago—it was on August 10th,
1879,—there gathered at Breslau a large number of
Rabbis and laymen, in honor of a scholar who has
done more, perhaps, to advance Hebrew culture,
and to acquaint the literary world with Jewish
thought, than any living representative of his race.
If Leopold Zunz was the earliest pioneer, Graetz
has been the most successful worker in unfolding
the treasures of Jewish history to the reading-
public of his time. It was the celebration of the
25th anniversary of the Jewish Theological Seminary, and of Dr. Graetz's connection with that Institution. On the occasion he became the recipient of
distinguished marks of esteem, in which his admirers
and disciples, in Germany, Austria, France, Den-
mark, Holland, England, and America alike joined.

Prof. Dr. Hirsch Graetz was born at Xions, in the
Duchy of Posen, Prussian Poland, on the 5th of November, 1817. He shared, as did many other famous
scholars, the hard struggles of a needy *Bachur*. Early
initiated into the study of the Talmud, his special

* This sketch is from the able pen of Dr. Abram S. Isaacs.

literary taste was fortunately not hampered by the pilpulistic method then in vogue. Trained for the Rabbinate, he displayed no great aptitude for preaching, and he was engaged as private teacher by Samson Raphael Hirsch, then Rabbi of Nicolsburg, Moravia, to whom the grateful friend dedicated his first work, " Gnosticism and Judaism " (Krotoschin: 1846). It is noteworthy, that in after days Hirsch, the present venerable Rabbi of Frankfort, and Graetz, the Seminary Professor, occupied opposing stand-points in the controversy which agitated German Judaism.

The appearance of his maiden-work, gave Graetz at once a name in the realms of Jewish literature, and inquiries were rapidly made as to the brilliant writer, who was to earn for some years a scanty livelihood at Berlin, giving lessons at a few *groschen* an hour. The style, the thought, the erudition exhibited in that little work of one hundred and thirty-two pages, which has not yet become antiquated, were full of promise of the future. His contributions, too, principally to Frankel's magazine, in 1845, 1846, 1848, 1852, 1853 and 1854, on such themes as the Septuagint in the Talmud, introductions to the Talmud, chronology and topography of the Talmud, and particularly his Jewish historical studies, which early displayed the bent of his mind, secured the writer so wide a reputation that on the opening of the Seminary in 1854, he was selected by Dr. Frankel to be Professor of Jewish history and Bible Exegesis.

His twenty-five years of activity have been blessed with the richest fruits. Working in constant harmony with Frankel,—whose views he shared, and reverence for whom often checked his natural impulsiveness—he has never failed to leave the impress of his strong individuality on all the young men with whom he has come in contact. Not restricting his subjects of instruction to history and the Bible, but teaching Talmud as well, with all the side-lights of comparative philology, archæology and historical illustration, he, with Frankel, has given the Seminary its world-wide reputation, and he still seizes all opportunities to influence it for good.

It was in 1852 that Graetz began to issue his famous " History of the Jews," from the earliest times to our day. In 1876 the series was finished, in eleven volumes, for which a second and third edition have been called. Single volumes have been published in English, French and Hebrew. Of this work, in whose preparation Graetz consulted not only the principal libraries in Europe, but also made a special trip to Palestine, it may safely be asserted that, as a whole, it is one of the most brilliant and comprehensive histories that have ever appeared. While critics have fastened upon an expression here, and a view there, with a relentless grasp, and accused Graetz of violent partisanship and flimsy theorizing,—no one has refused to award high praise for the unremitting industry, the extensive erudition, the broad sympathies, and the marvelous unravelling of characters and circumstances, joined to a glowing and picturesque style, which have won for Graetz the title of father of Jewish history, and have given him a place next to Mommsen, Curtius, Ranke, and other leading historians. A thinker of decided views, and blunt in their expression, he has his detractors, who charge him with prejudices and distortions. But he stands out like a giant, among the host of pigmies and pilferers who raise an outcry against him. Out of the mist of dim tradition he has lifted the Jewish people and placed them, with all their faults and virtues, before the reader. He has frankly shown that as men suffering degradation and intolerance, hypocrisy, narrowness, and ignorance ruled some of the Hebrews; but as heroes, filled with a divine ideal, the heart of our race throbbed with resolute effort, undying courage, reverence for the household and the house of God, and a desire for knowledge in its best sense.

The production of his History did not exhaust Graetz's literary powers; it only spurred them on to further endeavors. As fruit, in part, of his lectures in connection with the University of Breslau—at which he was appointed an Honorary Professor, by the King of Prussia—and at the Seminary—he has published exe-

getical works on *Koheleth, Shir-ha-Shirim*, and smaller
brochures on subjects connected with history and the
Bible, while his essays in Dr. Frankel's magazine, conducted for some years past by himself, number more
than one hundred, and stretch themselves over the entire field of Jewish literature.   Add to the prodigious
amount of work thus displayed, the fact that he has
lectured, by invitation, in Berlin, Posen, Hamburg,
Frankfort, Pesth, and Lemberg ; that he has travelled
to Palestine ; that he takes an active interest in the
Alliance Israélite Universelle ; that he lectures two
hours daily at the Seminary, and two or three hours
weekly at the University; and edits a magazine besides ;—and some idea may be formed of the Titanic
strength required to perform with unvarying ability
the duties of his position.

Age has not led Dr. Graetz to relax from his work.
Loving to his friends, a tender husband, and an affec-
tionate father, the idol of his home circle, whose pleas-
ures he participates in as though he were a child,—so
simple and unassuming is his nature,—Graetz is a
merciless antagonist of hypocrisy and ignorance, and
gives blow for blow.   For years yet, may he be spared
in continued health and usefulness.

REBECCA GRATZ.

What can effect nobler ends than an unrestrained exercise of the good qualities in human nature? Where the mind and the heart work in unison, blessed results alone must follow. This fact has been clearly exemplified in the lives of men whose names have reached posterity, surrounded with a halo of sanctity. Yet woman bears the palm in whatsoever calls into requisition thoughtful tenderness, merciful endurance, and calmness, amid irritating causes. Truly it has been said, that woman is the crowning work of the Creator. See what comfort she gives the sorrowful, how she ministers to the sick; mark the hopes she breathes into the oppressed, and the peace she restores to the agitated. There stands the princess of philanthropy, Florence Nightingale; Lady Judith Montefiore and Lady Burdett-Coutts closely follow her footsteps. The lady, to whose character attention is drawn, was not so widely known, but the inestimable services she rendered, in a comparatively narrow sphere, have endeared her memory to many, specially to her co-religionists.

Rebecca Gratz was born at Philadelphia, on March 4th, 1782, of a wealthy and intelligent family. She received such an education as was accessible at the time. But her innate faculties soon shone forth. Very handsome, most graceful and polished, possessing abilities above the common average, she attracted and retained warm friends. She did not, however, allow flattery or praise to damage the traits for which she was distinguished. Unostentatious demeanor ever remained a noticeable characteristic in Miss Gratz.

Strict in her adherence to the ancestral religion, she went in quest of opportunities for assisting in the spread of knowledge among her fellow-believers. The earnest Jewess perceived that, to bring the young together, and familiarize them with some essentials in the faith, would be productive of permanent good, and she was the first to carry out the idea. She founded the Hebrew Sunday School of Philadelphia in 1838, the oldest institution of the kind in America, and served as its Superintendent and First Directress for a period of thirty-two years. The Female Hebrew Benevolent Society, the Jewish Foster Home, the Fuel Society, and the Sewing Society reckoned Miss Gratz among their originators, and she held the office of Secretary of the first-named association for several decades.

But though Miss Gratz considered it a duty to direct her utmost efforts to the furtherance of every object of a Jewish nature, she was broad-minded in her views. In the dispensing of her benevolence, she recognized neither sect nor creed. Gentiles as well as Hebrews were made the recipients of the same

kindness. At the Philadelphia Orphan Asylum, the
Widows' Asylum, and wherever she labored, the zeal
exhibited met with the hearty appreciation of her
colleagues, and the gratitude of her beneficiaries.

But to the people whose descent and doctrines
formed her pride, Rebecca Gratz was invaluable.
For she offered them a bright example, not only by
good acts, but by a piety almost rare in one of her
condition and social standing. Never, throughout
her entire career, would she sanction the least viola-
tion of the law and precepts. Regular in her attend-
ance at the Synagogue, devout in worshiping her
Maker, she imparted to the beholders a feeling of
awe for the house of prayer and the divine service.

The attractiveness of Miss Gratz's conversational
powers, and her dignified mien, contributed to create
around her a very choice circle. She became acquainted with Washington Irving, Sully, the artist,
and other celebrities. But the respect shown her
by Christians, did not tend to lessen a whit her attachment to Judaism. Many and severe may have
been her trials to hold fast to principles, but she
arose above them all.

It is related that Washington Irving, while paying
a visit to Sir Walter Scott, at his home in Scotland,
learnt from the latter that his novel of "Ivanhoe"
was in course of preparation, and that a Jewish
female character would be introduced. Whereupon

the former remarked, that he knew of a lady who would suit admirably. He proceeded to describe, in glowing terms, Rebecca Gratz, her acquirements and suavity of manners, and her unyielding devotion to Israel's God. Scott attentively listened to the interesting narrative, and when he had finished "Ivanhoe," he sent the first copy to Irving, inquiring whether the "Rebecca" he had pictured, compared well with the pattern given.

Miss Gratz, in the pursuit of her educational designs, induced the writing and compilation of text-books for instruction in the Jewish faith. The Rev. Isaac Leeser dedicated his catechism to her, as a mark of esteem and veneration for a Jewess so exemplary, and so eager to promote religious knowledge.

To the end of her days, Rebecca Gratz followed the same righteous course, "doing justice, loving mercy, and walking humbly with her God." On August 27th, 1869, at the ripe age of eighty-seven years, her pure life was brought to a close in the city of her birth. "Give her of the fruit of her hands, and let her own works praise her in the gates."

JACQUES FRANÇOIS FROMENTAL ÉLIE HALEVY.

France occupies an enviable position for the height she has reached in literature, art and science. Specially in the last-named branch of knowledge she has excelled many enlightened nations. But the products of her musical genius have also added considerably to the fame she has won. Of truly great composers France has given but few, yet those she can claim, have so clearly evinced superior abilities that they have enhanced the reputation of their country. Persons possessed of a musical training will agree that attractive operas, more than classical, are in demand at the present day, and that they always meet with unqualified success. In the production of such operas, the French have surely come up to the standard. It cannot, however, be denied that the subject of this sketch, while fully alive to the requirements of the times, offered the world compositions well worthy of a great master.

Jacques François Fromental Élie Halevy was born at Paris, France, on the 27th of May, 1799. At the age of ten years, his parents placed him under musical instruction, at the conservatory. Cherubini, his favorite tutor, ever remained his warm friend.

Halevy, when only twenty, obtained the first prize

for composition at the Academy of Fine Arts, an honor which entitled him to a pensionary residence of two years at Rome, and whereof he availed himself. Returning to France in 1822, he for five years in vain besought the managers to put upon the stage, either his grand opera *Pygmalion*, or his comic opera *Les Deux Pavillons*. In 1827, however, his one-act opera *L'Artisan* was brought out with moderate success at the *Théatre Feydeau*. In 1829 his three-act opera *Clari* was produced at the *Théatre Italien* and well received, since Malibran assumed the principal role. A grand ballet in three acts, *Manon Lescaut*, the text written by Scribe, made its appearance in 1830.

Halevy's masterpiece, *La Juive*, came forth in 1835, and by it he achieved a wide-spread fame. Replete with charming music and depth of sentiment, it has affixed to the name of the author the title of *Maestro*. To this day that ever popular opera holds the stage. It was first represented at the Royal Academy of Music, and it has been heard at the principal opera-houses throughout the world.

Of some of the other productions of our composer that added to his celebrity, are: *L'Eclair*, *La Reine de Chypre*, *Charles VI.*, *Les Mousquetaires de la Reine*, *Le val d'Andorre*, *Le Juif Errant*, *Jaquarita*, and *La Magicienne*. It is needless to say that all of Halevy's operas have left a profound impression of his musical skill and the beauty of his melody. He wrote more than thirty operas, five or six of which are constantly set before the public.

Halevy also distinguished himself as a graceful writer on musical subjects. His *Leçons de lecture musicale* has been adopted as a text-book in the schools of .Paris. There were published besides, *Souvenirs et Portraits, études sur les Beaux-Arts*, and, as a posthumous work, *Derniers Souvenirs et Portraits*.

Halevy succeeded Fétis, as professor of composition at the conservatory, and perpetual secretary of the Academy of Fine Arts. He died at Nice, France, on the 17th of March, 1862. In recognition of his valuable services, and untiring energy to further the progress of musical science, the French Government bestowed upon his widow an annuity of 5,000 francs.

Of the Halevy family, Leon, brother of the composer, was a cultured author. He wrote a number of learned works, among them an introduction to *Opinions littéraires, philosophiques et industrielles*, of Saint-Simon, to whose principles he had become a votary; *Fables; Fables Nouvelles;* and *La Gréce Tragique*, in three volumes. Some of these productions won prizes from the Academy.

Leon Halevy held several literary stations under

the French Government. It may be of importance to mention that he issued *Résumé de l'Histoire des Juifs*, (A Summary of Jewish History) in two volumes; a translation of " Macbeth ; " and several tragedies and dramatic pieces.

His son, Ludovic, is also known as a dramatist. He has written the *libretti* for some of the *bouffe* operas of Offenbach and others. Of his recent works are the comedy *Tricochet et Cacolet*, the vaudeville *Réveillon*, and a collection of equivocal sketches, including *Madame et Monsieur Cardinal*.

The Halevys are, doubtless, entitled to a more detailed delineation of their splendid endeavors, especially the most noted who enriched, by his genius, the soul-captivating art. But the subject presents singular difficulties to non-adepts, and it has, therefore, to be left incomplete. Awarding to one the glory all have accorded to him, the reader is referred to the printed works of the two of whom a passing mention was made, so that an unbiased opinion may be formed of their respective merits.

JOSEPH HALEVY.

Remarkable is the determination with which some prosecute their plans. Nothing seems to deter them. The severer the obstacles, the greater the perseverance. Men of that calibre launch into perplexing subjects, and force intricacies to yield to their mighty will. A moral courage they muster which would be called heroic, if the world had learnt to apply terms in a truthful sense. An instance of that heroism is given in the archæologist and traveler, Joseph Halevy. We propose to offer a faint outline of his arduous, but successful labors.

Joseph Halevy was born at Adrianople, Turkey in Europe, on the 15th of September, 1827. The study of languages appears to have possessed an extraordinary attraction for the boy. Fitted by nature for it, he laid down as a design, which he must execute, the acquisition of Semitic tongues, their dialects and literature. This became the polar star of his life, whereby he was, · indeed, led safely to regions where few had ventured to set foot.

For a lengthy period, Halevy superintended con-gregational schools, first at his native city, and af-terwards at Bucharest, Roumania. Meanwhile he tried to earn a name, inditing Hebrew poems and articles which appeared in journals, published in the sacred tongue.

But M. Halevy's most effective activity dates from 1867. In that year he went to France, where he has since resided. The *Alliance Israélite Universelle* had long felt the necessity of learning more than what had been reported about the Falashas, as the Jews of Abyssinia are called. Who better than

Halevy could procure the desired information? Not only linguistic attainments, but a disposition for what savored of the romantic had admirably fitted him for the mission. He was therefore charged with it. He was to study the characteristics and habits, the religious tenets and practices of those distant Hebrews. The result of his investigations, as reported to the Central Committee on July 30th, 1868, is of profound interest. He details the condition and customs of that wonderful people, preserved to Judaism after astounding vicissitudes.*

In 1869, at the request of the French Minister of Instruction, M. Halevy set out for Yemen. Six hundred and eighty-six inscriptions he deciphered in that ancient spot in Arabia.

Of the writings of Joseph Halevy there are: "The Language in which the book of Enoch was Compiled"—a work he translated from Ethiopian into Hebrew; "New Suggestions about the Inscriptions at Marseilles;" "Studies on the Sabeans;" "Letter to M. D'Abbadie on the Language of Mahri or Ehkili;" "Report of an Archæological Voyage to Yemen;" "The Language of the Falashas;" "Miscellany of Semitic Archæology and Epigraphy;" "Critical Researches into the Origin of Babylonian Civilization;" and "Prayers of the Falashas, or Jews of Abyssinia."

*See *The Occident and American Jewish Advocate*, of November, 1868.

The names suffice to point out the abilities exercised in presenting a complete analysis of the subjects. They significantly tell of the merit due to unflagging energy, and they claim for him, who brought to light what had long been hidden, distinguished honors in the republic of letters.

NUMA EDWARD HARTOG.

Not as a writer did the subject of the present sketch gain distinction, but as a youth who sanctified his talents, by devoting them to the exaltation of his revered belief. The lectures and essays he delivered were of no mean order, but his good name rests firmly upon the exceptional line of conduct pursued at Colleges and Universities he had been allowed to frequent.

Numa Edward Hartog was born at London, England, on May 20th, 1846. His father, Monsieur Alphonse Hartog, then Professor of French at the Jews' College, and his mother, Mrs. Marion Hartog—widely known for her various works, among which " The Romance of Jewish History," issued in conjunction with her sister, Mrs. Levetus, " The Siege of Jotapata," and " The Prophet's Daughter," deserve special mention—superintended their child's education.

It is readily seen that young Hartog enjoyed a great advantage in the nature of his descent. He had sprung from a stock of more than ordinary worth. Home training and social surroundings must needs have nurtured and fostered latent qualities. The boy first attended a commercial school, where his inborn capacities began to clearly develop. The evidence of what lay hidden within and was destined to unfold in a splendid manner, is a certificate received when only eight years of age. This step led to a higher one. · He obtained a diploma from the College of Preceptors, as a testimony of proficiency and assiduity.

Shortly after that event, the lad entered the University College School. There he soon became a conspicuous figure, having won a high prize for signal advancement in mathematics. Young Hartog passed into the college proper, and the certificates of his progress, and the praises awarded to his diligence and devotion to learning, were flattering in the extreme. "Onward and upward," became the student's motto. It was not personal vanity that impelled him, but the desire to reach a point, never before attained by an Israelite in the United Kingdom; he aimed at consigning to oblivion, illiberal laws against his fellow-believers. Examined for matriculation at the University of London, his familiarity with the classics, not less than with mathematics, earned for him tokens of distinction. At the first *Bachelor of Arts'* examination, honors were conferred on the young Israelite, by reason of his knowledge of several foreign languages, in addition to that of mathematics and the classics. But it was at the second B. A. examination, so searching and thorough, that he acquitted himself nobly. He created universal amazement by carrying off the prize in Physiology, and scholarships in other branches.

In 1865 Numa Hartog entered Trinity College, Cambridge. In his second year, he was elected Foundation Scholar. In 1869, however, he achieved the crowning reward of all his endeavors, viz : that of being elevated to the position of Senior Wrangler, a height no Israelite had yet reached.

The London *Jewish Chronicle* of February 5th, 1869, thus remarks:—"A Senior Wrangler always stands alone. He is never found bracketed with another so near as not to be separable from him. . . . . The telegraph has flashed the news through the Kingdom, because it ranks as an event, the profound significancy of which is recognized on all hands." The Jew had scaled the wall of prejudice, and torn it down. The degree of *Bachelor of Arts* was conferred on young Hartog, in the following form : " *Auctoritate mihi commissa admitto te ad titulum Baccalaurei in Artibus designate,*" the objectionable words " *In nomine Patris et Filii et Spiritus Sancti,*" being omitted. With the same propriety, the administering of the thirty-nine articles of faith, to which as a Hebrew he could not subscribe, was set aside.

Hartog returned to London, after having been placed second for the Smith prize, and began to study law. While thus engaged, he was appointed to an office in the Treasury, which he held for some time, but finally resigned. He lectured before various associations among those of his own creed, and manifested a lively interest in the mental improvement of all his co-religionists. As a member of the Council of the Jews' College, and as one of the Honorary Secretaries of the Society of Hebrew Literature, he discharged his duties faithfully, and exerted himself to extend the usefulness of both organizations. Pious he was, and anxious to contribute by his example to enkindle a sentiment of love and reverence for the observances of the ancestral faith.

Scarce had the flower blossomed, and begun to emit its sweet fragrance, than it withered and was cut down. Numa Edward Hartog fell a victim to a virulent disease, on June 19th, 1871, after a short existence of twenty-five years. He had trodden the path once beaten by the illustrious Philoxene Luzzatto and Arthur Lumley Davids, and, like them, was too early removed from a sphere of most promising labors.

ISAAC HAYS.

While it must be conceded that Europe has set the foundation-stone to the structure of modern medical science, America has furnished more than her share of builders. Not quite so much, perhaps, in the theoretical department, but in the practical, our country has certainly elevated that edifice to a lofty pinnacle. An unbroken line of stupendous achievements can be unfolded to view, both in the clinical and the surgical school. Among physicians whose renown is enduring for invaluable services, reflecting lustre on the profession, Isaac Hays deservedly claims honorable mention.

Isaac Hays, M. D., was born at Philadelphia, on July 5th, 1796. After receiving elementary instruction, he attended the University of Pennsylvania, and graduated from the Department of Arts in 1816, and from the Medical school in 1820. He studied under Dr. Nathaniel Chapman, and began his career as a general practitioner. Though not limited to any specialty, he soon obtained a wide reputation as an oculist, which circumstance alone, speaks volumes for his skill, since he had mastered a knowledge, by which he could cure the ailments of the most delicate of human organs.

But besides a large practice, Dr. Hays devoted a considerable portion of his time to literary matters. His connection with the *American Journal of the Medical Sciences*, dates from February, 1827.   He continued on its staff for a period of fifty-two years, making him, therefore, at his death, the oldest living editor in the United States.   The paper originally called the *Philadelphia Journal of Medical and Physical Sciences*, started in 1820, was given the name of the *American Journal of the Medical Sciences*, when Dr. Hays assumed entire control, after the retirement of Dr. Goodman.   In 1869 Dr. Hays associated with him, his son, Dr. I. Minis Hays, who now edits the periodical.   That the Doctor's journalistic efforts have been successful may be proven from the fact that, in 1843, he established a monthly, entitled the *Medical News*, and, in 1874, the *Monthly Abstract of Medical Science*.   The motto of the *Journal* when the Doctor first took charge of it, was "What does the world yet owe to American physicians or surgeons?" a theme often discussed with much vigor in its editorial columns.

In addition to these duties, Dr. Hays edited Hall's edition of "Wilson's American Ornithology," in eight volumes, published in 1828; "Hoblyn's Dictionary of Medical Terms," in 1846; "Lawrence on Diseases of the Eye," in 1847; and "Arnott's Elements of Physics," in 1848. He also attended regularly the meetings of a vast number of medical and scientific societies, being among the founders or directors of many, and the surgeon and visiting physician to several hospitals.

The Doctor was a prominent member of the American Philosophical Society, and of the Academy of Natural Sciences. In the latter institution, he filled the office of President, from 1865–'9. Very active in the Philadelphia College of Physicians, a valued member of the Franklin Institute, and the oldest at his demise, energetic on the staff of Will's Eye Hospital, and one of the principal originators of the American Medical Association, his usefulness was clearly perceptible. For the last-named, he composed a code of ethics, which inculcated the relations of the medical profession to each other, and to the profession at large, and which has been adopted by every State and county medical society in the Union.

Dr. Hays' fame was by no means confined to the United States. The Philadelphia physician became known in Europe, and of the numerous organizations to which he belonged, were the Royal Society for Northern Antiquities of Copenhagen, the Medical Society of Hamburg, and the *Université D'Ophthalmologie*, of Paris.

Among those whose acquaintance Dr. Hays enjoyed, were such noted persons as Horace Binney, William M. Meredith, John Sergeant, General George Cadwalader, Dr. Caspar Wistar, John K. Kane, Henry

C. Carey, Dr. George B. Wood and Prof. Bates.   The
lamented poet and scholar, William Cullen Bryant,
alluding to one of Dr. Hays' recent works, in an
editorial, in the New York *Evening Post*, in 1875,
observed, that, next to himself, the Doctor was the
oldest living editor in continuous service in America.

Not the least of the merits of Dr. Hays, was the
gentleness with which he discharged his professional
functions.   On April 12th, 1879, an exceptional
career of·eighty-three years closed, and both the
people and the press attested to the moral qualities
of a Philadelphian, rich with intellectual gifts.

PHINEAS MENDEL HEILPRIN.

Within late years, many of the brightest stars in
the Jewish horizon have disappeared from view, leaving a ·void to be deeply deplored. All that love
Hebrew literature must sincerely hope that the remaining few of a glorious band of Israel's scholars
will long be spared to elevate their brethren before
the world. It is our purpose to set forth a. short
account of the life of one endowed with mental excellencies. He never attained the distinction due to
his superior talents, because real modesty and an
unyielding attachment to religious truths, made him
shrink from a notoriety to which principles are at
times sacrificed.

Phineas Mendel Heilprin was born at Lublin, Russian Poland, in November, 1801. He belonged to a cultured and pious family. As customary with the Polish Jews, he devoted himself, almost from infancy, to the study of the Talmud. This course he pursued for several years, scarcely applying himself to aught else. But after a time he took to other books, particularly the writings of Maimonides, whose views he adopted, as a guide in thinking and acting. He subsequently studied the works of Aristotle, Plato, Mendelssohn, Kant, Fichte and other philosophers, and they contributed largely in giving the proper bent to his thoughts. Lessing, however, was his great favorite. Established in a small but comparatively flourishing town of Russian Poland as a wool merchant and cloth manufacturer, he devoted a large portion of his time to reading, to learned conversation, and the education of his children.

Heilprin became attached to the Sephardic school, which he considered the only true exponent of Judaism, and he freely criticized the doctrines of the French and German Rabbis of the Middle Ages, whom he charged with slavish adherence to the text and words, instead of the spirit, of the Talmud and Scriptures. Believing the Talmud to be badly disfigured by clerical errors and interpolations, he labored to purify and harmonize the original through emendations suggested by his inquiring mind, and in these endeavors he evinced erudition, ingenuity and boldness. Nor did he refrain from similar attempts in regard to the Bible. He soon formed, thereby, an acquaintance with well-known *savants*, as Zunz, Geiger, Frankel and Rapoport, carrying on with the latter a learned correspondence. As much as he esteemed the honored Chief Rabbi of Prague, just as strong and undisguised was his contempt for some of the German preachers of Reform. The notions they disseminated soon led him into a hot contest. In 1845 he came forth with a Hebrew pamphlet, entitled "Responses to Men of Evil," containing thirteen letters, principally directed against Dr. Holdheim. Heilprin did not measure words when attacking those whom he styled "false prophets" and "hypocrites." The work which, like all his writings, appeared anonymously, was extensively and fairly reviewed by the historian, Dr. Jost, in Fürst's *Orient*. Shortly after, Heilprin published his "Touchstone" and "Good Sense," works in which he exhibited specimens of his critical attempts in dealing with the mediæval writings, and he sharply assailed Geiger, whom he charged with being the foremost representative of a movement more apt to destroy than to reform and purify Judaism. He also prepared an attack on Prof. Luzzatto, in which he defended Maimonides from the aspersions of the Italian author.

Heilprin wrote all his productions in Hebrew, a

language which he handled with masterly skill, and, when the subject allowed it, with admirable elegance. He was, however, generally inclined to blend Biblical sentences with Talmudical phrases. All the treasures hidden in "the sea of the Talmud" were not only known to him, but he could always apply them with facility. He would recite, by heart, entire passages as fluently and accurately as though he read them from a book. Rigorously strict in his religious obser-vances, but philosophically independent in his views, he never allowed his convictions to waver. Judaism, in its pure, unadulterated form, as he understood it, was his ideal of purity; his teacher of the love of God and man; hence his vehement opposition to inno-vations which he believed detrimental to its preser-vation.

In his political opinions, Heilprin was inclined to radicalism. Growing Russian oppression determined him, in 1842, to quit Poland, and he emigrated with his household to Hungary. When, after the failure of the revolution of 1848, despotism had fully estab-lished itself there, he left for America, arriving in 1859. All his family had preceded him in this second emigration for the sake of liberty. He resided suc-cessively in several cities of the United States, and finally took up his abode in Washington, where, on the 30th of January, 1863, he breathed his last. While in this country, he passed his days in retire-

ment, but displayed warm interest in the cause of
the Union and emancipation.

Of Heilprin's two sons, the elder, Michael, born in
1823, ardently espoused the cause of the Hungarian
revolution in 1848. He was, by Kossuth's prime-
minister, Szemere, attached to the literary bureau of
the Department of the Interior in 1849. He came to
this country in 1856. The ripe scholar has largely
contributed to the *New American Cyclopædia*, the
New York *Nation*, and other publications. He is
associate editor of the *American Cyclopædia* and *Condensed American Cyclopædia*. In 1879 he issued the
first volume of " The Historical Poetry of the Ancient Hebrews, translated and critically examined."

Michael Heilprin's two sons, Louis and Angelo,
and his nephew, Fabian Franklin, have made successful *débuts* as contributors to American literature and
science in the respective fields of history, paleontology
and mathematics.

MICHAEL . HENRY.

As serious as are the responsibilities of a journalist, so must his qualifications be varied and numerous. To communicate that which is useful, to
create a taste for that which enlightens and refines,
to expose wrong and vindicate right, requires a
pure heart and a well-trained mind. The late

Michael Henry gave unmistakable evidences of having possessed the requisites of his vocation.

Michael Henry was born at Kennington, England, in February, 1830. After receiving an education in the City of London School, he proceeded to Paris, where he found employment in a counting-house. Thence he returned to London, and entered the office of the *Mechanics' Magazine*.

On the demise of the editor of that periodical, Mr. James Robertson, Henry assumed the management of the business, which he carried on from 1857 until his death.

Before speaking of Mr. Henry's connection with the *Jewish Chronicle*, it may not be out of place to cast a glance at the condition of Jewish journalism in England. From the beginning of the present century, attempts were made to establish an organ that would serve the interests of Judaism. The *Hebrew Intelligencer*, a monthly paper, appeared in 1823, but, after the issue of three numbers, it came to an untimely end. In 1834 Dr. M. J. Raphall bought out his *Hebrew Review and Magazine of Rabbinical Literature*, which, though admirably conducted, became extinct, after a short existence, for the lack of support. The *Voice of Jacob*, originated in 1841, continued five years, but it also ceased, owing to general apathy and pecuniary losses. After the *Jewish Chronicle* had, for some time, remained alone in the field, strenuous efforts were again brought about, by which the *Hebrew Observer*, the *Hebrew National* and the *Jewish Record* appeared, but none lived long. However, the *Jewish World*, more recently started, shows signs of permanent stability, and it is rapidly gaining favor.

The *Jewish Chronicle* saw its first days in 1841, meeting at the outset a lukewarm reception. It languished for awhile, but in 1844 Mr. Mitchell revived it, and secured the services of Mr. M. A. Bresslau, a man of unquestionable attainments. Shortly after Mitchell's death, however, the journal passed into the hands of Dr. Abraham Benisch, with whom Michael Henry subsequently associated himself. When Dr. Benisch vacated the editorial chair in 1868, Mr. Henry became his successor. While in charge of the *Chronicle*, he exerted his powers to obtain for his brethren a recognition of their equality of rights, and raised his Weekly to such a high degree of excellence, that both its popularity and circulation steadily increased, standing now foremost of all the journals of its class.

During the course of his life, Mr. Henry wrote several poems and tales, and composed prayers for his own use. The founder of benevolent and educational institutions, he indefatigably labored for the welfare of his fellow-believers. And, therewithal, he was modest and unassuming. His cordiality and suavity of manners, won for him scores of friends.

In June, 1875, when just in the fulness of his mental and physical strength, Michael Henry died the victim of a lamentable accident. The direction of the *Jewish Chronicle* reverted to Dr. Benisch. But lately the Jewish community have sustained a great loss in the removal from their midst of also this celebrated scholar. His memory will be perpetuated, as that of another of Israel's noble sons.

The *Jewish Chronicle* has built for itself a solid foundation, which will ensure its future success as a leading journal of the Hebrew people.

LEVI HERZFELD.

The eventful history of the Jews in Post-Biblical times has suggested numerous works. In these, the religious and social condition of the inhabitants of the Holy Land, while tributaries to foreign governments, has been pictured with various success. The prolixity of some writers has taxed the mind, the brevity of others has withheld important information. Though the remarkable production of Flavius Josephus —a production that is really the source from which all have largely drawn—must ever be perused with satisfaction, works of great merit embodying facts which that fertile genius has given us, can now be cited. We desire to introduce to the reader, in a few words, a man who has acted his part well as

a Jewish annalist, and has extended the boundaries
of literature.

Rabbi Levi Herzfeld was born at Ellrich, in the
Hartz Mountains, Germany, on the 27th of December, 1818.   He studied Bible and Talmud at the
Gymnasium of Nordhausen, and subsequently pursued a course of philosophy, and classical and oriental philology, at the University of Breslau.   Making
rapid progress, he acquired a large fund of knowledge.

Graduating at Breslau, Herzfeld took up again the
Talmud, under Rabbi Egers, of Brunswick, whose
adjunct he became in 1842.   Later, he was chosen
Rabbi of Brunswick.   From 1861-'73 he served
as one of the managers of the Jewish Literary Association, founded by Dr. Philippson.

From his entrance to manhood, Rabbi Herzfeld
has constantly been active in literary circles.   As
early as 1838 there appeared his "Translation and
Explanations of Ecclesiastes," which gave at once
bright promise of the young man's future.   "Pro-
positions for a Reform of the Jewish Marriage-Laws,"
in 1846, and "A Revision of the Prayer-Book," in
1855, show the author's turn of mind.   The researches into the history of commerce among the
Ancient Hebrews (1863-'5), reveal much that was
unknown, and an extraordinary comprehensiveness
of views.   "Lectures on the Art-Productions of the

Hebrews" (1864), is a work replete with original and sound thought.

The principal merits of Herzfeld lie in his "History of the People of Israel, from the Destruction of the Temple to the Elevation of the Maccabean Simon, as High-Priest and Prince," in three volumes (1847-'55-'57). In this production, the incidents connected with the periods dilated upon are treated in a masterly manner. The stirring occurrences in Jewish annals are reviewed, and learned expositions and annotations enrich the writing; the whole being derived from the very best sources. The Rabbi's fame may worthily rest upon this one effort, for it tells loudly of the author's learning and industry. An abridgment of this work was published in 1870.

A succinct account is all that has been in our power to offer of the life of one who must be regarded as an unquestionable authority on all topics bearing on Jewish history.

ISRAEL HILDESHEIMER.

The system which governs the Jewish ritual, and the regulations pertaining to public worship, have undergone, within the last few decades, such vicissitudes that a presentation of causes and effects may well be left to the future historian. He will be able to dispassionately lay down facts, and do justice to the main actors in the exciting events. Still, in honor to truth it must be said that, among the bold leaders who have striven to preserve the Jewish religion as handed down by the fathers, the name of Israel Hildesheimer will shine forth resplendent.

Dr. Israel Hildesheimer was born at Halberstadt, Prussia, on the 20th of May, 1820. His father, a Hebrew scholar of eminence, died, leaving the boy quite young. But, under the care of his mother, who encouraged him to study diligently, the lad's talents were so well cultivated that he early became the pupil of the famous Jacob Ettlinger, Rabbi of Altona. Hildesheimer fathomed the depths of the great Talmudic ocean, and all its flowing streams. He likewise turned his thoughts to knowledge of a secular nature, and went to the University of Berlin, and afterward to that of Halle. At the latter, he received the degree of *Doctor of Philosophy*, in 1846.

On his return home, the learning of the new teacher spread fast. Scholars came from other cities to slake their thirst for rare information at a fountain so copious.

In 1851 the Doctor accepted a call from Eisenstadt in Hungary, a place where many distinguished divines had officiated. There his school flourished, and a large number of students obtained an insight, not only into Rabbinical literature, but also into philosophy and science—the best evidence of the teacher's popularity and remarkable abilities. As the Rabbi of Eisenstadt, he made himself powerfully felt in religious and educational affairs.

On the formation of the Orthodox Congregation *Adath Israel* of Berlin, in 1869, Rabbi Hildesheimer received an urgent invitation to become its spiritual guide. Now all his efforts were centred to the accomplishment of one design—to fight Reform. The sharp-pointed arrows he hurled against innovations, clearly revealed the position he had assumed. He would not yield an iota; he would not sanction the breach of the slightest law or custom; but, despite the bitterest opposition encountered in the course he has maintained, all give him credit for honesty.

Among the Rabbis taught by Dr. Hildesheimer, and who imbibed his ideas, may be mentioned Dr. Mayer Lehmann, editor of *Der Israelit*, of Mayence; Dr. Ehrmann, of Trier; Dr. Kahn, of Wiesbaden; Dr. Carlebach, of Lubeck; Dr. Marx, of Darmstadt; and Dr. Cahn, of Fulda. In 1875 the subject of our sketch founded a Rabbinical College, which is yet in a prosperous condition, numbering about fifty attendants.

Dr. Hildesheimer's untiring activity in the field of beneficence might alone suffice to call forth praise. He has collected large sums for the poor and oppressed of Palestine, Persia, Russia and other countries; and he rendered excellent service during the late Franco-Prussian war, when, with his wife, he visited and provided for the wounded and dying, alleviating the sufferings of the victims of a fierce struggle.

On the 6th of September, 1876, Dr. Hildesheimer celebrated the twenty-fifth anniversary of his career as a Rabbi, and a becoming recognition of his worth was offered by many who regarded themselves his beneficiaries.

The Doctor has won general affection by the sterling qualities he has exhibited. While his ardent zeal has set him against modifications in any of the anciently accepted rules of the Jewish creed, his enthusiasm and devotion to principles deserve to be recorded as an instance seldom met in our days.

SAMSON RAPHAEL HIRSCH.

Conspicuous, not solely as one of the acknowledged champions of Conservative Judaism, but as a profound theologian, and an active worker in Hebrew literature, is the venerable Rabbi, Samson Raphael Hirsch. Many years have seen this divine faithfully labor in the sacred trust confided to his guardianship. The lasting services he has rendered the Jewish community are significantly illustrated by schools and educational institutions that foster and disseminate religious knowledge. But an honest and uncompromising adherence to the principles of Judaism he believes in, and a dauntless defence thereof, entitle the Rabbi to the highest commendation.

Samson Raphael Hirsch was born at Hamburg, Germany, in 1807. His parents had designed him for a merchant. That he should choose the ministry was far from their thoughts. But, evidently, business offered him no attraction. He felt drawn to the college and the pulpit, and openly avowed the bent of his mind. Accordingly, he proceeded to Manheim, where he began theological studies under Rabbi Ettlinger. He attended the lectures at the University of Bonn, and, having completed his course, he was, in 1830, ordained Chief Rabbi of Oldenburg. Splendid must have been the qualifications which gave their possessor. a claim to so high a position at the early age of twenty-three.

From that time forward, Rabbi Hirsch became a central pillar of the ancient fabric of Orthodoxy. About the period of his election to the Rabbinate, strenuous efforts were being made to remodel the ritual, discard doctrines deemed heretofore inviolable, reduce the number of observances, and present the worship in an entirely new form. On the whole, a thorough reconstruction of historical Judaism was contemplated. The movement had gained, in the lapse of a few years, such strength, that to grapple with it, required the combined energies of many who advocated the opposite views. Rabbi Hirsch, at once realizing the situation, prepared to meet the enemy. With fiery zeal he assailed the Reform camp. The Rabbi's " Nineteen Letters," pleading for old Judaism, and written under the *nom de plume* of *Ben Usiel*, created much enthusiasm, and in so able and masterly a manner were the questions handled, that scholars were puzzled as to their authorship, until the name casually leaked out.

Shortly after the last production had appeared, Rabbi Hirsch brought forth another learned work, called " Horeb," which treats of the duties of Israelites. He had accepted a call from Emden in Hanover, but he subsequently became the ecclesiastical head of the Jews of Nicolsburg in Moravia. While there, he encountered the political storm of 1848, raging throughout Europe, and he had to endure many troubles from attending circumstances. The Rabbi obtained popularity, however, to such a degree, that he was elected a member of the Austrian Parliament. In that body he labored assiduously, and struggled hard to secure the rights of his fellow-believers, and the recognition of their equality with other classes of society. In Nicolsburg, Rabbi Hirsch devoted many hours to imparting instruction in the Rabbinical seminary, and goodly were the fruits that sprung from his planting.

In 1851 a number of Israelites seceded from the Congregation at Frankfort-on-the-Main, owing to the tendencies exhibited towards Reform. They organized, and invited Rabbi Hirsch to be their spiritual guide. Determined to serve the cause he had espoused, the Rabbi consented to go, notwithstanding the honorable stations occupied at Nicolsburg and the entreaties of friends to remain. He had not been long at Frankfort, ere he effected a thorough revival in religious affairs. The Jewish community rose to a flourishing condition under his guidance. On the 17th of September, 1876, Rabbi Hirsch celebrated the twenty-fifth anniversary of his induction into office, and general festivities were held.

As to his literary works, in addition to the writings already mentioned, Rabbi Hirsch commenced issuing, in 1854, *Jeshurun*, a monthly periodical, devoted to Hebrew religion and literature. But the most noteworthy of all his publications is a commentary on the Pentateuch, which has just been finished, and bears the name of "The Pentateuch translated and elucidated." It affords decided evidences of the author's towering intellect, and the depth of his research.

Though the Rabbi has passed the allotted three score years and ten, he still takes an earnest participation in every measure for the welfare of Israelites. All may not look upon his opinions, touching certain points in Judaism, with reverence, but every one must admit that Samson Raphael Hirsch is richly deserving of the fame earned by a consistent and upright career.

SOLOMON HIRSCHEL.

From the period that the Rev. Dr. Solomon Hirschel was elected Chief Rabbi of the Great (German) Synagoge, the affairs of the English Jews assumed much importance. The few incidents to be narrated will clearly show the rapid strides taken by our British brethren since that time; and, as they are all inseparably connected with the career of Rabbi Hirschel, it is fit to mention them here.

The Rev. Dr. Solomon Hirschel, though born in England, in 1761, received his education in Germany and Poland. Hence the reason for the lack of a thorough acquaintance with his native language. The father of the Doctor, Zebi Hirschel, had been a former Chief Rabbi of the German Congregation.

Dr. Hirschel, for nine years, occupied the position of Rabbi of Prenzlau, in Prussia. In 1802 he was called to minister at the Duke's Place Synagogue, London. Endowed with keen perception, accurate scholarship and sound judgment, Dr. Hirschel did not remain indifferent to the many wants of his fellow-believers. He noticed the division existing between congregations that would not have the slightest connection with each other, either by reason of ritual differences, or by the prevalence of jealousy and personal bias. A remedy must at once be applied, and Dr. Hirschel found it, in the amalgamation of the entire German congregations of England, thus placing them under one head. The Portuguese Jews, who had long kept aloof from their German brethren, must be reconciled, and to accomplish this, no little difficulty presented itself. But the work was brought to a successful issue, and, ever since, both communities have labored together for their general well-being.

The notable events of Dr. Hirschel's Rabbinate were the establishment of useful institutions, as the Jews' Hospital, and the Jews' Free School; the memorable journey of Sir Moses Montefiore to the East, in 1840; and the unfortunate schism in some congregations, which terminated in the Reform movement and the formation of the West London Synagogue, in 1842, with the Rev. Prof. D. W. Marks as its pastor.* It is said that, were it not for the

---

*For a full account of this separation, see Picciotto's " Sketches of Anglo-Jewish History," Chapters L. and LI.

infirmities attendant upon old age, Dr. Hirschel would have been able to avert the sad rupture ; for his influence was always powerfully felt, and he might have granted concessions effecting a reconciliation, without proving detrimental to Orthodoxy. But the Elders of the various congregations refused to entertain any of the demands of the secessionists. Hence the result which caused heart-burnings and ill-will. But these ritual differences have happily not impaired the political condition of the British Jews. They have stood nobly together when questions of great moment, bearing on their rights, arose. And now animosities have subsided, and the entire Hebrew community are eventually being drawn into closer contact.

Private troubles, together with congregational dissensions, sorely grieved Dr. Hirschel's spirit. In his last days, he could not enjoy repose. Broken down in mind and body, he was rendered unfit for service. Fasting and other deprivations had told severely upon his constitution. The Rabbi met besides with two severe accidents that tended to shorten his existence. He died October 31st, 1842, at the advanced age of eighty-one.

The funeral of Dr. Hirschel, on November 2d, was attended with imposing ceremonies. All Jewish places of business remained closed, and the utmost respect was shown to the memory of a man, who, for forty years, had guided his flock in the path of righteousness.

SAMUEL HOLDHEIM.

A movement that aimed at the introduction of radical changes in the Jewish ritual, originated in Germany, over fifty years ago. At first, it did not make great headway; but, as the idea continued to be agitated by its upholders, it soon took a tangible form, and assumed large proportions. It bears the name of Reform. To descant upon its history and progress, and the opposition it created, would be to write a book. A brief sketch of an individual who is generally regarded as the head and front of Radicalism, is all that is here attempted.

Dr. Samuel Holdheim was born at Kempen, in the province of Posen, Prussian Poland, in 1806. His early education did not extend further than a familiarity with the Bible and the Talmud. The great proficiency obtained in the latter, brought him to notice when yet a young man. At the Universities of Prague and Berlin, he pursued, with ardor, various studies, but his limited preparation for a collegiate course, made it impossible for him to graduate at those institutions. Nevertheless, he acquired, within a short space of time, a remarkable amount of knowledge, so that he could step before the world, possessed of abilities superior to those of many of the Rabbis of his day.

In 1836 Holdheim received a call from Frankfort on the Oder, whither he proceeded. There, his first efforts were directed to advance the political interests of his fellow-believers, and to gain for them liberal concessions. He delivered a number of sermons in behalf of this cause, which were given publication. In 1839 he issued *Gottesdienstliche Vorträge*, in which he treats of the Jewish holy days, usages, etc. This work was the subject of polemics in the leading Jewish periodicals.

Holdheim's scholarly attainments secured public recognition in 1840, when the University of Leipzig conferred on him the degree of *Doctor of Philosophy*. In the same year, he was tendered the position of Chief Rabbi of Mecklenburg-Schwerin, which he accepted. In this new field his influence increased rapidly, and the plans he had in view excited eager expectations.

The first of Dr. Holdheim's writings, that showed a strong tendency to extreme notions, was his *Über d. Autonomie d. Rabbinen u. d. Princip. der jüd. Ehe*, which came from the press in 1843. In it he urges upon Jews the importance of submitting matrimonial questions to the law of the land in which they sojourn. The Rabbi argues from his own standpoint, and tries to show that adherence to the prescribed ordinances would conflict with the duties of citizenship, and become antagonistic to liberal principles. To quote a writer's words: " He held, first, that the autonomy of the Rabbins must cease; secondly, that the religious obligations should be distinct from the political and civil, and should yield to the latter, as of higher authority; and, thirdly, that marriage is, according to the Jewish law, a civil act, and consequently an act independent of Jewish authorities."

Über d. Beschneidung zunächst in religiös-dogmat. Beziehung, came forth in 1844, wherein the author treats of the question whether circumcision is essential to Jewish membership, and expresses radical opinions as to the efficacy of the Abrahamic covenant. The promulgation of this theory aroused the wrath of formidable opponents, in nearly every noted Rabbi of Europe. But even those who condemn Holdheim's attacks on Jewish customs and rites, cannot fail to admire the perseverance with which he prosecuted his designs. For he stood almost alone, facing the battle waged against him by a host of scholars of the highest rank. He grew not faint by the loss of supporters, but continued to tenaciously maintain his principles. To this circumstance, we may principally attribute the success of Reform.

Dr. Holdheim was a prominent member of the Jewish councils, held from 1843 to 1846. In 1847 he removed to Berlin, to become the leading spirit of the Jewish Reform Society of that city; an association composed of persons who, on account of their pronounced hostility to Conservatism, had seceded from the body of the community. Here, he did not relax in his work. In addition to a number of short treatises, in pamphlet form, written in defence of his position, and against the advocates of traditional Judaism, there appeared *Religions u. Sittenlehren d. Mischnah z. Gebrauch b. Religions-unterricht i. jüd. Religions-schulen*, on the moral and religious teachings of the Mishna, in 1854; *Gesch. der. jüd. Reformgemeinde*, on the history of Jewish Reform, in 1857; followed, in the same year, by *Jüd. Glaubens u. Sittenlehre*, on Jewish faith and customs; and *Gebete und Gesänge für das Neujahrs-u. Versöhnungsfest*, or prayers and hymns for the New Year and the Day of Atonement, in 1859. A number of his sermons were separately published after his death.

Dr. Holdheim lived to see his labors accomplish the ends he wished to carry out, viz: a gradual extension of the system for whose victory he had long fought. He died at Berlin, Prussia, August 22d, 1860.

Notwithstanding the denunciation and forcible condemnation which the new *régime* has met, we would not deny its mighty defender a claim to sincerity. He may have believed that the emancipation of his German co-religionists from notions which

a state of proscription had engendered, demanded their
breaking loose from all ritual restraints, and he imagined that the time called upon him to lead in
the change. Whatever the verdict of posterity may
be on the question at issue, all will acknowledge
that Samuel Holdheim was talented and energetic,
and that he had the courage of his opinions.

REBEKAH HYNEMAN.

A lady who, though not born in the Sinaic
law, did much to entitle her to a place by the
side of Israel's illustrious daughters, was Mrs. Rebekah
Hyneman.   Her varied effusions breathe devotion
to the belief she eagerly embraced in her woman-
hood; such a devotion, that it alone might commend the character of the authoress to the respect of the Hebrew community.   But she combined
a clear intellect with a pure heart, and both were
directed to a righteous end.

Rebekah Hyneman, *née* Gumpert, was born in
the city of Philadelphia, on September 8th, 1812.
When yet a child, she evinced a strong desire for
knowledge, and so diligently she applied herself to
study, that, in a few years, without the aid of a
regular instructor, she not only mastered English
composition, but gained a correct idea of the
French and German languages.   This enabled her

afterward to translate several pieces, embodied in her published work, and of which notice will be taken.

In 1835 Miss Gumpert was wedded to Benjamin Hyneman, brother of Leon Hyneman, the well-known writer on Free-Masonry, and for many years editor of the *Masonic Mirror and Keystone*. Constitutionally weak, Mrs. Hyneman was destined to grow still feebler through untoward circumstances which sorely tried her faith. She was left a widow, after having enjoyed but five years of married life. One of her sons, who had inherited his mother's natural enthusiasm, enlisted in the Union army during the late Civil War, and died in the rebel prison at Andersonville from sheer starvation. The other son, having long endured bodily sufferings, sank to an early grave. The death of her sister Sarah, wife of Leon Hyneman, intensified her sorrows. Still the bereaved woman arose above gloom, and turned her mind to the task of communicating to others her godly sentiments.

Mrs. Hyneman was a constant contributor to the *Masonic Mirror and Keystone*. She wrote for it a number of original stories, essays on multifarious subjects, fugitive pieces of poetry, and frequently presented translations from the works of different foreign authors. "The Leper and Other Poems," appeared in 1853. Many of the subjects are Scriptural, and show, in vivid colors, the feelings she entertained for the religion of her choice. The most notable poems, beside "The Leper," are "Zara," "Livia," "The Muses," and some beautiful delineations of the Women of the Bible and the Apocrypha. We reproduce the piece, descriptive of the drowning of Pharaoh and his host in the Red Sea, written as an introduction to "Miriam's Song:"

> Retire, ye waves! roll back your crested heads—
> Presume not to approach the royal host,
> That presses onward to your bosom now,
> In glittering pomp and panoply of war.
> See how they tower, those lordly, swelling waves,
> And form a pathway walled on either side—
> Rides the king safely now?
>
>   The billows roll,
> But not in sport, nor as when tempests lash
> Their angry heads, but with a sullen sound,
> Murmuringly and low—moaning, as if in pain,
> They heave and rise, then slowly sink again,
> Impatient for the word to set them free.
>
> But what has he, that kingly one, to fear?
> Have they not passed in safety o'er the path—
> They, his hereditary bondsmen?
> And shall he, a monarch, a crowned King,
> With all his glittering host of armed men,
> Yield to base coward fear? Perish the thought!
> He comes to conquer—hear ye not that shout?
> It tells of victory already won.
> But see! the strange commotion in that mass;
> They turn, they flee! Oh! gods of Egypt, help!
> Vain prayer! wild shrieks burst on th' affrighted ear,
> And the mad billows triumph o'er the sound.
> Whose voice thus echoes o'er the raging waste?

> Who calls for help in that wild surging sea?
> Mighty and dreaded Pharaoh, is it thou?
> Thou! why the very waves laugh thee to scorn;
> And of thy train, the meanest follower
> Claims brotherhood with Egypt's haughty King,
> And boasts as lordly sepulture. Sad sight—
> Chariot, and horse, and rider, each alike
> Engulfed in one vast grave.

As a prose writer, Mrs. Hyneman must be also assigned a prominent station. In addition to quite a number of miscellaneous compositions, she produced her "Tales for Children," which, together with other emanations from her pen, will soon be issued in book-form. It is conceded that writing for the young presents singular difficulties. The ideas must be conveyed in the simplest style, and, to accomplish the object, a perfect familiarity with the habits of children is required. Mrs. Hyneman is said to display in her "Tales" a great adaptability to the topic, and a grace and originality that cannot fail to give her stories an enduring place in the memory of their juvenile readers.

Mild of disposition and endowed with rare conversational powers, Mrs. Hyneman possessed a large and select circle of friends who sympathized with her in the tribulations she was doomed to bear. From this affection she derived a fresh impulse to divert her thoughts from the painful to the useful; and, when under intense agony from a chronic disease, she received the attention which genuine attachment and esteem alone can offer. But her strength slowly ebbed away, and on September 10th, 1875, the spirit of Rebekah Hyneman passed into the abode set apart for the just.

She was truly a woman whose example may well be imitated by every daughter of the race of Abraham.

SAMUEL MYER ISAACS.

The stability of Judaism in America is supremely due to the endeavors of a few ministers of foreign birth, who labored with singleness of purpose. Half a century ago the communal condition of the Hebrews in this country, was somewhat like a wild, uncultivated plain. It required skilful hands to weed, to prune, and to plant anew; and that work became the all-absorbing object of several spiritual leaders. They sought no self-aggrandizement, no popular ovations, but the satisfaction of having done right by elevating the character of their co-religionists, and drawing them into a closer union. The subject of the present sketch is entitled to rank among those ardent laborers.

The Rev. Samuel Myer Isaacs was born at Leeuwarden, in Friesland, Holland, on the 4th of January, 1804. His father, a banker, had lost his property by unfortunate speculations, and the family emigrated to England in 1814, where young Isaacs received his education. Of five sons, four entered the ministry, viz: Isaac, Jacob, David and Samuel.

After completing his studies, Mr. Isaacs occupied the position of Principal of a charitable and educational institution, known as *Nevè Tsédek*, until 1839, when he set sail for New York, to assume the ministerial charge of the Congregation *B'nai Jeshurun*, then worshiping in Elm street. The healthful effect of the selection at once exhibited itself. A revival took place in the religious affairs of the metropolis, and the weekly sermons of Mr. Isaacs aroused the lethargic spirit of the community, and greatly added to the number of attendants at his Synagogue.

In 1845 circumstances occasioned a division, by which the Congregation *Shaarè Tefila* was called into existence with Mr. Isaacs as its pastor. His energies now found a wider scope. The zealous divine well understood that, with the growth of population, more institutions, tending to advance Jewish ends, and specially, to stem the current of denominational prejudices, were needed. He, therefore, used his powers as a speaker, to advocate the establishment of organizations that might supply the various wants of his fellow-believers. Thus hospitals, asylums, and beneficial and educational societies were founded.

Co-operating with such men as Leeser and Raphall, Mr. Isaacs extended his usefulness in every direction. He took a prominent part in the formation of the Board of Delegates of American Israelites—an association now merged with the Union of American Hebrew Congregations, and whose influence has been felt in far-off lands—and he never ceased to give his counsel and personal aid to the furtherance of its noble aims. He visited different cities of the United States, in the interest of his brethren; lectured before Yale College, and spoke frequently, beyond his own pulpit, to large assemblies.

While Mr. Isaacs proceeded in an even way towards the continuance of accepted practices, a movement, looking to radical changes in the Jewish Church, was being made with more or less success. Reform attacked Conservatism, thereby compelling its adherents to stand on the defensive. Mr. Isaacs could not remain indifferent to innovations which he deemed unlawful. He openly condemned the new school, and employed the columns of his weekly paper, the *Jewish Messenger*, (started in 1857), to denounce a system in which he saw the downfall of traditional Judaism. Whether Mr. Isaacs gained what he strove for or not, is a question which it would be idle to discuss.

The *Jewish Messenger* has won deserved support for its consistency, and for the excellent manner in which it has been conducted. During the Civil War it upheld the North, and attacked the institution of slavery. This course led to the temporary loss of a large number of subscribers to the journal. Mr. Isaacs' characteristic remarks are well worthy of reproduction : "We want subscribers, for without them we cannot publish a paper, and Judaism needs an organ; but we want much more truth and loyalty, and for them, we are ready, if we must, to sacrifice all other considerations." Mr. Isaacs enjoyed the esteem of some of the most eminent Americans, and of foreigners, the great philanthropist, Sir Moses Montefiore, with whom he frequently corresponded, regarding measures for the amelioration of the Jews of Palestine. Mr. Isaacs' charity was as notable as were his pious habits. He distributed of his own to the poor, and devoted a large portion of his time to succor the afflicted.

The venerable minister of the *Shaaré Tefila* Congregation, retired from office about a year prior to his death. One of his last public duties was to officiate at the funeral of his lamented colleague, the Rev. Jacques J. Lyons, who died in August, 1878. But Jewish affairs ever engaged Mr. Isaacs' thoughts and feelings, and his interest therein was manifested to the last.

The long and useful life of the Rev. Samuel Myer Isaacs closed on the 19th of May, 1878. Hebrews throughout the Union hastened to pay a tribute of respect to the memory of one whose purity of character and steadfastness of purpose, endeared his name to young and old; to those who shared his sentiments, and to others who differed.

Mr. Isaacs contributed largely, by his writings, to the spread of Jewish literature in America, while his brother the Rev. Prof. David Myer Isaacs, who died in the spring of 1879, disseminated learning in England, and became widely known for his eloquence and choice diction. The four sons of the deceased New York divine, Myer, Jacob, Isaac, and Abram, the last named of whom is the present editor of the *Jewish Messenger*, are respected alike as citizens and Israelites.

ADOLPH JELLINEK.

Pulpit oratory is comparatively new among Hebrews. Disquisitions on some Scriptural or Talmudical passage, which were wont to satisfy the fathers, failed to attract their children. Hence a method more in accordance with the taste of the age had to be adopted. The need was felt for the presentation of theological truths in a systematic manner, and it did not long remain unsupplied. In Prague a Kaempf, in Breslau a Joel, and in Vienna a Jellinek, fill to-day positions which would not suffer in comparison with those held by noted dignitaries of the Church. But the last-named possibly bears the palm for vivid imagery, felicitous conceptions, and admirable delivery.

The Rev. Dr. Adolph Jellinek was born at Drslowitz, in Moravia, Austria, on the 26th of June, 1821. When still young he studied Talmud. Later, he followed a course of philosophy and Oriental languages at Prague, and finally at Leipsic. His aptitude for learning was readily discerned in the thoroughness with which he acquired the knowledge imparted.

The Jewish community soon became aware of Jellinek's talents, and, in 1845, he was chosen preacher at Leipsic. Then the latent fire broke forth in burning thoughts which kindled enthusiasm. The influence which the divine exerted in religious matters kept pace with his popularity. Feeling that he must address throngs, he urged the erection of the new Synagogue, begun in 1855.

In 1856 Dr. Jellinek went to Vienna, where he has since officiated as Rabbi-Preacher. In that capacity, both his voice and his pen have ever been brought into requisition for the advancement of Judaism and its literature. A great feature in Jellinek is, that he evidences intense earnestness in all he says and writes. None who have heard his sermons, or read his effusions, can fail to notice that elocution and well-rounded sentences are not the only merits of the Doctor. His discourses carry conviction through their pervading sincerity, and his productions create profound impressions, because they emanate from love of the cause espoused.

As a writer, Dr. Jellinek has issued works of intrinsic value. He has searched into the dark labyrinths of the Cabbala, and has brought forth original and striking facts of special interest to the votaries of that mystic system. Among the Doctor's numerous productions are: a translation of Prof. Adolphe Franck's "Cabbala, or Religious Philosophy of the Hebrews," 1844; *Sefat Chachamim*, explanations of Persian and Arabian words occurring in the Talmud, Targumim and Midrashim—1846; "Elisha ben Abuya, called Achér," 1847; "Moses ben Shem-Tob De Leon and his Connection with the Zohar," 1851; "Contributions to the History of the Cabbala," 1851; "Thomas Aquinas in Jewish Literature," 1853; *Beth ha-Midrash*, a collection of many, and, among them, rare Midrashim, in three volumes, 1853-'5; Philosophy and Cabbala," 1854; a revised edition of *Rashbam's* (Rabbi Samuel ben Meïr) commentaries on Canticles and Ecclesiastes, 1855; "Commentaries on Esther, Ruth and Lamentations, based on the Exegetical Method of the French School," 1855; "*Shaar ha-Schamayim* of Rabbi Joseph ibn Lattif," a contribution to the history of the Religio-Philosophical movement in the thirteenth century, with a historical introduction—1865; and "Studies and Sketches," 1869. Jellinek has also furnished articles to different publications.

It may not be amiss to say that the Doctor lost a gifted brother during the political upheaval of 1848. Hermann Jellinek had already risen to a conspicuous rank, as a terse and polished writer, and he bid fair to reach an extraordinary eminence. But the reaction in the affairs of government, which brought Metternich again into power, doomed the outspoken and freedom-loving Hebrew to a premature grave.

GEORGE JESSEL.

Long was Great Briain in learning that a liberal policy is not alone the most just, but the most profitable. For centuries she held her gates tight-shut against the Hebrew, and when permitting him at length to pass through, she waved over his head an iron rod. But the once proscriptive England has made *amende honorable.* She stretches forth her hand, and generously welcomes Israel within her territories. Nowhere is the people, whilom greatly despised, more exalted than in the United Kingdom and its dependencies. Nor is the honor unappreciated or unrequited. Jewish loyalty and patriotism cannot be excelled—Prof. Goldwin Smith's assertions to the contrary notwithstanding. In all departments those traits are noticeable, and, therefore, most delicate and responsible positions are filled by the descendants of the Patriarchs. A very prominent character among our English Brethren is the present Master of the Rolls, the first Anglo-Jew to occupy a seat on the judicial bench.

The Right Hon. Sir George Jessel, M. P., Q. C., son of the late Mr. Zachariah Nathaniel Jessel, a merchant of Putney, was born at London, England, in 1824. Having remarkably benefited by the tuition received in his boyhood, he gained admission to University College, London, graduating *Bachelor of Arts* in 1843. In the following year he was made *Master of Arts*, being awarded a gold medal in mathematics.

Mr. Jessel commenced the study of the law, and, in May 1847, he was called to the Bar at Lincoln's Inn. His legal talents attracted the favorable notice of the Government, and, in 1865, earned for him the appointment of Queen's Counsel and a Bencher of his Inn. Elected a Senator of the University of London, he was also returned to Parliament in 1868 by the Liberals, as one of the representatives for the borough of Dover. In all these offices, Mr. Jessel's demeanor redounded to the general advantage, as well as to his own credit. But exertions wisely directed were destined to a glorious lot.

The subject of our sketch became Solicitor-

General in November, 1871, under the Right Hon. W. E. Gladstone's administration, and, on February 21st, 1872, his services were publicly rewarded by his elevation to the knighthood. In August, 1873, on the recommendation of Mr. Gladstone, he was chosen Master of the Rolls, to succeed Lord Romilly, being at the same time sworn as a member of the Privy Council.

An experience of seven years has amply justified the choice. With firmness and ability are the laws enforced. The discipline maintained in the Court over which Sir George presides, was shown recently by the expulsion of an individual who disturbed the proceedings. The offended man—discovered, however, to be of unsound mind—attempted the life of the judge. Fortunately for the would-be assassin, he lived under the shades of the Court of St. James, and not at St. Petersburg.

Sir George's co-religionists have found in him one truly deserving of their respect, on account of his open adherence to the ancestral religion and warm advocacy of their interests. The feelings thus nurtured are growing stronger with the lapse of time, and in proportion as the country recognizes in the man who fears Israel's God, one eminently fitted for his high station, through acumen, soundness of judgment, and equanimity.*

----

*Sir George is said to be the greatest equity lawyer who has sat in the Master of the Rolls' Court during the present generation.

The career of Sir George Jessel has hitherto been stamped with the seal of universal commendation, and Israelites everywhere may well wish that, to its very end, it may bear the same distinguishing impress.

JOSEPH JOACHIM.

The violin is everywhere considered one of the favorite musical instruments. Its sound, when airs are discoursed by acknowledged masters, enchains the thoughts. Music may really be regarded an inspired gift. How it wields a power which affects even inferior animals, is beyond human description. But to avoid a discussion of the merits of this wonderful art, it may be merely said, by way of introduction, that Joachim stands foremost among living violinists.

Joseph Joachim was born at Keczel, a small village near Presburg, Hungary, July 15th, 1831. At a very early age, he displayed a fondness for music. One day the child visited an inn where a band of gypsies was playing, and listened to the strange melody with wonder and delight. He eyed curiously the fiddle-sticks, gliding and skipping across the strings, from which escaped such singularly weird and merry tunes. Returning home he took an old guitar, and began knocking on the strings, trying to produce the sounds he had heard. This amused his father, who presented the boy with a violin.

From that moment, young Joachim's future life was mapped out. He soon commenced studying under several musicians, and in his seventh year created, by his playing, a sensation destined to be nevermore forgotton. At the Vienna Conservatory, Helmesberger and Böhm afforded him instruction. He afterwards went to Leipsic, performing at a concert, and evoking a storm of applause. Appearing in London, he at once convinced the English people that he was above the class known as "youthful prodigies."

In 1850 Joachim accepted, at the solicitation of Liszt, the post of Concert-Master at Weimar. This situation was exchanged in 1853, for a similar one at Hanover. In 1866 he became Director of the Academy of Music of Berlin, where he still remains. He makes frequent visits to England, Holland and Belgium, but a natural reluctance to being lionized, has led him to decline numerous offers for a concert tour in the United States. The Cambridge University recently honored him with the title of *Doctor Musica.*

The chief points of Joachim's excellence are (we quote): " purity and fulness of tone, perfect intonation, absolute mastery of all the technical difficulties of the instrument, and the closest sympathy with the classical composers, whose works he interprets." Though Joachim has written compositions of a high order, both for violin and orchestra, his fame is principally due to his qualities as a player, and to the great worth of his performances.

MICHAEL JOSEPHS.

In the various walks of life, individuals may be found who, notwithstanding their remarkable talents, have never attained popularity. This is generally attributed to the modest and unostentatious demeanor characterizing them. Another cause may be the indiscriminate praise often bestowed upon persons of ordinary abilities, inducing the truly deserving to remain in retirement. This discouraging fact should not, however, deter the historian from seeking where merit exists, and according it commendation. Those who have labored to elevate humanity are entitled to public notice, be they ever so humble or unassuming. A memoir of one who rendered great service to Anglo-Judaism may be of interest.

Michael Josephs was born at Königsberg, Prussia, in 1763. His young years were employed in studying the Bible and collateral works. On leaving for England, when but sixteen, he already possessed a store of Hebrew knowledge. About the time of his departure from Germany, the educational movement, led by Mendelssohn, had gained much ground, and Mr. Josephs became at once convinced of its practicability and usefulness.

Shortly after his arrival in Great Britain, Mr. Josephs brought forth several Hebrew poems, and other productions in prose. Their avowed worth elicited frequent requests that the author would prepare odes and anniversary poems for different Jewish associations. Quite a number of minor pieces proceeded from the same source, and they were read with eagerness by the lovers of Hebrew literature. But Mr. Josephs' reputation increased very considerably, when his principal work, a Hebrew and English Lexicon, appeared. It was dedicated to his Royal Highness, the Duke of Sussex,—a patron of Hebrew lore, and so cleverly arranged as to materially assist the student of Biblical and Post-Biblical writings.

Mr. Josephs was also active among organizations of learning. He took part, in 1830, in forming a Hebrew Literary Society, and though, as a merchant, business consumed a large portion of his time, many hours were devoted to aid intellectual progress. Perfectly familiar with all matters relating to Hebrew composition, his opinion upon the subject was consulted by celebrated Rabbis. Mr. Josephs is regarded as the first to have urged the propriety of refuting the aspersions cast on the books of Jewish traditions in " M'Caul's Old Paths;" a suggestion which was afterwards carried out.

Strict in his religious observances, he was tolerant and careful in judging of the motives of those who did not adhere to the strict letter of the law. Thoughtful and discreet, he would, like Socrates, often say, " Let us sacrifice a cock to Æsculapius." Mr. Josephs freely employed his pecuniary means to benefit his fellow-creatures. He was summoned before his Maker in 1849, having attained the ripe age of eighty-six. In him we have a bright illustration of a man who directed his mind and substance to a channel whence his brethren might draw vast advantages.

ISAAC MARCUS JOST.

The works of Zacuto and of Gans are invaluable, when consideration is made to the times in which they were written, and to the knowledge within reach of their authors. But, for a systematic, comprehensive, and carefully collated history of the Jewish people and its literature, the largest debt of gratitude is due to German Israelites. Of modern workers in this department, Jost was, it is conceded, the pioneer, for he pointed out the way, in following which, others have excelled. It is, therefore, right that his name should be first in the thought of all who value that which his pen has popularized.

Dr. Isaac Marcus Jost was born at Bernburg, Germany, February 22d, 1793. During the same year, his father became totally blind, and Isaac, when only five years of age, had to labor for the support of a large family. After the death of his father, in 1803, he resided with his grandfather at Wolfenbüttel.

Dr. Jost received his first education at the Hebrew school in Bernburg. Soon, however, he was admitted into the Samson Institute, where he made the acquaintance of that great *savant*, Dr. Leopold Zunz, and the two scholars became intimate associates. Both made rapid progress, and were promoted to the highest class. In 1813 Jost entered the University of Göttingen, where, for one year and a half, he pursued studies in history, philology, philosophy and theology; and removed, in 1814, to the University of Berlin, from which he graduated in 1816. Shortly after, he opened a school at Berlin, that Christians, as well as Jews attended. He accepted, in 1835, the head-mastership of the Jewish Normal School, at Frankfort-on-the-Main, in which capacity he spent the remainder of his days.

Now to speak of the literary labors of Dr. Jost. While at college, he penned several minor compositions of great excellence. But the first work that attracted general attention is the one upon which rests his fame. "History of the Israelites," in twelve volumes,—nine of which appeared in the years 1819-1827, and the remaining three in 1845—is the first of its own kind issued complete since the days of Josephus, and the result of gigantic labors on the part of its author. The vast amount of reading and research necessary to the accomplishment of such a prodigious task, baffles description.

It must futhermore be remembered that there were then fewer sources from which to derive information, than are now opened to the student of history. The perseverance of Dr. Jost in the prosecution of his work, must have been, indeed, wonderful. In 1831-1834 were published a "General History of the Jewish Nation," in two volumes, being an abridgment of the former work; a German translation of the "Mishna," with a Rabbinical exposition, etc.

Dr. Jost edited a weekly journal from 1839 to 1841, called *The Israelitish Annals*, which numbered among its contributors some of the ablest Jewish writers, and furnished its readers with articles of rare literary merit. On its discontinuance, he started, in conjunction with his friend, Creiznach, a periodical in Hebrew, entitled *Zion*, of which two volumes appeared.

It was but a short time ere the German scholar brought forth another great production, in the shape of a " History of Judaism and its Sects," in three volumes, and which, a writer says, " may fitly make the top stone of the great historical edifice, he had reared so perfectly from the outset."

Dr. Jost indited a large number of miscellaneous essays and criticisms, and contributed to various journals and magazines.*   His labors effectively tended to elevate the moral status of Judaism.

Dr. Jost's philanthropic efforts also deserve notice. He became the " father of the fatherless," in establishing an asylum for the protection and care of orphans. The means he acquired were liberally spent in alleviating the miseries of his fellow-beings, until death put an end to his kind ministrations, on the 20th of November, 1860.

A sympathetic disposition and a courteous demeanor, combined with commanding talents, were brilliant features in the character of Dr. Jost.   They should inspire universal admiration for a man whose whole life was an exemplification of what well-directed energies can achieve.

MARCUS M. KALISCH.

An inestimable debt of gratitude is due to the humble-minded philosopher of Dessau.   For he set

---

*Dr. Jost published in 1830, his " Explanatory Dictionary to Shakspeare's Plays."

the wheel in motion, which still rolls on with unabated celerity. Since the days of the immortal Mendelssohn, Germany has become a new Attica, and her Jewish denizens have a primary title to distinction. Into the vast sea of literary research they have dived deeply, and into that which pertains to Hebrew knowledge their investigations are singularly profound. The number of scholars that first saw the light of day in that section of Europe, has multiplied in a manner which makes one almost shrink at the thought of drawing an outline of the life and deeds of even the smallest minority. Still, what a scion of the ancient race has done must be told, so that many may be induced to obtain a familiarity with the emanations of a fertile brain.

Marcus M. Kalisch, M. A., Ph. D., was born at Trepton, in the province of Pomerania, Prussia, on the 16th of May, 1828. Educated at Berlin, first in the Grammar School, directed by Dr. Ribbeck, and then at the University, he profited well by what had been imparted. At college, he studied classical philology under Boekh and Laihmann, and the Semitic languages and Biblical sciences under Petermann, Benary, Kingstenburg, Vatke, and others. Much of his time was also given to the Talmud, both in private and at the Rabbinical Institute. In 1848 he received several degrees at Berlin and at Halle.

In the following year, political disturbances led

Dr. Kalisch to bid farewell to his native country. He proceeded to England, where he took up a permanent residence. Immediately on his arrival at the metropolis, he engaged in literary pursuits. While contributing to periodicals of Great Britain and the Continent, he also delivered lectures on secular and theological topics. His thorough culture and versatile powers, enabled him to master philosophy, which he applied to Biblical exegesis. Thus he attracted the notice of the religious authorities of his fellow-believers, and served in the capacity of Secretary to Chief Rabbi Adler.

But Dr. Kalisch was bent on the attainment of a special object,—that of reviewing the Scriptures with unsparing criticism. To that end, he relinquished all other occupations. Supported by the Rothschilds, with whom he stood in very friendly relations, he worked with indefatigable energy, and in 1855 published his first volume, entitled " A Historical and Critical Commentary on the Old Testament, with a new Translation—Exodus." The second, " Genesis," appeared in 1858; the third, " Leviticus, Part I., containing Chapters I. to X., with Treatises on Sacrifices and the Hebrew Priesthood," in 1867; and the fourth, " Leviticus, Part II., containing Chapters XI. to XXVII., with Treatises," in 1872. It is asserted that, while lucidness and erudition are constantly displayed in these commentaries, radical opinions are set forth as to the authenticity and correctness of certain texts and chapters of Holy Writ.

Dr. Kalisch has also composed a Hebrew Grammar. Toward the close of 1872 he was prostrated by a severe illness, which hindered his labors for a lengthy period. When partially recovered, in 1876, he resumed them with earnestness. In 1877 he issued the first part of "Bible Studies," comprising annotations on "The Prophecies of Balaam." The second part, on "The Book of Jonah, preceded by a Treatise on the Hebrew and the Stranger," has lately been offered.

As no intelligent person would like to check an instinct which stimulates the brightest minds to soar above their ken, so it would be wrong to deprecate the attempts to subject the revealed books to the same process of investigation as writings of of human creation. Anything possessing the elements of truth will come forth unhurt from the searching test. Dr. Kalisch may, therefore, be wished unimpeded success in the prosecution of his aims, and the continuance of health to proceed without interruption.

MOSES KAYSERLING.

That the preservation of sacred literature is a great boon, admits of no question. In learning how much has been accomplished in the past, the mind will retain its elasticity, and the heart will feel prompted to cherish and set off the real object of our boast. How many, now prominent before the world, might have lived and died in obscurity, but for the sentiments aroused by a knowledge of the endeavors of a choice band of ardent laborers? To such feelings may be due the restless activity of one of the most prolific writers; one who very nigh rivals the illustrious Steinschneider. True, his efforts have not taken the immense range which that master's herculean work embraces. But the painstaking, accuracy, and the conscientiousness which have been made to subserve a vast erudition, will, doubtless, be employed to increase the number of Moses Kayserling's works. To our readers we say: do not judge of the merits of the man by the space devoted to his biography.

Dr. Moses Kayserling was born at Hanover, Germany, on June 17th, 1829. He obtained elementary, and subsequently higher, instruction in his native city. Declared fit for a collegiate education, he attended the University of Berlin. There, after a course of difficult studies, he graduated.

Kayserling did not exhibit in early life the marked aptitude for which some of his contemporaries have been distinguished. But he thoroughly compensated for that in later years. A feeling of humility may have held him back; modesty may have counseled slowness, to avoid a fall on the high road to learning. Hence his comparative tardiness in appearing as an author. But he gathered experience, and gave us in manhood the ripe fruits of his meditation.

In 1861 the Government of Aargau appointed Dr. Kayserling Rabbi of the Swiss Jews. In that office, he used his exertions to secure religious and political privileges, until then denied, in many Cantons of the Helvetic Confederacy, to the adherents of Mosaism. In 1870 he was chosen Rabbi and Preacher of the influential Jewish community of Pesth, Hungary. His versatile knowledge is attested by the able discharge of his ministerial duties, as well as by the productions of his pen.

Dr. Kayserling has issued numerous works which will ever interest, by reason of the topics discussed and the tone pervading them. All his writings are in the German language. An ardent admirer of the scholars to whom the Iberian peninsula gave birth during the Middle Ages, he has bestowed his attention specially, and with acknowledged success, on Sephardic literature. "Romanic Poetry of the Jews of Spain," came out in 1859; "A Holiday at Madrid—A Chapter of the History of the Spanish and Portuguese Jews," in 1859; History of the Jews of Spain and Portugal," in 1860; "The

Life and Writings of Menasseh ben Israel," in 1861 ; "History of the Jews of England," in 1861 ; "The Life and Writings of Moses Mendelssohn," in 1862; and "The Poet, Ephraim Kuh—A Contribution to the History of German Literature," in 1867. "Select Library of a Jewish Preacher," begun in 1870, will comprise several volumes when completed. The Doctor has largely contributed to German publications, and he has also given us valuable works on the history of eminent sons and daughters of Israel, from the earliest to the present day.

There can be no doubt that any one conversant with the diction and spirit of both languages, who should undertake the translation of Dr. Kayserling's writings into our vernacular, would confer a benefit on English-speaking Israelites, and earn an enviable notoriety.

MINNA KLEEBERG.

Those who admire the poetry of the fatherland of Goethe, will be stirred by the effusions of a Jewess glowing with enthusiasm for the good and true. A short time ago the pen which gave form to heavenly thoughts was guided by a pure hand. And now Death holds that hand in its cold grasp. But the fell destroyer could not extinguish the fire which burnt within the soul. It still emits brilliant sparks, in writings of touching loveliness. Our only regret is, that we cannot enkindle therewith those whose mother-tongue is English, for Minna Kleeberg wrote in German. Did we even possess the ability, we would not venture upon a version which might mar natural beauty. The works, entitled to eminence, because of the sympathy they awaken for the sufferer, and the reverence they inspire for the merciful, will partly be mentioned without comment. But it is our earnest wish that they may find, in the original, the number of readers which their intrinsic value deserves.

Minna Kleeberg was born at Elmshorn, in the province of Holstein, Germany, on July 21st, 1841. The daughter of Dr. Cohen, a physician of note, her natural talents soon told of what they were capable. Under the guidance of her father, she enjoyed the advantage of a careful training, and thus acquired a surprising amount of information on general topics, long before arriving at maturity. While yet a young girl, she devoured works of a poetical and scientific character, in German, French and English. Her attachment to the sublime art soon manifested itself. Attentive to household duties, she still kept her mind continually alive upon subjects, in the treatment of which she so excelled in after years. When a child, she traced lines indicative of the future in store for her abilities.

In 1862 Miss Cohen married the Rev. Dr. L. Kleeberg. Up to that year, her verses did not claim attention outside of the Jewish circles of her native town. But now she began to send forth words that could not fail to challenge the applause of multitudes. The learned sought her acquaintance, and among them the poet Rittershaus was numbered.

Shortly after Mrs. Kleeberg had written *Das Lied vom Salz*, a poem on the oppressive tax imposed on salt by Prussia, a convention of literary celebrities took place at Frankfort-on-the-Main. Discussions as to the merits of certain productions elicited the remark that Jewish authors lacked patriotism, and that they did not properly understand how to give effect to their utterances. Thereupon Rittershaus read to the assembly the composition above-mentioned. All listened breathlessly. The piece was pronounced a model. The surprise may well be imagined, when the faith of the authoress was disclosed. No more would the hearers dare cast reflections on the ancient people, for the words, "The one who thus feels and writes is a Jewess," shamed them into perfect silence.

Mrs. Kleeberg thus earned an extensive fame, which increased when, during the late Franco-German war, she heightened the zeal of many, by her generous outpourings in behalf of her native country.

The strength of her religious convictions forced her to publicly repel the malicious accusations of Richard Wagner and Prof. Billroth against her race. Her emanations gained the well-timed praise of such personages as Prince Bismarck and Herr Lasker, who sent letters expressive of their thanks.

When Mrs. Kleeberg came to the United States, the reputation which had preceded her drew towards the poetess some of the ablest representatives of literature in its various branches. She was chosen a member of several societies, composed of individuals conspicuous in the ranks of letters, science and the fine arts.

Prominent among the poems of Minna Kleeberg are *Die West Mauer des Tempels*, *In Gottes Namen*, *Bar-Mizva*, *Dima ben Nethina*, *Im Ebenbilde Gottes*, *Schach*, and *Dichterweihe*. Most of these, besides others we omit naming, were contributed to Dr. L. Stein's *Freitag Abend*, of Frankfort-on-the-Main. The writings of Mrs. Kleeberg have been collected and published.

Painful it is to record that strides taken in the career of honor and usefulness were suddenly stopped short. The gifted authoress was not permitted to fully reap the harvest of her sowing. When not thirty-eight years of age, Minna Kleeberg sadly bade farewell to the world, in which so much that she yearned and craved for, remained. A solemn scene

was that which closed a life's mission, at New
Haven, Connecticut, on the last day of the year
1878—a scene indelibly impressed on the hearts
of relatives and friends, such as will be thought of
with sorrowful emotions, by all who will have learnt,
from the effusions of the German Jewess, how deep
were the sentiments that pervaded her breast.

NACHMAN KROCHMAL.

We are told that in bygone ages business and
Talmudical studies were associated. But the system has not altogether fallen into disuse. Of this
we have assurance in late accounts. Examples
are given of merchants who, after fulfilling their
daily occupations, repaired to the spot where Rabbinical writings were expounded. But towards the
close of the last century, and in the first quarter of
the present, it was more frequent for fathers to place
before their sons the ponderous volumes, embodying
the discussions of the Sages, beside the Journal and
Ledger. Rather than neglect the former, the latter
would be set aside. Under these influences Nachman
Krochmal was reared. Parental wealth did not occasion any deviation from the usual plan. It will
be seen how this affected his career.

Nachman Krochmal was born at Brody, in Galicia,
Austria, on the 18th of February, 1780. Nothing

of importance is recorded of his youth, save that he entered the mercantile profession, struggling, at the same time, to attain a secular education, in the pursuit of which he encountered severe obstacles. From the wonderful knowledge he afterwards displayed, we may fairly presume that a large portion of his time was spent in deep study and research.

To undertake the prodigious task which Krochmal performed—that of investigating the Bible, with a view of ascertaining the origin, unity, and date of each book, as well as to characterize its peculiarity of style and language—required a combination of intellectual powers, possessed by only a few of the greatest scholars. A subject of so wide a range, presenting many difficulties in the way of exposition, needed the ability and perseverance of one who could search into its intricacies, and set all forth in a clear and satisfactory light. In his endeavors to accomplish his purpose, Krochmal was subjected to adverse strictures, aspersions, and virulent attacks. Especially did he meet with strenuous opposition from those who held fast to accepted traditions, in his theories on the authorship and ages of the respective Scriptural writings. Undaunted, however, he pursued his investigations, and the results that followed will be referred to.

On account of feeble health, and physical infirmities, Krochmal published but little during his life. His principal works have since appeared, and, it is conceded, they evince immense learning. His interest in philosophy is shown in a production entitled, *Moré Nebuché Ha-Zemán* (A Guide to the Erring of the Present Age), which the renowned Dr. Leopold Zunz edited and published at Lemberg, in 1851.

Krochmal was an intimate associate of that prince of Jewish literators, Rapoport, and he enjoyed the respect, nay, the veneration of many illustrious personages. He died at Tarnopol, in Galicia, Austria, on the 31st of July, 1840. Those who have profited by the fruit of his labors, need not be told what a loss was experienced on that day.

The chief writings of Nachman Krochmal are on "The Sacred Antiquities and Their Import." They partly appeared in the Hebrew Annual, called *Kérem Chémed*, whose editor, Samuel Loeb Goldenberg, was distinguished alike for his scholarship and the sound judgment employed in conducting his excellent periodical. The subjects herein treated by Krochmal are (we quote the words of a writer): " 1. On the age of the comforting promises in the second part of Isaiah, chap. 40–66, in which he tries to demonstrate the late date of this part of the volume, and to show that Aben Ezra was of the same opinion, only that he veiled it in enigmatical language.

2. On the date and composition of Ezra and Chronicles, with an investigation of the ancient statement on this subject, contained in the Talmud, *Baba Bathra*, 14, *b*, which is very important. He tries to trace and analyze the different parts of which these books are composed, and to show that they extend to the destruction of the Persian Empire. 3. On the date and composition of Ezekiel, the Minor Prophets, Daniel and Esther, with an examination of the ancient statement on this subject, contained in the same passage of the Talmud, which is still more important, inasmuch as Krochmal shows here what is meant by *The Great Synagogue*, and tries to demonstrate that some portions of the Minor Prophets, belong to the period of the Greek Empire. 4. On the origin and date of Ecclesiastes, in which he insists that it is the latest composition in the canon."

Speaking of his personal traits, an author asserts that Krochmal's acquaintances, whether youths or men, derived much from his intercourse. To some he would afford a taste for the sublime outpourings of German or Hebrew poets; to others he would offer abundant light on geometry or mathematics. At one time he would explain passages in the philosophical writings of Maimonides; and again on the comments of Aben Ezra, into which he had dived with his acute mental vision. Such a character is truly inestimable.

EDWARD LASKER.

Civilization has wrought many wonderful changes in the moral, social and political condition of man. Thus, governments, once absolutely despotic, are now limited monarchies or republics. Men have struck for equal rights, and have largely obtained them. The followers of whatever creed are declared qualified to take part in state and national affairs.

The tidal-wave did not stop short, when nearing the banks of the Rhine, and futile will prove the combined attempts of reactionists to force it back. The anti-Semitic league, which would fain ostracize the emancipated Israelite, will be overwhelmed by the swelling current. A Jew, dreaded in the Reichstag, because of his trenchant speech, may be denied a re-nomination, but the leader of liberalism—our Lasker—will yet assert his power.

Edward Lasker was born at Jarocin, in Posen, Prussian Poland, October 14th, 1829. After receiving a preliminary education, he attended the seminary at Breslau, and obtained a knowledge of jurisprudence and mathematics. For three years he resided in England, studying the constitution and laws of that country. In 1856 he was appointed to an office under the Prussian Government; but his religion, as also his political views which he set forth in several excellent papers, prevented further advancement.

However, his election to the House of Deputies, as a member from Berlin, in 1865, met with approval. From his entrance therein, Lasker manifested an active interest in all important matters. He was several times re-elected to represent various districts, and his energies continued unabated. Conspicuous and foremost in everything, his popularity steadily increased.

Herr Lasker was one of the founders of the National Liberal party, but he is not wedded to any, save to that which upholds justice, and, therefore, on more than one occasion, he voted with the Progressive party.

For a considerable length of time, Lasker warmly supported Prince Bismarck's administration. But the introduction of a bill, aiming to limit the freedom of speech in Parliament, found in him a decided antagonist. The sagacious commoner, foresaw a direct hindrance to liberty in the Prime Minister's arbitrary and tyrannic measure, and forthwith directed a fiery attack upon it. This boldness brought on a rupture, of which the astute Prince took advantage to unseat his uncompromising opponent. Lasker's defeat at the election in 1879, is thus spoken of by a writer. " One of the strangest of recent occurrences in Germany is the compulsory withdrawal from the political arena of Lasker, the Liberal Parliamentary leader. Lasker has been one of the best and most popular orators of the Empire, and is conceded even by his opponents to be in character pure and above suspicion. He is . . . . poor, notwithstanding opportunities to become rich, and content to remain poor, rather than depart from his convictions, or soil his hands. He has beaten in fair, open Parliamentary fight more than one bitter enemy of his party, his race, and himself, and he threw the gauntlet many a time at Bismarck himself and had no difficulty in matching him. . . . For years Lasker was idolized by his party, and it was never supposed that he could possibly be shelved, but in the signal Conservative victory that the recent elections won for Bismarck, Lasker was wrecked. . . . The German Liberal press is filled with lamentations for his loss, which it hopes may be but temporary."

Herr Lasker was chosen an attorney-at-law in 1870. His erudite work on the constitutional history of Prussia, (New Edition, Leipsic, 1873), shows him a gentleman of brave mettle, an acute observer, and a far-sighted statesman.

EMMA LAZARUS.

The history of American Hebrews is of comparatively recent date. Nevertheless it presents the record of women who have honored their people, by employing their native language in a manner that has elicited favorable comment. Thus, to cite one instance, Miss Penina Moïse has received the deserved acknowledgment of her fellow-believers for the devotional poems and stirring hymns she has written for the Synagogue in Charleston, S. C. But it is of a poetess who has left an impress on English and American literature, recognized far beyond the city of her birth, that more than some passing remarks are suggested. Eminent scholars have publicly attested the intrinsic worth of her productions.

Emma Lazarus was born in the city of New York, July 22d, 1849. After being instructed in the rudiments of knowledge, she applied herself to reading. The discrimination she exercised in the choice of such books as would tend to cultivate her mental powers, became apparent on the appearance of her own works. Miss Lazarus displayed a particular fondness for poetry, and her skill in the rhythmic art was disclosed at an early date.

In 1866 Miss Lazarus brought forth the first volume of her poems, written between the ages of fourteen and seventeen. It exhibits precocity of genius in the rich imagery with which it teems, and a remarkable command of language. The soul of the authoress is in her work, hence the labor is doubly appreciated. Miss Lazarus issued a second volume in 1871, entitled "Admetus and Other Poems," which met with an enthusiastic reception, especially at the hands of English critics. The best notices appeared in the *Westminster Review*, the *Athenæum*, and the *Illustrated London News*, and from the last-named periodical we cull the following : "Miss Lazarus must be hailed by impartial literary criticism as a poet of rare original power. She has unconsciously caught from admiring perusal more, perhaps, of the style of Tennyson's Arthurian Idylls, in her narrative and dramatic pieces, than would seem fitly to attend the perfectly fresh and independent stream of her thought. But her conceptions of each theme, and the whole compass of her ideas and emotions, differ essentially from those of preceding or contemporary poets. In her treatment of the story of Alcestis and Admetus, one of the two Greek subjects among the poems in this volume, she is far happier than Mr. Browning in his half adaptation of Euripides. The motive of Alcestis in dying to preserve the life of her lord, is here not a mere blind womanly fondness. It is rather an exalted persuasion that he, as the best of men and kings, the saviour and wise ruler of his country, as a person honored of the gods, as a monarch gratefully and trustfully obeyed by the people, is an object most worthy of her noble self-sacrifice. Admetus, for his part, still refuses to let her die for him; but the solemn act is consummated by the intervention of Phœbus, his divine guest, and former assistant in his winning of Alcestis to be his wife. The conflict afterwards between Hercules and 'Death, and the return of life to Alcestis, are represented with more force, as well as more grace, in this poem than in that of Mr. Browning. Let the reader judge of this:

'Then from the dying woman's couch again
Her voice was heard, but with strange sudden tones.
" Lo, I awake—the light comes back to me.
What miracle is this?" And thunders shook
The air, and clouds of mighty darkness fell,
And the earth trembled, and weird horrid sounds
Were heard of rushing wings and flying feet,
And groans; and all were silent, dumb with awe,
Saving the king, who paused not in his prayer,
" Have mercy, gods!" and then again, " O gods,
Have mercy!"
    Through the open casement poured
Bright. floods of sunny light; the air was soft,
Clear, delicate, as though a summer storm
Had passed away, and those there standing saw,
Afar upon the plain, Death fleeing thence;
And at the doorway, weary, wellnigh spent,
Alcides, flushed with victory.' "

The same volume contains other beautiful poems, such as " Orpheus," " Tannhauser," "The Garden of Adonis," and " Regret;" also several patriotic pieces devoted to the cause of the Union in the late Civil War, as " Heroes," and " The Day of Dead Soldiers." The narrow limits of this sketch will, we regret to say, prevent even detached quotations from any of these thrilling poetical effusions.

A prose work by Miss Lazarus, entitled " Alide, —an Episode of Goethe's Life," was published in 1874. She has favored different journals and magazines with miscellaneous compositions. Her lines on the Jewish Synagogue at Newport, are full of pathos and religious sentiment. Of Miss Lazarus' contributions to the *Jewish Messenger*, there is one printed in an issue of October, 1877, which, we think, will interest Israelites, and it is therefore reproduced. The poem was written on the death of the Rev. Jacques J. Lyons, minister of the congregation *Shearith Israel*, of New York:

THE NEW YEAR.

The golden harvest-tide is here, the corn
Bows its proud tops beneath the reaper's hand.
Ripe orchards' plenteous yields enrich the land;
Bring the first fruits and offer them this morn,
With the stored sweetness of all summer hours,
The amber honey sucked from myriad flowers,
And sacrifice your best, first fruits to-day,
With fainting hearts and hands forespent with toil.
Offer the mellow harvest's splendid spoil,
To Him who gives and Him who takes away.

Bring timbrels, bring the harp of sweet accord,
And in a pleasant psalm your voice attune,
And blow the cornet greeting the new moon.
Sing, holy, holy, holy, is the Lord,
Who killeth and who quickeneth again,
Who woundeth, and who healeth mortal pain,
Whose hand afflicts us, and who sends us peace.
Hail thou slim arc of promise in the West,
Thou pledge of certain plenty, peace and rest.
With the spent year, may the year's sorrows cease.

For there is mourning now in Israel,
The crown, the garland of the branching tree
Is plucked and withered. Ripe of years was he,
The priest, the good old man who wrought so well
Upon his chosen glebe. For he was one
Who at his seed-plot toiled through rain and sun.
Morn found him not as one who slumbereth,
Noon saw him faithful, and the restful night
Stole o'er him at his labors to requite
The just man's service with the just man's death.

What shall be said when such as he do pass?
Go to the hill-side neath the cypress-trees,
Fall midst that peopled silence on your knees,
And weep that man must wither as the grass.
But mourn him not whose blameless life complete
Rounded its perfect orb, whose sleep is sweet,
Whom we must follow, but may not recall.
Salute with solemn trumpets the New Year,
And offer honeyed fruits as were he here,
Though ye be sick with wormwood and with gall.

Miss Lazarus has double claims to the recognition of her co-religionists, because the brilliant talents for which she is distinguished are now devoted to illustrate, in the English tongue, the outpourings of those immortal bards of Spain who beautified the Sephardic ritual. There will shortly appear in book-form, a series of essays on the Jewish poets of the Iberian peninsula in the Middle Ages. This will comprise copious extracts, translated from the works of grand old masters, affording no doubt a clear insight into the inimitable productions of Gabirol, Halevy, and Aben Ezra.

We have attempted to give simply a bird's-eye

view of the life and writings of Emma Lazarus. A broad vista, revealing the character and abilities of our authoress, will be open to those who unclasp the volumes with which she has enriched literature.

MORITZ LAZARUS.

In the knowledge of the various branches of speculative science, our German co-religionists have risen to the highest standard. A glance at any of the modern researches into subjects most abstruse and perplexing, will disclose the important part played by Israelites. To withhold from them praise, would be to wilfully tear out some of the brightest pages in the history of this wonderful age. Let the career of a mighty leader in metaphysics and transcendental philosophy confirm our position.

Prof. Dr. Moritz Lazarus was born at Filehne, in Posen, Prussian Poland, on the 15th of September, 1824. His father, Aaron Levin Lazarus, a distinguished Talmudist, and pupil of the celebrated Rabbi Akiba Eger, departed this life only a few years since, at an advanced age. His brother, L. Lazarus, Ph. D., also an eminent Rabbi and scholar, and Director of the Jewish Theological Seminary at Breslau, died in 1879.

Young Lazarus attended the congregational school in his native city, and received private instruction from his uncle, Abraham Waldenberg, (father of Prof. Waldenberg, of Berlin). With his father, he chiefly studied Rabbinical writings. When sixteen, he entered a mercantile house where he remained three years, and then returned to science, his favorite pursuit. From the gymnasium at Brunswick he passed to the University of Berlin, ending his collegiate course when twenty-two years old.

No one could doubt but that the mind of Dr. Lazarus commanded a very wide range. But any possible misgiving was dispelled by works on abstract topics, in which new ideas are evolved, and philosophical truths presented in a clear light. A passing allusion will be made to some of them. First, however, we shall speak of Lazarus as a Professor.

In 1860 a flattering admission of the Doctor's vast acquirements was made by his election to a professorship at the University of Berne, Switzerland. The satisfaction given by an untiring devotion to duty, led to his appointment as Dean of the Faculty of Philosophy, in 1863. One year later he was elevated to the rank of Rector of the University.

Thus, in the lapse of four years he attained stations that could only be filled by the very ablest and most profound scholars. Nor did the honors he gathered terminate there. In 1867 Prof. Lazarus became Instructor in Philosophy, at the Royal

Military Academy of Berlin. The climax was reached in 1873, by his being chosen Professor of Philosophy at the University of Berlin. The reader may judge of the qualifications of a man who, surrounded, as it were, by a constellation of shining lights, finds himself preferred to all others; for to occupy such a chair in such a college is, indeed, a recognition of preëminent talents.

Prof. Lazarus has displayed warm interest in Jewish matters. Twice he presided over important conferences; the Israelitish Synods held at Leipzig and Augsburg, in 1869 and 1871 respectively. He is one of the founders of the High School for the Science of Judaism, and since 1872 he has been President of its Directory. As head of the Society for assisting Jewish Students, he has shown an ardent desire for the spread of education among his fellow-believers; and as an Honorary Member of the Directory of the Union of German Hebrew Congregations, his influence has been sensibly felt. Other organizations reckon him among their directors.

Now to mention some of Lazarus' productions. His work "On the Moral Justification of Prussia and Germany," appeared in 1850. It was followed, in 1851, by an essay, "On the Idea and the Feasibility of a Science of National Psychology," in which originated the term, and the science of, National Psychology. Since 1859, the Doctor has issued, in

conjunction with his brother-in-law, Prof. Dr. H. Steinthal, the *Journal of National Psychology and Philology*. "The Life of the Soul," thus far in two volumes, contains various articles under different titles,
and it has passed through two editions—1877–'8.
"Ideal Problems" was published in 1878. "The
Origin of Morals," "The Theory of Sense-Illusions,"
and "Ideas in History," are writings replete with
suggestive thoughts. Of the first and the last, three
editions have appeared.

A scientific critic may review the emanations of
a pen so fertile; he may offer salient points, descriptive of their nature. We can merely name them.
Thus a conception, perchance, may be formed of the
mental labor those works must have entailed upon
their author, who, with energy and perseverance, has
set them all in array before the world.

ISAAC LEESER.

There is probably no name so familiar to American Israelites, as that of Isaac Leeser; and none
will ever say that the fame acquired was not justly
earned. Indeed, few persons can bear comparison
with him who is revered for his self-sacrificing devotion and unremitting labor. The present advanced
condition of Hebrews in this land of freedom must
be chiefly attributed to his ceaseless exertions for

their moral and spiritual welfare. In fact, the history of American Judaism and that of Isaac Leeser are one and the same.

The Rev. Isaac Leeser was born at Neuenkirchen, in the province of Westphalia, Prussia, on the 12th of December, 1806. His parents' pious disposition, early led the child to a proper understanding of his religion. He received a preliminary education, and remained for some time at the college at Münster, acquitting himself with honor. At the request of his uncle, Zalma Rehiné, who resided in Richmond, Virginia, Isaac, in his eighteenth year, left home for America, where he arrived in May, 1824. Taking up his abode with his uncle, he attended school, which, however, he soon left to engage in business. Though closely occupied during the day, he still found time to devote to mental culture, and his evenings were constantly spent in literary pursuits. He early evinced interest in religious affairs, as shown by the assistance given to the Rev. Isaac B. Seixas, in gratuitously teaching the younger portion of the Jewish community of Richmond.

It was not, however, until 1828 that Mr. Leeser attracted public notice. In that year, the London *Quarterly Review* came out with articles tending to defame the character of Jews and Judaism. On reading these slanderous productions, Mr. Leeser, decided at once to stand up for his fellow-believers, and he set forth a vindication in the columns of a Richmond newspaper. His remarks, couched in excellent language, and displaying much earnestness, produced a marked impression. When Mr. Leeser penned the reply he had resided but four years in this country, and his surprising acquaintance with English, in so brief a period, proves the aptitude he possessed for linguistic knowledge. The circumstance related clearly indicates the state of religious learning in America, when the defence of Judaism had to be assumed by an obscure young man.

The Congregation *Mickvé Israel*, of Philadelphia, had long needed the services of a pastor, and Mr. Leeser was at once set forward for the position. Though hesitating to enter upon such a task, he yielded to the wishes of his uncle and many friends, and was elected to the office in 1829. As spiritual leader of one of the most important congregations in the United States, a wide field was opened to his future efforts. Mr. Leeser added to official duties the delivery of English addresses and discourses to his flock, the first being pronounced on June 2d, 1830. Prior to that time no attempt to that effect, worthy of note, had been made in America, and the new system, meeting with favor, spread much farther than the city in which it was introduced.

Notwithstanding this self-imposed addition to

Mr. Leeser's obligations, his literary labors proceeded unchecked. In 1830 appeared his translation of Johlson's "Instruction in the Mosaic Religion," and, in 1833, a work entitled, "The Jews and the Mosaic Law," containing also the articles first written in defence of the Jews. In 1834 Mr. Leeser suffered from a severe attack of small-pox, which prostrated him for a while, but did not eventually weaken his inborn energies. Early in 1837 he issued some of his sermons, in two volumes, and in 1838 his Spelling-Book. A series of articles, written in 1839 and 1840 for the Philadelphia *Gazette*, against the strictures of the London *Quarterly Review* concerning Hebrews, was published in 1841, under the title of "The Claims of the Jews to an Equality of Rights." In 1839 Mr. Leeser brought out a Catechism, and other volumes of his sermons followed from time to time. He also edited several of the works of Miss Aguilar; the Dias Letters; "The Inquisition and Judaism;" and "Meditations and Prayers," by Mrs. Hesther Rothschild, etc.

In 1843 Mr. Leeser began the monthly magazine, known as *The Occident and American Jewish Advocate*, in the interest of Judaism, which he carried on until his death, having completed twenty-five volumes. Its publication was continued for twelve months, by Mayer Sulzberger, Esq., one of his executors. During one year of Mr. Leeser's editorship, *The Occident* came forth weekly, in the shape of an eight-page newspaper. Throughout its whole existence the periodical was ably conducted, always abounding with instructive and valuable reading matter. A thoroughly conservative organ, *The Occident* did not once deviate from its adopted course.

Mr. Leeser issued his edition of the Pentateuch in Hebrew and English in 1845, and afterwards the Daily Prayers, agreeably to both the German and the Portuguese customs. There was also published his translation of the complete set of Prayers for the Jewish Holidays, in accordance with the Portuguese ritual.

In 1850 Mr. Leeser retired from the ministry in the *Mickvé Israel* Synagogue, and on the formation of the Congregation *Beth-El-Emeth*, of Philadelphia, by some of his friends, in 1857, he was chosen its pastor, and he served in that capacity during the remainder of his life. Mr. Leeser gained much of his reputation by travelling. He visited various parts of the United States, everywhere exhibiting his eloquence, obviously to the spiritual advantage of his hearers.

Space will not permit even a cursory review of the multifarious labors of this famous divine. Many organizations, having for their object the improvement or temporal benefit of Israelites, were projected by him. The Hebrew Education Society, the Board of Hebrew Ministers, the Jewish Hospital, the Maimonides College, all of. Philadelphia, owe their foundation to the active efforts of Mr. Leeser. The Board of Delegates of American Israelites, the American Jewish Publication Society, and other institutions, are also greatly indebted to him for their creation. He advocated a union of the divers charities of Philadelphia, which was consummated some years after his decease in the present Society of the United Hebrew Charities.

When the Maimonides College opened at Philadelphia in October, 1867, Mr. Leeser, in acknowledgment of his endeavors for the cause, was elected Provost or President of the Faculty, his branch being Homiletics, Belles-Lettres and Comparative Theology.

Among Mr. Leeser's other published works, were renditions into English of Rabbi Joseph Schwarz's Geography of Palestine, and Moses Mendelssohn's "Jerusalem." But the production by which he is best known, and which would have sufficed to give him immortality, is a translation into the vernacular of the Hebrew Bible. Besides all these services to Judaism, Mr. Leeser was ever watchful of attacks from hostile camps, and many times did he enter the lists to combat for his co-religionists.

When considering the immense achievements, in a literary sphere, of a single individual, we are astounded at the power of human perseverance. Mr. Leeser's memory was marvellous. He could recognize, and even recollect the names of, persons whom he had not seen for many years. With a quick comprehension, he could perceive almost instantly the point of difficult questions. Though not educated as a Rabbi, he had some acquaintance with the numerous writings of the Sages, and his peculiarly retentive faculties enabled him to study much in a short time. As a speaker he commanded general admiration, and most of his addresses were delivered extempore.

The indefatigable industry of Mr. Leeser often occasioned spells of sickness, and towards the end of the year 1867 he was seized with an illness which proved fatal on the 1st of February, 1868. Thus, the Hebrews of America were deprived of a bold champion, a staunch friend, and a great benefactor, whom coming generations will hold in grateful remembrance.

MAXIMILIAN LETTERIS.

The beauties of Hebrew literature have been ably set forth by a countless number of prose writers, who labored to explain and critically delineate

the contents of Biblical and Post-Biblical compositions. To them we are beholden for the intellectual
development of Jewish communities. But we must
not forget our indebtedness to those who, through
the ardor of real poetry, have expressed their
thoughts in "words that burn." Notably, the bards
of the Middle Ages occupy lofty seats in the world
of letters. Nor is the present century destitute of
individuals who are in truth more than rhymsters.
Poland alone has given us splendid specimens of genius, and few have equalled, in depth of poetic sentiment, and grandeur of style, him of whom we
shall speak.

Dr. Maximilian Letteris was born at Ziolkiev,
Poland, on the 13th of September, 1800. His father, Rabbi Gershon Letteris, enjoyed much esteem
as a Talmudical scholar, and as the possessor of exceptional abilities. Having lost twelve of his children, Maximilian only being left, he determined to
do his utmost that the future of his son might be
worthy of a great man. Bent on that object, he
engaged in the task with unabated vigor, and the
results must have surely been encouraging to the
loving father.

When but a mere boy, Maximilian showed a remarkable acquaintance with the Bible and the Talmud. Desiring to obtain a more extensive knowledge than simply that of Hebrew, he devoted his

attention to German, and other modern languages, and their literature. But his parent did not favor this course, as he feared that his son might disregard the law; therefore he forbade secular studies altogether. The youth, who had already acquired a different taste, found it impossible to obey the injunction; hence he continued his favorite studies by stealth.

Young Letteris was, at an early age, placed under the charge of the celebrated Rabbi Nachman Krochmal, who enriched the mind of his pupil with the fruits of his own vast learning. Receiving instruction from so great a preceptor, it is not surprising that Letteris afterwards rose to a high station in literary circles. While yet in his youth, he gave unmistakable indications of the divine afflatus stirring within his breast. He wrote poems that charmed the reader, and served as a prognostic of a brilliant career.

In 1819 Letteris at last secured his father's consent to go where he deemed best in search of a wider range of knowledge. Accordingly, he entered the University of Vienna, and the year 1820 found him an assiduous student at that college.

In 1822 Dr. Letteris published his *Dibrè Shir* (Words of Song), a collection of poems, some from his pen, and others as translations. The reputation gained acted as a stimulus to more strenuous efforts. Letteris belonged to the school of Lyric Poetry, in which Hebrews have excelled. In fact, he may be deemed the most prolific of that class among his native fellow-believers.

In addition to sundry poems and prose-essays in German, as well as in Hebrew, there appeared *Gézang Yishaï*, a paraphrase of Racine's "Athalie," which met with an enthusiastic reception; *Sheloin Estér*, a version of Racine's "Esther," admired still more; and *Ben Abuyah*, Letteris' masterpiece, which alone would suffice to encircle his brow with the laurels of immortality. For the soul of a great poet is reflected therein. Every line is music. To the lover of Hebrew verse, this effusion is an echo of Andalusian songs. So invaluable was this production considered, that the French Academy seized the first opportunity to procure it. Almost as famous as the work just mentioned, is the elegy entitled *Yonah Homiyah* (The Moaning Dove), so full of pathos and intensity of religious' feeling. Concerning it, the Rev. Dr. H. Vidaver thus remarks: "I shall never forget until my last hour, what profound emotions of love for Judaism and Israel, did the song *Yonah Homiyah* awaken in my heart, when yet in my tender boyhood! I never saw this patriotic Jewish poem in print; it used to be traditionally delivered from one to another, and accompanied with a melody. We boys in Poland used to sing it, and our tears were all the time gushing from our eyes!"

Dr. Letteris was appointed, in 1831, corrector and proof-reader in one of the largest Hebrew printing-houses in Vienna, and he worked in the same capacity during the greater portion of his life. For the writings which elicited so much encomium were by no means of pecuniary advantage. Their author lived in poverty, and it was with considerable difficulty that he obtained the wherewith to support existence. He died at Vienna, Austria, on the 4th of June, 1871.

The literary success of Maximilian Letteris may be ascribed to the fact that he steadily followed the object in view, notwithstanding serious impediments. A bright light in our horizon might never have shone, if the Polish scholar had allowed the prejudices of the time, and the frowns of Fortune to prevail. His resolve to pursue the adopted course, despite all obstacles, earned him the name which is familiar to all but pretenders in the knowledge of modern Hebrew literature.

URIAH PHILLIPS LEVY.

The subject of the present sketch offers an illustration of an American Jew who did not allow official promotion to lower, in his estimation, the faith in which he had been born and reared, nor to erase from his heart his affection for his co-religionists.

He owed the respect paid him by his countrymen
to personal efforts, coupled with firmness of character, and the esteem of his brethren to a determined
attachment to the main principles of Judaism. It
will be our province to refer to the manifold services he rendered his native-land, when endeavoring
to reform the United States Navy, and to the dignity with which he upheld his office—never swerv-
ing from the line of duty.

Uriah Phillips Levy was born at Philadelphia,
April 22d, 1792. After pursuing a course of instruction, he entered the Navy, October 23d, 1812.
The United States, at that period, was engaged in
a war with Great Britain, and Levy served as an
officer on the brig *Argus*, which ran the blockade
to France, with Mr. Crawford, the American Minister to that country, on board. The vessel, after accomplishing her mission, ravaged the English Channel, destroying twenty-one British merchantmen, one
of which alone was worth $625,000. But the *Argus*
being finally captured, Levy and his shipmates were
held as British prisoners for two years.

In recognition of his gallant conduct, Mr. Levy
was created a Lieutenant on March 5th, 1817, and
subsequently a Commodore on February 9th, 1837.
He received the appointment of Post-Captain on
March 29th, 1844.

Captain Levy made many cruises into foreign

waters, the last of which, in 1858, as Flag Officer of the Mediterranean Squadron. His meritorious demeanor and bravery, had raised him to the highest station in the Navy.*

But more than for the undaunted courage which characterized the discharge of his obligations; more even than for the patriotism which raised him in the general esteem, Uriah Phillips Levy deserves to be ever remembered as a humanitarian. The great system he inaugurated has been adopted by many civilized nations; we mean, the abolition of corporal punishment to seamen, which put an end to cruelties that subordinate officers were compelled to endure. Ruthless practices had been indulged in to a fearful extent. Captain Levy saw that their continuance compromised the honor of his country, cast a stigma on Freedom, and outraged nature. Accordingly, he devised a scheme which recognized no superiority, but that which belongs to a well-earned elevation in the ranks. This plan would not suffer the least abuse of power by naval commanders. So noble a conception met, and will eternally meet, with the heartiest approval of the right-thinking.

One of the distinguishing traits of Commodore Levy's character was his admiration of Thomas Jefferson, whose family-seat at Monticello, Virginia, he

---

* It must be borne in mind that the office of Admiral was not created until the Civil War.

purchased. This property was confiscated by the Confederate Government, during the Rebellion.

Mr. Levy died at New York City, March 22d, 1862, in the full fruition of national honors. The monument erected to the memory of this worthy Hebrew, may be seen in that portion of the Cypress Hills Cemetery in use by the Congregation *Shearith Israel*, of New York.

As a lover of his country and a generous benefactor, Uriah Phillips Levy has been marked out a place in the annals of free America.

LOUIS LOEWE.

"There is a power behind the throne," is a common saying. Applied more widely than in its literal sense, it means that unseen influences are at work for good or for evil. Sir Moses Montefiore, whose name cannot be too often mentioned, is the recipient of letters, applications, memorials, and books of all sorts, from all parts of the world. He must of necessity advise with, and employ persons on whose abilities he may rely, to relieve him of the burden of correspondence. To the man who mostly stands by his side, and whose suggestions are practically felt by many of the philanthropist's beneficiaries, these lines are devoted.

The Rev. Dr. Louis Loewe was born at Zülz, in the province of Silesia, Prussia, in 1809. At the Academy of Rosenburg, in Silesia, he obtained a more than ordinary education. But to perfect his knowledge, he attended the colleges of Lissa, Nicolsburg, and Presburg, where he steadfastly pursued studies in theology, the Oriental languages, and scientific branches. When Dr. Loewe finally came forth from the University of Berlin, he was possessed of a remarkable fund of knowledge, that enabled him to take his stand by the side of the most cultured.

Repairing to England, Dr. Loewe became known to the Duke of Sussex and Admiral Sir Sydney Smith, under whose auspices he travelled, in the years 1836, 1837, and 1838, in Egypt, Nubia, part of Ethiopia, Syria, Palestine, Turkey, Asia Minor, and Greece, for the cultivation of the study of the Arabic, Coptic, Nubian, Turkish and Circassian languages and their literature. In 1839 the Duke of Sussex appointed the Doctor his lecturer on the Oriental tongues. He had, prior to this, been chosen Sir Moses Montefiore's private secretary. In that capacity, he made several journeys, with the venerated Baronet, to the East, on behalf of his oppressed co-religionists.

Dr. Loewe assumed the position of Head-Master of the Jews' College, Finsbury Square, in 1856; and

Examiner for Oriental Languages to the Royal College of Preceptors, in 1858. When, in 1868, Sir Moses Montefiore founded a Theological College, at Ramsgate, he selected his secretary as Principal and Director,—a fitting choice, for the Doctor's capacities are unquestionably great. The ease with which he reads the epistles, in a number of languages, sent to the Baronet, would serve as a proof. But, independent of that, he bears the reputation of an Orientalist. It is, moreover, averred that his lightning-like comprehension of the most abstruse topics astonishes even those who have been brought into close connection with him.

We will refer to some writings that have emanated from his prolific pen. A translation of J. B. Levinsohn's *Efes Dammim*, being a series of conversations between a Patriarch of the Greek Church and a Chief Rabbi of the Jews, was published in 1841, and followed, in 1849, by "Observations on a Unique Gold Coin," issued by Al-Âamir Beâkhcám Allah, Abû Ali Manzour Ben Mustali, tenth Caliph of the Fatimite dynasty. There also appeared "A Dictionary of the Circassian language," in 1854; "Origin of the Egyptian language"; "Letters from the East"; and a rendition into English, in 1872, of Rabbi David Nieto's *Matteh Dan*, which is a kind of supplement to the *Cuzari*, of Rabbi Jehudah Halevy, having for its object a vindication of the Oral

Law; besides numerous "Discourses," and papers in the transactions of learned associations.

Dr. Loewe is a member of the Royal Society of Great Britain and Ireland, and the Asiatic Society of Paris. A recent contribution to the *Jewish Messenger*, descriptive of a visit to the Samaritans of Naplouse, and of adventures among the Druzes, inspires a strong wish that this accomplished writer may allow his name to be brought more frequently before the public, so that the ripe fruits of his experience may become a source of literary pleasure to many who have enjoyed his past efforts.

SAMUEL DAVID LUZZATTO.

When attempting to dilate upon the careers of individuals whose talents and acquirements have created wonder, and excited the deepest veneration, one must keenly feel that he will fall short of the undertaking. Samuel David Luzzatto may be safely said to have excelled all his contemporaries as a Hebraist. We make this assertion with a boldness warranted by the testimony of profound critics. How it was given to a man to accomplish single-handed what might have scarcely been expected from the combined energies of many, is a marvel to scholars.

Samuel David Luzzatto, the descendant of a very

learned family, was born at Trieste, Austria-Italy, on the 22d of August, 1800. Among his ancestors, Moses Hayim and Ephraim Luzzatto are names not unknown to fame. Hezekiah Luzzatto, the father of Samuel, though a turner by trade, possessed such knowledge of the Scriptures and Rabbinical writings as assisted him very materially in furthering the boy's education. When three years old, Samuel was sent to school, where, incredible as it may seem, he began to read and translate the Pentateuch. At four and a half he went to the *Talmud Torah* institution, remaining there a number of years, and exhibiting a proficiency which entitled him to frequent promotion. Then Rabbi Mark Isaac Cologna took charge of the lad, and taught him Hebrew Grammar. At the same time, and for five years, young Luzzatto received instruction in Talmud from Abraham Eliezer Levy, Chief Rabbi of Trieste; and he also pursued the study of classical and modern languages, and of secular branches of literature.

Very early in life, Luzzatto evinced a taste for poetry, and he would try his hand at rhymes, both in Italian and Hebrew. When only eleven years, he commenced to write a Hebrew grammar, and, at twelve, he translated the life of Æsop from his native language into the sacred tongue, and even ventured to commit to paper some observations on the Five Books of Moses. Having obtained as a prize at school the celebrated work of Montesquieu, *Considerations sur les Causes de la Grandeur des Romains et de leur Decadence*, he eagerly devoured its contents, and ascribed to it a considerable influence in the moulding of his mental faculties.

In 1813 Luzzatto rendered into Italian some difficult portions of the ritual of the German Jews. Encouraged by a natural aversion for the mystical interpretation of Holy Writ, then in vogue, he would engage in discussing Cabbalism with his father, trying to show its fallacies. It might appear impossible that a youth could convince his parent, already advanced in age, of the falsity of a system to which he had been wedded, and which counted adherents among the most polished literators; but the father did yield to his son's arguments, and gave up the study of the Cabbala. The subject of our sketch now took up philosophy and logic, and, notwithstanding that straitened means compelled him to attend to household duties, he still kept at Locke and Condillac.

The first of Luzzatto's productions, a volume of poems, called *Kinor Nangim* (Sweet Harp), was indited in 1815. It contains thirty-seven pieces, one of which is descriptive of the service of the High Priest on the Day of Atonement, and another of the national misfortune by the destruction of Jerusalem. But lately a second and

large-sized volume of poems under the same title
has been issued. In 1817 Luzzatto wrote *Maa-
mar Hannickud*, a pamphlet on Hebrew punctuation, aiming at a denial of the authenticity of
the *Zohar*, the principal Cabbalistic work. This
was followed the next year by *Torah- Nidréshet*,
(The Law Examined),—now published in an Italian
translation by Rabbi M. C. Porto, —a philosophico-
theological treatise, tending to prove the authorship of the Pentateuch by Moses; and *Chélek
Kechélek Yochélu*, a short poem, in vindication of
the ways of Providence.

But despite all that Luzzatto had written, he
continued unknown to his co-religionists until 1818.
The following incident served to introduce him into that circle where he was destined to sit a
monarch: On the 9th of June of the year mentioned, a daughter of an Israelite of high standing
was married at Trieste. The celebration of the
wedding had elicited the composing of an enigma,
copies of which had, as usual, been handed to
the learned for a solution. Luzzatto's father obtained one of these, and endeavored in vain to
discover the answer. At last the son, to relieve
his parent, requested to be allowed a short time
for reflection. He solved the enigma, and added
thereto a few lines in verse. This incident was the
foundation of his fame.

Yet with all, the material advancement of the author was not secured. The elder Luzzatto wished his son to follow some trade, or mechanical pursuit; but the young man very strongly objected, feeling that he possessed the qualities to make his mark as a writer. At first, he was employed as tutor in a number of private families, and he contributed to the *Bikkuré Haittim*, a Hebrew periodical, published at Vienna. The deep learning of Samuel David Luzzatto soon attracted attention abroad. His capacities shone forth so brilliantly, that he was deservedly placed among the most renowned Jewish *literati*.

In 1829 the Rabbinical college at Padua was opened, and Luzzatto became the Professor of Biblical Literature. While he lived, that seminary grew in reputation as a model university. But it did not long survive the Professor. With his death, the interest once evinced by the community ceased.

It was, while fulfilling the onerous requirements of this position, that Luzzatto penned the works which stamped him as a real genius. The industry and research he used in the preparation of his books are truly amazing. Nor did the fruits of early and painful exertions fail to appear in all their splendor. Scholars hastened to pay their obeisance to a man whom they were proud to own as master. What can be added to the grand

tribute of Prof. Dr. H. Graetz, who says : " If Krochmal and Rapoport were the fathers of Jewish history,
Luzzatto must be acknowledged as her mother." *

Only a passing reference to the most noted
writings of the Padua Professor can here be made.
Besides innumerable articles in nearly every Jewish
journal and magazine in Europe, there were published, " Dialogues on the Cabbala, the Zohar,
the Antiquity of the Vowel-Points and Accents
of the Bible," seeking to gainsay the Cabbala,
and to show that the *Zohar* dates from the thirteenth century, the vowel-points from the fifth,
and the accents, probably, from the sixth; *Prole-
gomeni ad una Grammatica Ragionata della Lin-
gua Ebraica*, on Hebrew Grammar; *Oheb Gér*, on
the Aramaic version of Onkelos; " Moral Theology;" "Dogmatic Theology;" "French Notes on
Isaiah," written at the request of Rosenmüller;
"Italian Translation of, and Hebrew Commentary
on, the Pentateuch, with a Critical and Hermen-
eutical Introduction;" "Isaiah," translated into Italian, with a Hebrew comment, and considered by
some, Luzzatto's master-piece; an Italian rendition
of Job; " Historico-Religious Discourses;" annotations on a collection of inedited poems by Rabbi
Jehudah Halevy, entitled *Betulath Bath Jehudah*;
and an Italian version of almost the entire Hebrew Bible.

---

* *Geschichte der Juden*, XI. 502.

Prof. Luzzatto also carried on an exceedingly large correspondence with Rapoport, Munk, Krochmal, Reggio, Jost, Geiger, Albert Cohn, Zunz, Carmoly, Dukes, Fürst, Sachs, Letteris, Pinsker, Kayserling, Frankel, Graetz, Steinschneider, Kirchheim, Jellinek, and a host of other celebrities. To his last days he was busily occupied, even devoting hours of the night to literary labors.

On the 30th of September, 1865, "the Sabbath of Sabbaths," Samuel David Luzzatto breathed his last at Padua, Italy. The news of his demise spread like wild-fire, and sent a thrill into the hearts of thousands who had learned to honor him whose life's design had been the glorification of Judaism; a man of whom it may be said he was "One of the few, the immortal names, that were not born to die."

Prof. Luzzatto's eldest son, Philoxene, deceased, whose mental excellencies cannot be too highly praised, is spoken of in the succeeding sketch; the second, Isaiah, is at present actively engaged in editing the posthumous works of his revered father. Of the two other sons, Joseph is a lawyer, and an eminent political economist; and Benjamin is a celebrated physician, lately appointed Professor of Pathology, in the University of Padua.

PHILOXENE LUZZATTO.

In the array of notabilities which this series has so far set to view, there will have been seen youths whose continued achievements predicted a splendid future, but whose careers were cut short by an untimely death. Davids and Hartog—the one through the well-directed use of his precocious talents; the other through his industry and genuine devotion to religious principles—will, perforce, fasten themselves on the memory of posterity. But admiration changes into veritable reverence when we look at the character of a young man, who, in his own sphere, stands alone in the annals of Judaism of our century. That no hyperbole is indulged in, an outline of the history of this real genius will confirm.

Philoxene Luzzatto was born at Trieste, Austria-Italy, on July 10th, 1829. No sooner was he able to read than his innate tendencies became visible. What presented the greatest difficulties chiefly arrested his attention. Thus naturally inclined, he overcame linguistic perplexities almost by intuition. Like Italian—his native language—French, German, and afterwards English were brought under his absolute control. But he also mastered Hebrew, Aramaic, Syriac, and Arabic; then Latin, Greek, and Sanscrit; and finally Ethiopian.

When only thirteen, young Luzzatto deciphered

some old inscriptions on tombstones in the Padua Cemetery, the meaning of which had baffled the understanding of eminent scholars. This effected an introduction to a class of men, with whom he thereafter closely associated. How nobly he devoted the advantage thus obtained! His intercourse and correspondence with the literators of the age were solely in the interest of Judaic science.

When fifteen, Philoxene read a narrative of travels in Abyssinia, by a Frenchman, M. D'Abbadie, in which more satisfactory accounts than those formerly received were given of Israelites in that far-off land. He immediately wrote to the author, and to the chiefs of the Jews dwelling in the distant region, to obtain accurate information on the subject. After waiting long, replies came, and the welcome help, together with the notices he had gathered from various writings on the topic, enabled him to set at once to work on a history of the *Falashas*, as the Abyssinian Hebrews are called.

Philoxene's delineation of the cuneiform inscriptions at Nineveh displays acumen and ingenuity. Noticing a similarity between them and the Sanscrit, he published *Le Sanscritisme de la Langue Assyrienne*, in 1849; and *Études sur les Inscriptions Assyriennes de Persèpolis, Hamadan, Van et Khorsabad*, in 1850. Then followed, in 1852, *Notice sur Abou-Iousouf Hasdaï Ibn-Schaprout*, on a Hebrew statesman of Spain, in the tenth century, a generous patron of literature. *Mémoire sur les Juifs D'Abyssinie ou Falashas*, on the Jews of Abyssinia or Falashas, appeared in the *Archives Israélites*, of Paris, after the author's death.

Young Luzzatto's fame had spread abroad, and he was honored by an election as member of the Oriental Society of Germany, as well as of the Academy of Padua. The benefit derived from studying at the Rabbinical College, wherein his father taught, was evidenced in his Italian translation of, and splendid Hebrew commentary on, eighteen chapters of Ezekiel. Furnished with a talisman by his surname, he undertook a tour through Germany and France, where he examined ancient manuscripts in museums and academies. Wherever he journeyed, an enthusiastic reception was tendered him by the *savants*.

Of Philoxene Luzzatto's minor productions, his remarks on the existence of an Assyrian god, named Semiramis, and on the inscriptions on the ruins of the Israelitish Cemetery of Paris, are of special importance.

The life of young Luzzatto was, unhappily, destined to be meteor-like, most luminous, but transient. While on his travels a disease overtook him, and he endured for many months excruciating pains. At length he arrived at Padua, but only to die. Even during intense suffering, his mind was bent on literary objects. The last pages of his work on the Falashas, he dictated when near his end. On January 25th, 1854, the spirit returned to its Maker. "The bowl was broken, the silver chord was loosed."

All may not soar so high as Philoxene Luzzatto, for towering were his capacities. But everyone can usefully apply the divine gifts of intelligence and reason; and, what is most essential for an Israelite, he can employ those Providential blessings to uphold the glory of his faith.

ROBERT LYON.

For many years, Hebrews lived in America in almost total silence, indifferent, to all appearances, to the absence of an organ through which their voices could be heard. But as years rolled on, it became obvious to some, that the establishment of a medium for the presentation of Jewish ideas, the diffusion of Jewish knowledge, and the upholding of the Jewish religion, would greatly enhance the status of Israelites in this country. Such a conviction, however, assumed no tangible form until 1843, when the Rev. Isaac Leeser brought out *The Occident and American Jewish Advocate*, as a monthly magazine. But the first weekly paper, published in the interest of Judaism, was *The Asmoncan*, of whose editor we will briefly speak.

Robert Lyon was born at London, England, on January 15th, 1810. Though early destined for mercantile pursuits, he gave himself up to study, and, before reaching manhood, he had written essays for different journals. Shortly after starting in business at London, Mr. Lyon joined the Synagogue in Maiden Lane, where his talents and integrity soon gained him the good-will of the congregation, and he was elected its Treasurer. On the marriage of Queen Victoria, in 1840, Mr. Lyon accompanied Baron de Goldsmid, as a delegate, to present a congratulatory address to her Majesty, in person.

Mr. Lyon arrived in the United States in 1844, and engaged in a manufacturing enterprise, but without success. Turning his attention to the Jews of New York, he felt that such an important, numerous, and wealthy community ought not to be without a journal setting forth its claims. Still, no one was willing to supply the want. Then Mr. Lyon took the matter in hand, and, on the 26th of October, 1849, he began the publication of *The Asmonean*. For nearly nine years he conducted the paper with dignity and ability, numbering among his contributors several gentlemen well-known for their scholarship. Mr. Lyon edited, at the same time, the New York *Mercantile Journal*, devoted to commerce.

Irreproachable in his private character, cultured and refined, Robert Lyon might have long enjoyed public confidence, but a sudden illness cut him off in the middle of his days, on March 10th 1858.

Neither *The Asmonean*, nor the New York *Mercantile Journal*, held out long after their editor's death. But from the seeds planted by the first have sprung the *American Israelite*, the *Jewish Messenger*, the *Hebrew Leader*, the *Jewish Record*, the *American Hebrew*, and other periodicals of a similar nature. May they always labor for the welfare of our co-religionists, and for the maintenance of those sublime principles given to Israel's safe-keeping.

DAVID WOOLF MARKS.

It is not our purpose to trace the origin of Jewish Reform in Great Britain. But as names, not unfrequently, fail to convey correct ideas, a few remarks may be deemed pertinent. To confound Reform in England with that in Germany and America, would be an error. The movement that gave prominence to the subject of this sketch, opposed the traditions of Judaism only in a very moderate degree. No departure from the ceremonial ordinances of the Mosaic code, and its moral tenets was attempted. This we are impelled to say in obedience to historical truth. Still the ritual innovations opened a sore which is not yet entirely healed, and which, for a time, rankled and festered to the injury of a great religious body.

The Israelite to whom attention is drawn, has led Anglo-Jewish Reform from its incipient stage.

The Rev. Prof. David Woolf Marks was born at London, England, in 1811. He attended the Jews' Free School, obtaining instruction in the rudiments of knowledge. His father died leaving him young, and the support of the family materially devolved upon the lad. All his leisure moments, however, were assiduously devoted to study.

Employed to read prayers in the houses of wealthy people, the youth's appearance and voice impressed many with favor. To this circumstance must be attributed his rising to the position of assistant reader in the Duke's Place (German) Synagogue. After having filled that office for a number of years, Mr. Marks was appointed Secretary of the old Orthodox Congregation of Liverpool. In the prosecution of his duties, he gathered around him a host of friends who bore testimony to his industry and efficiency. But subsequent events showed Mr. Marks' talents to the best advantage.

Prior to the year 1840, numerous petitions, couched in respectful language, had been sent to the Wardens of the Bevis Marks (Portuguese) Synagogue, urging alterations in the ritual, and the preservation of more order and decorum in the Divine worship. The establishment of a House of Prayer at the west end of London, by reason of the distance of a number of members from the sacred precincts, was also pressingly solicited. But these memorials, though they did occasion considerable discussion on the part of the Elders, were never acted upon. Exhausting every means to accomplish their objects, several gentlemen of high standing, both of the *Sephardim* and *Ashkenazim*, convened together, and determined to secede, and form a new Congregation. Among the advocates of the plan were the widely-known families of Goldsmid, Mocatta, Henriques and Elkin. But all realized the difficulty of selecting, as a spiritual guide, a person equal to their needs. Mediocrity would not answer when a staunch defender of their views was demanded. At the suggestion of Dr. Joshua Van Oven, Mr. Marks was invited to London, to meet some Hebrews who had espoused the new cause. The interview resulted in his election. "The West London Congregation of British Jews," as the body was called, consecrated its first Place of Worship, in Burton street, on January 28th, 1843. The Rev. Mr. Marks conducted the service, and delivered the dedicatory address. In 1851 a removal was made to an edifice in Margaret Street, Cavendish Square, and in 1868 to the present handsome Synagogue in Berkeley Street.

Naturally, this separation could not be regarded with indifference. The Elders of the Portuguese Congregation, at their meetings of February 26th, and March 4th, 1842, proclaimed the ban of excommunication or *Hérem* against the separatists, Mr. Marks, and every Jew who acknowledged his ministration, being included in the writ.

Happily, bitter animosities have subsided. A spirit of tolerance has worked a beneficial change. The real interests of the Jewish people are now watched over in England, by all who adore the God of Sinai. The anathema has never been revoked, but it has become a dead letter which none wish to resuscitate.

Mr. Marks' flock continue in their attachment to him. For the Pastor has labored thirty-eight years to make good the expectations formed on the qualifications early exhibited. Modest in his demeanor, he quietly performs obligations of the importance of which he early became sensible. His constituents declared pulpit instruction an essential, and, therefore, sermons are delivered at the Synagogue on each Sabbath. The Minister compiled the Prayer-Books in use, and arranged the order of the services.

Through the aid of Sir (then Mr.) Francis H. Goldsmid, the Congregation was recognized by Parliament, and allowed the rights pertaining to religious corporations. In 1857 a kindred institution was established at Manchester, and the Rev. Dr. Gustav Gottheil, at present, Rabbi of the "Temple Emanuel," of New York City, occupied the pulpit for several years. It is now under the ministerial charge of the Rev. L. M. Simmons, B. A.

Besides attending to the immediate wants of his congregation, Mr. Marks has been active in furthering educational designs. This fact, together with the abilities he was known to possess, gained him the Chair of Hebrew in the University College of London, in 1848, as the successor of the lamented Prof. Hyman Hurwitz. Recently he was honored by being chosen Dean of the Faculty of Arts and Sciences.

Prof. Marks is a director of several organizations, such as "The Anglo-Jewish Association," and "The Western Philanthropic Society." He often lectures before associations not of his people, and, as an orator, compares favorably with the best among the English clergy.

Of literary productions Prof. Marks has published two volumes of sermons, and a pamphlet, "The Law is Light," in addition to having done editorial work in Smith's "Dictionary of the Bible," and contributed to the press.

It has been held that his unseen influence with eminent statesmen considerably assisted in bringing about the passage of the Bill for the relief of Jewish disabilities in the British Empire—an intimate acquaintance with the foremost in that struggle for equal rights, gives support to this assertion.

A self-made man—as the Rev. Prof. Marks certainly is—may now look back on the past with satisfaction. His efforts have not gone unrewarded. They have

upheld the high social standing of that portion of the
community he has served, and have prepared the way
for a reconciliation which will strengthen the bonds of
Anglo-Jewish brotherhood.

ISAAC PESARO MAUROGONATO.

It has not been long over thirty years since the
gates of the narrow and unventilated quarters in
which the Jews of Rome had been ·confined for ages,
were thrown down.   But even after Pius IX., feigning
to respond to the demands of the time, granted a gra-
cious boon, and allowed his subjects, so caged in, to
leave the Ghetto, few ventured out of its limits.   They
knew that rooted prejudice would give them no rest beyond the horrid precincts.   The real liberation experienced under the popular King, Victor Emanuel II., in-
fused a new spirit into the Italian Hebrews.   With astounding rapidity they who were deemed the lowest,
forced themselves up to distinction by talents and character.   We find among them leaders in municipal and
national affairs, and the Italian Parliament shows a Mor-
purgo, a Luzzatti, a Maurogonato, and others whose
judgment is ripe and whose counsel is heeded —and
here the inestimable services of Samuel Alatri, the
champion of the Roman Jews, must be publicly acknowledged.   But it is of Maurogonato—aptly
styled by his countrymen, " an athlete in Parliamentary debate"—that some slight information is thought
to be opportune.

Isaac Pesaro Maurogonato was born at Venice, November 5th, 1817. When he began to apply his faculties to the study of the Law, he did it with an earnestness that finally secured to him the degree of *Doctor*. A maternal uncle, greatly attached to the youth, named him his heir, and bequeathed him a large fortune.

Maurogonato continued at his profession, while at the same time he displayed an active interest in politics. Having contracted a strong friendship for the renowned Daniel Manin, the Venetian Dictator, he labored with that patriot to effect reforms in the government of his native city.

During the stormy days of 1848, Maurogonato was appointed Postmaster-General of Venice, and shortly after he became a member of the financial commission. In 1849 he was called to the most delicate and trying office of Minister of Finance and Commerce. In this capacity the duty devolved upon him to provide Venice with food, the city being besieged by the Austrians. In that station his probity and civic virtues became objects of general admiration. Notwithstanding the great pressure on the public treasury, he retired from office leaving in it a larger sum than it contained on his assuming the ministry. After the fall of the Provisional·Government, and the return of the Austrians to Venice, one of the authorities, astonished to find accounts so scrupulously kept and minutely rendered, exclaimed, " I never would have thought that those Republican rebels could be so honest!"

Maurogonato, together with Manin and others, lived for some time in exile, and he afterwards made a short sojourn in the Ionian Islands. Returning home, he directed his attention to banking and insurance matters.

When Venice became a part of the kingdom of Italy, in 1860, Maurogonato was elected a deputy to Parljament, which position he filled with so much credit that popular will again placed him as high. He now ranks among the life-senators of his native country.

Maurogonato has published several essays, and has frequently contributed to various political organs. As a thorough financier, he has few equals throughout Italy. His private character is unblemished, his charity is without stint. It is important to mention that, while Maurogonato is an advocate of every measure that may benefit the State, he is neither forgetful of the interests of his fellow-believers, nor of the faith of his fathers.

RAPHAEL MELDOLA. .

The Portuguese Jews of Great Britain have had the fortune of obtaining as spiritual chiefs, ripe scholars and men of undoubted piety. Rabbi David

Nieto, the *Haham* during a portion of the eighteenth century, was distinguished as a philosopher, physician, poet, mathematician, astronomer and theologian. So rare a combination of learning could not fail to hand down his name to posterity. But in a lesser degree only than Nieto, Meldola exhibited capacities which marked him out as a divine of vast attainments.

The Rev. Dr. Raphael Meldola was born at Leghorn, Italy, in 1754. His father, Rabbi Moses Meldola, had occupied the position of Professor of Oriental Languages at the University of Paris, and gained renown by his literary productions. In fact, the Meldola family for many generations gave the world great and erudite Rabbis. Raphael Meldola pursued a regular course of studies, soon developing those latent talents destined to be brought into requisition for the benefit of the House of Israel, and for the glory of their possessor. When but fifteen, Meldola was permitted to take his seat in the first Rabbinical university. In 1803 he obtained the title of Rabbi; and, as such, was empowered to settle disputed cases, by *Din Torah*, or Mosaic and Talmudical laws, according to the custom then in vogue throughout Italy.

In 1805 Rabbi Meldola proceeded to London, whither he had been called, to fill the vacant office of *Haham* of the Portuguese community. During his ministration stirring events took place, in the course of which the Rabbi's abilities showed to great advantage.   Dr. Meldola cultivated the acquaintance of scholars, and enjoyed the esteem of Christians, not less than that of Israelites.   The sermons he occasionally delivered were in Spanish, and though the subject-matter was always excellent, the language of Spain, once universally understood by the congregation, had then become almost obsolete among the young, who naturally preferred their native language.   But the special characteristics of Dr. Meldola were his benevolence and generosity, which led him to sacrifice time and means for others, while his humble and unpretentious manners increased the respect entertained for the learning of the Rabbi.

Dr. Meldola died on the 1st of June, 1828, aged seventy-four years.   He was interred by the side of his countryman and predecessor, Rabbi David Nieto, an honor which he particularly craved.

To mention a few of Rabbi Meldola's writings: first appeared *Korban Minha*, explanatory of the service of the High Priest, read in the Portuguese Synagogues on the Day of Atonement.   In 1796 was issued *Hupat Hatanim*, which is said to display great knowledge of mathematics, as well as of Talmud.   Dr. Meldola left several works in manuscript, one of which, originally written in Hebrew, and translated by his son, the Rev. David Meldola, is entitled *Dérech Emunah*, (The Way of Faith).   It treats of Jewish doctrines, rites, etc.

The Rev. David Meldola, who, after his father's death, became presiding officer of the *Beth Din*, or Ecclesiastical Board of the *Sephardim*, acquired distinction for his abilities as a Hebraist and linguist. He was also a native of Leghorn, having emigrated with his parents, when rather young, to England. Mr. Meldola died in March, 1853, and with him closed a long line of eminent scholars who had successfully labored in the field of sacred literature.

GIACOMO MEYERBEER.

Years of study would be required to write understandingly on the origin, history, and modern development of the sublime art of Music. Therefore, in presenting what relates to the career of a great celebrity, we must beg the kind indulgence of our readers for attempting that which others, by their full knowledge of the subject, have effectually accomplished.

Giacomo Meyerbeer (properly Jakob Meyer Beer) was born at Berlin, Prussia, on the 5th of September, 1794, of a family some of whose members had become remarkable for their musical abilities. As early as his fifth year, he performed tunes on the piano spontaneously. After receiving instruction from various tutors, he was placed in the conservatory at Cassel, under the charge of that distinguished musician, the Abbé Vogler. He had already studied dramatic composition under Bernhard Anselm Weber. While at Cassel he formed the acquaintance and friendship of the renowned *maestro*, Carl Maria von Weber, with whom he competed in the production of church music.

Meyerbeer soon brought forth a *cantata*, " God and Nature." This was followed by his first opera, " Jephthah's Vow," which passed its trial on the Munich stage, in 1812. It failed, however, to arouse the audience, and, though warmly admired by Vogler, Weber, and others, it was considered a failure. Meyerbeer now proceeded to Vienna, where, at the express desire of the Court, he composed " The Two Caliphs." But it, unfortunately, met the fate of the previous opera.

Italian music was, at that time, in the ascendency, and, by the advice of Salieri, director of the Vienna opera, Meyerbeer visited Italy, where he became a convert to the new Italian school, and what he afterwards produced proved highly popular. " Romilda and Constanza" was greeted with deafening applause at Padua, in 1819. Then came " Semiramide," performed at Turin, the same year; " Emma of Resburg," at Venice, in 1820, and which created a *furor*; " Margaret of Anjou," " The Exiled of Granada," and " The Crusader." The success of the last work was immense. For many weeks it remained the standing programme of the theatres of Italy and Germany, and its softness and richness of tone, afforded the most decisive proofs of the wonderful capacities of its author. Meyerbeer now took up his residence at Paris, where, in 1831, after very active preparations, "Robert, the Devil," one of the grandest of his operas, was given to an expectant public. It excited the wildest enthusiasm throughout France, England, Italy, Austria and Russia. Meyerbeer may be said to have reached the climax of his fame on the appearance of "The Huguenots," though "The Pilgrimage to Ploermel," and "The Prophet," won universal encomiums. Among the other of our composer's operatic works may be mentioned "Peter the Great," "Dinorah," "The African," and "Almanzor;" the last-named having never been represented, by reason of the illness of the *Prima Donna* chosen to introduce it upon the stage. Meyerbeer likewise wrote a vast number of sacred and miscellaneous pieces, all of which clearly show the versatility of his genius.

The German poet, Heine, said of Meyerbeer: "He is the man of the times; his themes are those of the spirit of the times, and embody the struggles of modern history for liberty; the cry of desperation of the writhing century finds vent in *The Huguenots, The Prophet*, and *Robert*. The passions of a fettered and gagged generation send forth their shrieks and wailings, and utter their claims for sympathy in measured words, and the brazen sounds of the orchestra."

At Paris, France, on the 2d of May, 1864, Giacomo Meyerbeer, when nearly three score years and ten, was called to his final home. But those rich legacies, his musical productions, will be the laurels forever encircling his name.

Meyerbeer's brothers, Wilhelm, the astronomer, and Michael, the dramatist, did good service to the cause of progress, and their own labors bespeak the praise of the ·wise.

MOSES MONTEFIORE.

When the history of the Jews of our century shall be written, universal consent will assign the brightest page to the man whose name rises on every lip with a blessing. He needs not feel lowered from his eminence when looking back at the Hasdaïs and Hannagids of Spain—patrons of learning, defenders of their race; for his gold flows like a perennial stream ·to benefit the indigent, and encourage sacred knowledge. The days· of his existence have been of endless service to Israel and mankind. God destined that Hebrew as an exemplar of his age. To teach mercy, he was, like Moses of old, sent to Kings' palaces with Divine messages; to instil veneration for the revealed Law, he was made to withstand all the allurements which beset a princely station ; to point to the eternity of prophetic promises, he was inspired to inscribe JERUSALEM on his escutcheon.   Is there an Israelite that must be told to whom these imperfect utterances apply?   All know the deliverer.

Sir Moses Montefiore, Bart., F. R. S., was born at Leghorn, Italy, on the 24th of October, 1784, while his parents were there on a visit; but he was soon brought to London.   His father, Joseph E. Montefiore, Esq., a noted banker, controlled considerable means, which he freely used to give his children an excellent education.*

Our Moses soon rose to prominence as a successful merchant, and more so for his probity and benevolence. He evinced the liveliest interest in Jewish affairs, hence, in April, 1828, he was elected a member of the Board of Deputies of British Jews, an organization founded in 1760, and still commanding influence at home and abroad.

It must be remembered that when said association was formed, as a protection to Israelites, these could not take part in matters relating to the government of Great Britain.   An insuperable obstacle was the ceremony attending induction into office, such as being obliged to receive the sacrament of the Lord's Supper,

---

*Of the brothers of Sir Moses, Abraham was an important member of the Jewish community.

and to be sworn "On the true faith of a Christian," etc. The Board of Deputies labored long and strenuously to have the obnoxious acts repealed, but not till the year 1858 did the yearnings and strivings of zealous men prove successful.

On the resignation of Moses Mocatta, Esq., the efficient President, in 1835, Moses Montefiore, whose exalted character had ever imparted solemn dignity to the Board, sat as its chief. In 1837 this most popular Israelite was preferred to the office of Sheriff of London and Middlesex, and, in the same year, Queen Victoria, valuing a subject acknowledged to be one of nature's noblemen, created him a Baronet, with the privilege of using a coat-of-arms—an honor conferred only on peers of the realm. .

But in 1840 the foundation-stone of that greatness which will ever distinguish our champion was laid. When a cry of misery from Damascus wrung the soul of every Jew, Sir Moses, obedient to the impulses of his generous heart, stepped forward and took the lead in the defence of a persecuted people, maliciously charged with a heinous crime. He proceeded immediately to the East, in company with Lady Montefiore, M. Crémieux, Prof. Munk, Dr. Loewe, his Private Secretary, and other personages. Despite the reprehensible conduct of the French Government that sanctioned the wicked deeds of its Consul, Count Ratti Menton, the merciful mission met with a happy issue. Some time after his return, Sir Moses was presented with a testimonial by his British brethren, and, subsequently, with a handsome gift by the Jews of Germany, for the noble efforts made in behalf of our cause.

To tell what claims the English Baronet has on the gratitude of all who feel Jewishly, or, to be more correct, of all who feel humanely, would demand the unfolding of the history of this age, as it regards the status of Israelites in countries of misrule, of misery and of oppression. For to repeatedly remonstrate with tyrants, and to illimitably help the hapless, has been the task assumed, and magnificently achieved by Moses Montefiore. One illustration may be of interest. In 1858 the civilized world was convulsed by the discovery that Jewish children were being abducted, and forced to embrace the Catholic faith. The most startling instance was that of Edgar Mortara, stolen from his parents in Bologna, Italy. The act had been publicly sanctioned by His Holiness (?) Mastai-Ferretti, *who was anxious for the salvation of the lad's soul.* At the news of the outrage, Sir Moses hastened to Rome, and endeavored to obtain an audience with the *infallible* Pontiff. Our leading representative was refused, and Cardinal Antonelli was sent to inform him that interposition would be of no avail. Sadly did the benign messenger return to England, but not at all shaken in the determination to stand up as a bulwark of defence, and so he has continued without cessation.

Notwithstanding the dissuasion of his dearest friends, Sir Moses undertook a seventh voyage to Jerusalem in his ninety-second year, and he has given a narrative of it in a volume which imparts pleasing information about men and places.

The piety of Sir Moses exceeds all praise. To perform his devotions with the prescribed number, he supports the Synagogue erected at his expense, and attached to his country-residence at Ramsgate. Colleges, hospitals, asylums, and places of worship, which do not even belong to his persuasion, have been endowed by the Baronet, and the amount expended on these, as well as on poverty-stricken families in all climes, cannot be calculated.

It is the hope of millions, that this glory of Israel may endure still longer; that, though bordering on his hundredth year, Sir Moses Montefiore, may abide here in health, to mirror forth all that is good and noble in human nature.

JUDITH MONTEFIORE.

The author of the Book of Proverbs revealed the inspiration which led his pen, when he personified wisdom in the form of a woman. She is made to stand prominent, and she tells men that "the fear of the

Lord is to hate wrong, pride and arrogance, and an evil
way." The voice of woman thus raised to offer
godly counsel, possesses an all-penetrating force. Its
earnest tones, heard at the domestic fireside, cannot fail
to effect durable blessings. The consort of the great
Sir Moses Montefiore was a Jewess who felt her power
for good, by urging her husband on to marvellous
achievements, and actively participating in his grand
work.

Judith Montefiore, daughter of Barnet L. Cohen,
Esq., and sister of Baroness Hannah de Rothschild,
was born at London, England, in 1784. Her father did
not belong to the Portuguese community of Jews. He
worshipped with his brethren of German and Polish
extraction. The descendants of those who had settled
again in England, by permission of Oliver Cromwell,
looked upon their co-religionists of another ritual as
their inferiors. As a natural consequence, intermar-
riages were avoided ; a Portuguese deeming it deroga-
tory to his standing to take one for a wife from among
the females of a congregation whose genealogical tree
did not show the *Dons* or the *Hidalgos*. It needed a
moral courage not easily mustered to face the prejudice,
and break its backbone. Sir Moses was the man both
to attack and conquer it. On the 10th of June, 1812,
he wedded a Jewess who had not read her prayers in
the Bevis Marks Synagogue.

The choice was fortunate, for Miss Cohen was

endowed with intelligence and tender feelings, and she knew how to bring her qualities to bear on the furtherance of the philanthropist's designs.

Lady Judith accompanied Sir Moses on his numerous tours, undertaken in behalf of humanity, and rivalled his generosity by distributing of her own means. Observant of what occurred during her journeys, she wrote an interesting volume with the title, " Notes of a Private Journal of a Visit to Egypt and Palestine," printed for private circulation.

Like Sir Moses, Lady Montefiore performed her religious duties with unswerving strictness, and she visited schools promotive of Hebrew knowledge, rewarding meritorious pupils, and speaking encouragingly to teachers.

This noble woman, whose whole life did not belie the name of Judith (Jewess) she bore, believed that her mission was not fulfilled when caring only for those of her own faith, but she made the unfortunate of other creeds partake of her bounties.

On the 26th of September, 1862, Sir Moses was bereft of his dearest companion. Lady Montefiore died in her seventy-eighth year, and was interred in the burial-place which her husband had consecrated at Ramsgate. The tears of him she fondly loved moisten the earth that covers her mortal remains, and countless numbers lament the loss of their benefactress. " Many daughters have done virtuously, but thou hast excelled them all."

IGNAZ MOSCHELES.

The art of Music and that of writing are not necessarily twin-born. But it occasionally happens that the hand whose delicate touch evokes sweet strains can wield a graceful pen. This double acquirement adds lustre to the possessor, and *éclat* to his performances. But in Ignaz Moschèles three qualifications combined to render his name famous. He was admired as a player, a composer, and a scholar. True, many years were given him to reach the height he attained, but when very young he had already moved upward so rapidly, that all could predict his future greatness.

Ignaz Moscheles was born at Prague, in Bohemia, Austria, on the 30th of May, 1794. As early as his eighth year he received instruction in music from F. D. Weber, director of the conservatory. The boy's innate talents developed fast, and when eleven he performed on the piano with the ease and skill of a finished artist. His introduction to men of note naturally followed, and each hailed the rising genius.

While still a lad, Moscheles went to Vienna, and there formed the acquaintance of Haydn and Beethoven, who advised him to continue studying. He became the pupil of Albrechtsberger, under whom he made such progress as to create amazement. He competed with Hummel, then reputed the first pianist in Germany.

Moscheles now undertook an extensive continental

tour, his playing creating everywhere rapturous delight. In 1820 he removed to England, where he resided for twenty-six years. Here his abilities met with full recognition, his popularity increasing to so wide an extent, that, in 1825, he was appointed Professor in the Academy of London; also Conductor of the Philharmonic Concerts, holding both stations more than two decades. It must be borne in mind that few could obtain the latter position, it being granted only to a musician of the very highest order.

Moscheles rendered incalculable service to the musical world, by inducing the English to cultivate the compositions of Bach, Mozart, Beethoven, and other acknowledged masters. In fact, he brought more influence to bear upon this than any who preceded or succeeded him. His thorough knowledge of the pianoforte, and capacity to show forth its wonderful applications, mainly tended to the glory he achieved. Then, his rendition of Beethoven's *sonatas* and *concertos* left him without a superior, and, probably, an equal.

In 1846 Moscheles was chosen Director of the Conservatory of Leipsic, spending there the remainder of his life. As a composer, he wrote, for the piano, violin, and other instruments, pieces which are splendid specimens of classical music, and marvels of perfection and beauty.

Moscheles' cultured mind enabled him to search into matters other than those to which he specially devoted himself. His literary work, an English translation of Schindler's " Life of Beethoven," to which he added valuable notes, does him honor.

The career of Ignaz Moscheles ended at Leipsic, in Saxony, Germany, on the 10th of March, 1870. Productions of sterling merit will always declare their own praise, and he must be deaf to the voice of truth who does not hear the deserved eulogy.

SALOMON HERMANN MOSENTHAL.

The cultivation of the drama, and its adaptation to the requirements of an enlightened age, form a subject which has engaged the attention of some of the deepest thinkers. Not the presentation of spectacles so common among the ancient Greeks and Romans, and which mocked their boasted civilization, has been the labor of Shakspeare, and those who have followed in the wake of the immortal bard of Avon. Tragedies and comedies, of a nature calculated to afford both instruction and amusement, are now put upon the stage. Public sentiment also tends to raise them to a more elevated plane, so that even the fastidious may not interpose an objection. The prolific pen of Mosenthal has done much to forward this good movement. That man is conceded to have been a genuine dramatist, laboring to one laudable end, and giving the world magnificent results of his superior talents.

Dr. Salomon Hermann Mosenthal was born at Cassel, in Hesse-Cassel, Germany, on January 14th, 1821. Having obtained a preparatory training, he went to the Polytechnic School at Carlsruhe, where the study of natural sciences occupied his time. He afterwards proceeded to Marburg, and there received his diploma as *Doctor of Philosophy*, in 1842. All along, his progress had been rapid, foretokening a useful career.

Dr. Mosenthal, having repaired to Vienna, became private tutor in the family of a rich banker. He seized the opportunity of making the acquaintance of a number of literary celebrities, which circumstance materially aided in bringing him to public notice. Accordingly, in 1851, the Doctor was appointed archivist of the ministry of State and of public instruction.

Dr. Mosenthal's efforts had already begun to assume a determined shape. Diving into his resolute purpose, he brought forth, in 1850, what insured his fame,—"Deborah," a drama which Madame Ristori, known and acclaimed in both hemispheres, has been proud to play, and which has universally met with a glowing reception. Only an Israelite whose heart beats in unison with the oppressed of his race, could have given the world that touching drama. It is historically Jewish in the spirit pervading it, but forcibly carries away all who listen, intensifying the interest in each successive scene. The popular favor exhibited for this piece, paved the way for the success of a second, *Sonnenwendhof* —1856; and a third, "The German Comedians" —1863. The first two have been translated into English, Italian, Danish, Hungarian, and other modern languages. Their author also issued " Cecile of Albano," " Life of a German Poet," " The Goldsmith of Ulm," " Pietra," " Isabella Orsini," etc., etc.

As a poet, Dr. Mosenthal is entitled to a large share of praise; not only for the ideas underlying his dramas, but also for the art displayed in versification, as exemplified in his " Lyric Poems," and minor compositions.

Dr. Mosenthal died on February 17th, 1877. Time may ungraciously consign to forgetfulness some of the offerings of his rich intellect, but " Deborah " will ever remain alive and fresh in dramatic literature.

SALOMON MUNK.

From the twelfth century, when Benjamin de Tudela wrote his book of travels,—the statements in which have been strongly disputed and as vigorously defended, learned works on the geography and history of the Holy Land, and the habits, manners, and pursuits of its inhabitants, have issued from the pens of Israelites. But whoever desires to see the results of conscientious investigations of those subjects, advanced in a clear, comprehensive, and attractive style, must read Munk's " Palestine." When it will further on be made known what the subject of this sketch wrought among his contemporaries, respect will grow into affection.

Salomon Munk, the son of a poor Synagogue beadle, was born at Glogau, in the province of Silesia, Prussia, on May 14th, 1805. From childhood he applied himself assiduously to study. When only fifteen years of age he travelled to Berlin—part of the way on foot, for want of means—to be instructed in the Oriental languages. He afterwards went to Bonn, and gained a knowledge of the Arabic. Having made considerable progress in various branches of learning, he proceeded in 1828 to Paris, to attend the lectures of Sylvestre de Sacy, Abel Rémusat, and men of equal celebrity. Here he attained high distinction, for his thorough acquaintance with Persian, Sanscrit, Arabic, and other Eastern tongues.

The year 1835 found him in England, where he spent some time at the University of Oxford, making preparations for the issue of an edition of Maimonides' celebrated work, *Moré Nebuchim*. At the same period he contributed several essays to the *Journal Asiatique* and the *Dictionnaire des Sciences Philosophiques*, which attracted the attention of the learned. In 1838 Munk received the appointment of deputy-keeper of the Oriental MSS., in the Royal Library of Paris, which position added to his store of knowledge, and redounded to the advantage of the institution. The salary was hardly sufficient to support life, still the generous scholar would offer a number of poor children gratuitous instruction.

When Sir Moses Montefiore, M. Crémieux, Dr. Loewe, and others were about to visit the East, to put an end to the atrocities committed on the Jews of Damascus and Rhodes, Munk gladly accepted an invitation to accompany the philanthropists, and to make his knowledge aid in the vindication of justice. Before returning home, he visited Egypt, with M. Crémieux, and secured many interesting MSS., in Arabic, relating to the early literature of the Karaites, etc. Already before that time several of Munk's works had been published. "Reflections upon the Worship of the Ancient Hebrews, in its Connection with Other Worships," appeared in 1833; and "An Account of Rabbi Saadiah Gaon, and his Arabic version of Isaiah," in 1838. From 1842 to 1850 came in regular order, "Notes on Joseph Ben-Jehoudah;" "Commentary of Rabbi Tanhoum of Jerusalem, on the Book of Habakkuk;" "The Phœ-

nician Inscriptions at Marseilles;" "Notes on Aboul-
walid Merwan, Aben-Ganach;" and "Palestine," the
most obvious manifestation of Munk's erudition, and
which Prof. M. A. Levy, of Leipsic, has presented
in a German garb.

In 1852 Dr. Munk became totally blind; but this
unfortunate circumstance did not check his unceasing
labors. Some of his principal productions were, indeed, written after his loss of sight. On December
2d, 1858, in acknowledgment of his many services
to the cause of science, he was elected a member of
the Academy of Inscriptions and Belles-Lettres.
The celebrated French historian, M. Guizot, travelled
from Normandy to Paris solely to cast his vote for
the *savant*, whom he highly esteemed. Even rigid
Catholics and devout Protestants undisguisedly
favored the choice. Shortly after this, Munk became
the representative of the Israelites of Lyons in the
Central Consistory at Paris, and subsequently he
was decorated as Chevalier of the Legion of Honor.
Faithful to his duties in the several offices to which
he had been elevated, he nevertheless found time to
publish his writings. "Memoirs of the Hebrew
Grammarians of the Tenth and Eleventh Centuries"
appeared, and was followed by "Miscellanies on
Jewish and Arabic Philosophy," that part relating
to philosophy among the Jews having been translated into German by B. Beer. But Munk's *chef*

d'œuvre, and, at the same time, a monument of his skill in the Arabic language and its literature, is his composition, in three volumes, of the *Moré Nebuchim*, of Rabbi Moses Maimonides. This was issued in the original, with a French translation, and critical, literary and explanatory notes, bearing the title *La guide des égarés; traité de théologie et de philosophie*, ("A Guide to the Erring—a Treatise on Theology and Philosophy").

Munk's fame had now become world-wide, and he was universally looked upon as one of the most brilliant scholars of the day. Witness his having succeeded M. Renan, as Professor of Semitic Languages in the College of France, in 1865. How the selection was greeted may be perceived from the subjoined remarks of *L'Union*, a journal of ultramontane tendencies, which could have been hardly supposed to favor a Jew: "A weak, blind man, who, only by the sense of touch, can build up the world of his thoughts, traverses the centuries of nations, cities, idioms. What a spiritual power! He is an ornament to science, for he teaches the scholar how to love. France possesses in him the greatest philologist, and though a mysterious decision of a kind Providence has robbed him of his physical light, the renown which he has gained, and the greater name which he will yet earn, are sure to shine in splendor for all times, and the light which he has shed into the darkness of Phœnician knowledge will never die out."

On February 1st, 1865, Prof. Munk delivered his inaugural address on the Hebrew, Chaldaic and Syriac languages, in which he touchingly alluded to his blindness, and spoke of his effort in exceedingly modest terms. He occupied the station named until his death, on February 6th, 1867.

Among those who pronounced panegyrics on the life and deeds of the deceased were M. De Longperier, President of the Academy of Inscriptions and Belles-Lettres; M. Albert Cohn, the scholar and philanthropist; M. Adolphe Franck, of the Central Consistory, the philosopher and author; and M. Isidor, Grand Rabbi of France, who, as a Jewish divine, feelingly spoke of the departed. Rabbi Isidor pointed out Munk's devotion to duty, and related how the immortal writer had drawn the eyes of the world to the literature of the people with whom he had shared belief and aspirations.

SELIG NEWMAN.

The anomaly of employing a Jew to teach the Scriptures in the original text, and dubbing a Christian with the title " Professor of Hebrew," is not rarely met in the annals of the world. Thus two famous Universities in England have more than once listened to the expositions of scholars of our race who were nevertheless compelled to live in obscurity. For the learning of those who did not avow the Trinity could not receive public recognition. Happily the German Neubauer, and the Hungarian Schiller-Szinessy were not born when old England bent reverently before her cob-webbed statistical records; else neither would the one be esteemed at Oxford, nor the other at Cambridge.

But Selig Newman arrived in London upwards of sixty years ago. Therefore he was forced to " hide his light under a bushel," and, after having taught at a University, was morally compelled to emigrate in an humble condition to the United States.

Selig Newman was born at Posen, Prussian Poland, in 1788. He early disclosed remarkable talents, and a desire for Biblical knowledge which he gained to perfection. He was educated in the city of his birth, and made rapid progress in the different branches imparted.

Poland, many of whose Jewish inhabitants—notwithstanding the depressive effect of Russian despotism—are very apt scholars, lent Newman many earnest co-laborers, in the field he had chosen. But wishing to breathe more freely he betook himself to England when twenty-eight years old. There he received the appointment of minister of the congregation at Plymouth, while at the same time he taught Hebrew at the University of Oxford.

Newman possessed such knowledge in what belongs to sacred literature, that many distinguished Christian as well as Jewish ministers, were numbered among his pupils. But his faith unfortunately debarred him from being chosen to a high professorship with a liberal salary, in a college of universal repute.

While in London, Newman took part in a spirited debate with some Christians, on the Messianic prophecies, which he boldly described. as entirely foreign to the subject applied by Gentiles.   His arguments created a deep impression, and procured for him a name, if not a position of ease and comfort.

At a rather advanced age, Newman sailed for America, and made his home in New York.   He gained a livelihood by teaching, but did not relax in his activity as a writer.   In 1850 appeared a work entitled " The Challenge Accepted," consisting of a series of dialogues between a Jew and a Christian, respecting the accomplishment of the prophecies on the advent of the Messiah.   In this, Newman exhibits his thorough Bibical training.   " Emendations of the English Version of the Old Testament," a " Hebrew and English Lexicon," a " Hebrew Grammar," etc., were also published.   Some manuscripts ol a condensed translation of the Bible were found after his death.   Possibly the writer intended to produce a compendium of Holy Writ and the Apocrypha, like that issued by Jacob Levi Levinski, with the aid of the Rev. Dr. Henry Vidaver, and others.

Selig Newman died at Williamsburgh, New York, on February 20th, 1871, after a long and useful career of eighty-three years.

MORDECAI MANUEL NOAH..

American Israelites have not remained passive in that which concerns the political welfare of their country, yet, unaccountable as it may seem, few of them have been preferred to offices of distinction. Perhaps the motive may be attributed to a disposition of our people for retirement, which ages of persecution have engendered, or it may be the effect of prejudice, which, even in this goodly land of equality, has not altogether died. Nevertheless, now and then Hebrews are intrusted with responsible positions which they fill creditably to themselves and their fellow-believers. The case about to be cited is a noteworthy illustration.

Mordecai Manuel Noah was born at Philadelphia, on July 14th, 1785. He first applied himself to a trade, but soon abandoned it for the study of the law. Removing to Charleston, S. C., he grew popular as a local politician. In 1811, during the administration of President Madison, Mr. Noah received his first public appointment, as American Consul at Riga,

Russia. His conduct, while in that office, merited so much approval that, in 1813, he was selected as Consul-General at Tunis, bearing, at the same time, a mission to Algiers. The United States being then engaged in a war with Great Britain, the vessel in which Mr. Noah sailed was captured by a British frigate, and he remained a prisoner for several weeks.

While at Tunis, he succeeded in rescuing a number of Americans, held as slaves in the Barbary States. His outspoken protest against the payment of an annual tribute to the pirate Government of Morocco, for the security of our merchant marine, doubtless occasioned the demand for his recall. Some, however, ascribe the removal to Mr. Noah's religion, which, it was argued, might injuriously affect the diplomatic relations between the two countries.

After making a tour through portions of Continental Europe, Mr. Noah returned to America, and permanently settled in the city of New York. Turning his attention to journalism, he became identified with several leading newspapers. He founded, and edited successively, the *National Advertiser*, the New York *Courier and Inquirer*, and the *Evening Star*. These were followed by the *Sunday Times*, an influential organ, at present directed by Robert M. Noah, . Esq., son of its founder.

Mr. Noah's reputation as a journalist placed him high in the esteem of his contemporaries, but it did not tend to lessen his wonted zeal for politics. His influence was wholly exercised for a period, in the support of President Van Buren's administration.* The citizens of New York honored Mr. Noah, by electing him Surveyor of the Port, and, shortly after, Judge of the Court of Sessions. When acting in the capacity of Sheriff, the outcry was raised against a Jew's hanging a Christian, which called forth Mr. Noah's famous epigram, " Pretty Christians, forsooth, to deserve hanging."

The philanthropic efforts of Mr. Noah deserve universal praise. While the yellow fever raged on Manhattan Island, the law imprisoning debtors was relentlessly enforced. Many a poor creature was dying of the plague, when the Sheriff took upon himself to liquidate all obligations, and thus set the prisoners free. This generosity made him a bankrupt.

But the great scheme of Mr. Noah's life is yet to be mentioned. He entertained the idea of a permanent settlement of the Jéws at Grand Island, in the Niagara River. In 1820 he announced his undertaking, and attempted to induce an emigration to that place. But, though the project was not crowned with success, Mr. Noah's faith in its feasibility did not falter, and he erected on the designated spot a monument, with the inscription : " Ararat, a City of

---

* See " The life and Times of Martin Van Buren," by William L. Mackenzie.

Refuge for the Jews, founded by Mordecai M. Noah, in the month of Tishri, 5586 (September, 1825), and in the fiftieth year of American Independence." This memorial of the interest he manifested in the well-being of his people, has since crumbled to dust. But the name of Mordecai Manuel Noah will live as one of the noble types of an American and a Jew.

Mr. Noah died in New York, on May 22d, 1851. Among his published works are : " Travels in England, France, Spain, and the Barbary States ;" a translation of the " Book of Yashar ;" " Gleanings from a Gathered Harvest "—a collection of miscellaneous essays ; several dramas, which were put upon the stage with some success, and numberless contributions to political and local periodicals.

JACQUES OFFENBACH.

The increasing taste for musical compositions of a light and sparkling character has singularly contributed to the popularity of Offenbach. His operas attract and amuse uncritical audiences, and therefore command a patronage which the emanations of a Mozart or a Mendelssohn cannot secure. We would not, however, be charged with disparaging merit where it exists. Offenbach's works reveal a genius ; for it is not an easy undertaking which he has accomplished. To found a school of music, eminently adapted to furnish pleasing diversion to persons who seek enjoyment, still within the boundaries of the mysterious art; to offer a style essentially different from others in almost every particular, requires a courage and self-assertion which cannot be underrated, when accompanied with corresponding abilities. No hesitation is therefore felt to briefly sketch the career of an eminent exponent of the new system.

Jacques Offenbach was born at Cologne, Prussia, June 21st, 1819. After pursuing a course of instruction, he proceeded to the Paris Conservatory, where, from 1835 to 1837, he obtained a clear insight into the music of the time. He early began to play upon the violoncello, and his performances made a marked impression. Becoming known, he was appointed, in 1847, leader of the orchestra at the *Théâtre Français.*

In 1855 Offenbach established *Les Bouffes Parisiens* on the *Champs Élysées*, as a summer theatre, transferring his company in the winter to the *Théâtre de Comte*, in the passage *Choiseul.* With the opening of the first-named resort, his fame spread, and so rapidly that his prosperity was assured. In 1873 he assumed the directorship of the *Gaité* Theatre.

The productions of M. Offenbach are numerous. He published first La Fontaine's fables, set to music. *La Belle Hélène* appeared in 1864. This opera illustrated at once the novel method adopted by the composer. The general appreciation could not be misunderstood. But *Orphée aux Enfers* called forth positive enthusiasm. When first brought out, it ran for three hundred consecutive nights, with a success scarcely equalled in musical annals. *La Barbe Bleue* in 1866, was followed, in 1867, by *La Grande Duchesse*, perhaps the most effective of Offenbach's compositions. It has certainly achieved a triumph. *La Périchole*, *Geneviève de Brabant*, *Les Brigands*, *La Princesse de Trébizonde*, and *Roi Carotte*, were given to the public from 1868 to 1872. *La Jolie Parfumeuse* in 1873, and *Madame L' Archiduc* in 1874, have considerably enhanced the composer's reputation. For the copyright of his spectacular opera *bouffe*, " Whittington and his Cat," produced at the Alhambra Theatre, London, in 1874, M. Offenbach received £3,000.

There seems to be no waning in the interest displayed for his effusions. Most all of those mentioned still hold the stage throughout Europe and America, the mere announcement of their presentation being sufficient to draw throngs. M. Offenbach did make an attempt to work out music of an elevated standard, when he wrote *Barcouf* and " Robinson Crusoe." But timely discovering his unadaptability, he has wisely devoted his sole energies to that which is more calculated to meet the cravings of those who are carried away by the creations of a volatile genius.

M. Offenbach visited the United States a few years ago, and was tendered an ovation.

Admitting that Jacques Offenbach cannot be numbered with the great masters, he has vindicated his claims to the gratitude of the public whom during past years, he has amused. If he has not edified or improved his audiences, he has, at all events, helped them drive away dull care.

JULES OPPERT.

The Orient has furnished materials wherewith a wonderful history is being built. The edifice is still in course of erection, and new and skilful workmen supply the places left vacant by former operatives. What Champollion, and Rosellini, and Botta began, Rawlinson, and Layard, and Smith have continued, and our Jules Oppert is now perfecting. By universal consent, that son of the olden race may claim to be the most successful of laborers in searching among monuments that mouldered in the dust of ages, and in employing what he discovers to raise a more complete fabric.

Prof. Dr. Jules Oppert was born at Hamburg, Germany, on the 9th of July, 1825. Learning appears to have been a family inheritance, for his maternal uncle, Edward Gans, had achieved celebrity as a jurist. A thorough classical education preceded the youth's law studies at Heidelberg. Evincing a taste for philology, young Oppert went to the University of Bonn, and followed Freytag's course in Arabic, and Lassen's in Sanscrit. He next proceeded to Berlin, and in 1847 to Kiel, receiving a diploma in philology. He applied himself diligently to the Zend and the ancient Persian, with encouraging results.

Laws in Germany, prejudicial to Hebrews, were yet in force, when M. Oppert attained manhood. He found it impossible to pave his way to promotion in that country, and therefore determined to seek in France what was shut against him in the ungracious land of his birth. Arrived at Paris in 1847, he soon formed the acquaintance of the eminent *savants* Burnouf and Letronne, who immediately perceived the talents with which he was endowed. By their aid he obtained, in 1848, the professorship of German at Laval, and subsequently at Rheims.

Contributions to the *Asiatic Journal* and the *Archæological Review*, on the cuneiform characters at Persepolis, on the Persian language, and kindred subjects, drew towards M. Oppert the attention of the French Institute. It being announced that the Imperial Government intended sending a commission to Mesopotamia, under the lead of Fulgence Fresnel, the subject of our sketch was designated as a member thereof. Returning to France in 1854, he submitted plans for interpreting inscriptions at Babylon and elsewhere. At the same period he was naturalized. In the following year the Minister of Instruction charged him with a mission to England and Germany, to examine the inscriptions on Assyrian monuments contained in the different museums. The important revelations made, led to his appointment to the chair of Sanscrit in the school attached to the Imperial Library, and to his being awarded the decoration of the Legion of Honor.

In 1863 M. Oppert won, over numerous competitors, the great biennial prize offered a second time by the Institute, for the work most fitted to reflect honor upon the country. On the 1st of January, 1874, his efforts were duly recompensed by his being chosen Professor of Assyrian Philology and Archæology in the College of France.

In his productions, Oppert unfolds a new system of deciphering inscriptions, and its satisfactory application has most enhanced its value. Aside from articles in the *French Athenæum*, in the *Annals of Christian Philosophy*, and in English journals and magazines, the Professor has issued " The Criminal Laws of the Hindoos"—1847, the thesis of his examination for the degree of Ph. D.; " The Vowel-System of the Ancient Persians"—1847; "The Inscriptions of the Achemenides"—1852; "Assyrian Studies"—

1858; " Scientific Expedition to Mesopotamia, by order of the French Government "—1858, containing, in addition to the narrative of the voyage, some remarkable facts relative to the chronological history of the Assyrians, and of the Babylonians, and to the reading of the inscriptions, from an historical point of view, together with charts, plans, etc.; " Cuneiform Inscriptions Deciphered a Second Time"—1859; "Sanscrit Grammar"—1859; " Elements of the Assyrian Grammar"—1860; " The Present State of the Decipherment of the Cuneiform Inscriptions"—1861; " History of the Chaldean and Assyrian Empires"—1866; " The Immortality of the Soul Among the Chaldeans," followed by a translation of " The Descent of Istar Astarté into the Infernal Regions"—1875; etc., etc. The inscriptions of the Sargonides at Nineveh, and the great one at Khorsabad, have been treated upon in separate writings. The works mentioned are eagerly sought after, and perused with avidity.

It is not on a single occasion that Jews have reason to feel a just pride, but in the present instance they can point to a man within their fold, whose pen is authoritative, and to whose *dictum* masters of science bow in humble acknowledgment.

DANIEL LEVY MADURO PEIXOTTO.

A complete mastery of *Materia Medica* may be the boast, but is not the possession, of all practitioners. Only physicians who have. followed their. chosen profession with intensity of love have attained an enviable rank. The sentiments they nurtured incited them to overcome impediments. What one of these worthies achieved in a short existence of forty-three years, the annexed lines will briefly tell.

Daniel Levy Maduro Peixotto, M. D., the son of Moses L. M. Peixotto, merchant, and subsequently Minister of the Portuguese Congregation *Shearith Israel*, of New York, was born at Amsterdam, Holland, on July 18th, 1800. His mother, a highly cultured woman, first took charge of the boy's education, and instructed him in languages, history, and religion. Later, the Rev. Dr. Strasbeck took the lad under his charge, and finally John Ironsides, at New York, prepared him for Columbia College, whence he graduated in 1816.

In the same year, young Peixotto began his medical studies with Dr. David Hosack. He applied himself with earnestness, and profited greatly by attending the regular course of lectures. In 1819 the degree of M. D. was conferred upon the youth.

Ill health impelled Dr. Peixotto to seek warm climates. He visited the West Indies and Caraccas, and, during his stay in the latter place, advantageously exercised his vocation.   In 1823 he returned to New York, where many had recourse to his skill. The Doctor's activity gave him an exalted station by the side of the leading physicians of the day.

As a writer, Dr. Peixotto acquired fame by articles of acknowledged merit, and of considerable importance to the profession.   In 1825-'6, conjointly with Drs. Beck and Bell, he edited the New York *Medical and Physical Journal* and " Gregory's Practice."   All pertaining to medicine enchained his thoughts and quickened his pen.

But Dr. Peixotto did not entirely confine himself to his own private practice.   He was a public-spirited man, and he served as one of the Physicians of the old City Dispensary in 1827, and as President of the New York County Medical Society from 1830-'2. One of the projectors and organizers of the Society for Assisting the Widows and Orphans of Medical Men, he also urged the establishment of a Medical Library.

So much appreciated were the Doctor's endeavors that, in 1836, he received the appointment of Professor of Theory and Practice of Medicine and of Obstetrics, and also that of Honorary Member of the Medical Society of Lower Canada.

Possessed of a store of useful knowledge, which he continually brought to bear on the discharge of his duties; truly religious; liberal in his dealings with his fellow-men; and generous to a fault: Dr. Peixotto could not but command the affection of his brethren, and the esteem of all with whom he came in contact.

But too soon was a noble career destined to close. At New York City, on May 13th, 1843, Daniel L. M. Peixotto exchanged this transitory life for that of everlasting peace and happiness.

BENJAMIN FRANKLIN PEIXOTTO.

The history of a man whose devotion to the cause of humanity has made him as widely known on the Eastern as on the Western Continent, must surely be of interest to all lovers of their kind. It speaks of deeds of self-denial. It points to an exceptional Hebrew of America, who sacrificed the sanguine hopes of a brilliant future at home, to become a deliverer abroad, and thus advance civilization.

Benjamin Franklin Peixotto, born in the city of New York, on the 13th of November, 1834, is a son of Dr. Daniel L. M. Peixotto, an eminent physician. His parents removed to Ohio in 1837, but returned to New York in 1841, where Benjamin received an education. In his thirteenth year, shortly after his father's death, he settled at Cleveland. Endowed with a clear understanding and bright talents, he soon attracted public attention.

Mr. Peixotto studied law under the celebrated statesman, Stephen A. Douglas, for whom he showed a sincere attachment, which continued uninterrupted until the death of his preceptor in 1861. He early engaged in politics, and contributed articles to the *Cleveland Plaindealer*, for the success of Mr. Douglas' election as President of the United States. Conspicuous in literary circles, he associated with many distinguished scholars.

From youth, affairs pertaining to Israelites excited Mr. Peixotto's warmest interest. His voice often resounded in societies, and in the Jewish lodges. As a member of the Independent Order of *B'nai B'rith* (Sons of the Covenant), he did much to elevate the standing of that organization, and, in the year 1863, he was chosen Grand *Saar*, or Master. A small institution had increased so rapidly, that, at the period of Mr. Peixotto's election, the Order counted twelve thousand members, about one-half of its present number.

The idea of establishing an Orphan Asylum at Cleveland was first conceived by Mr. Peixotto, and his influence secured the passage of a bill which led to its foundation. Mr. Peixotto went back to his native city in 1866, but sailed for

California in 1867, and took up his residence in San Francisco, where he obtained a lucrative practice as a lawyer. This profession, while it demanded considerable of his time, did not check his zealous labors in behalf of his co-religionists.

Thus, in June, 1870, when the news of a frightful massacre of Jews in Roumania, followed by dire persecutions, was cabled across the Atlantic, Benjamin Franklin Peixotto, just in the prime of life, and in the enjoyment of ease, stood up a champion, and offered to go to the benighted province of Turkey in Europe, in the double capacity of representative of the United States, and messenger of happy tidings to his helpless brethren. He was nominated as Consul by President Grant, and unanimously confirmed by the Senate. The new official departed at once on his noble mission. Arriving at the Court of Prince Charles, of Roumania, he succeeded in allaying the sore distress under which his fellow-believers groaned. For over five years Mr. Peixotto remained at Bucharest, to avert oppression, which his absence would have encouraged. While there he effected a vast amount of good for the down-trodden; improving their moral condition, by the formation of associations of various natures, notably the Society styled "Zion," founded in 1872, with objects similar to the *B'nai B'rith* of this country.

Mr. Peixotto returned to the United States in

1876, leaving the Consulate in charge of Dr. Adolph Stern, who had filled the office of Vice-Consul, and given useful assistance to his principal. The honored Israelite was cordially received everywhere. The services he had rendered formed the topic of general conversation. Mr. Peixotto was requested to lecture in different parts of the Union. He addressed large assemblages, and exerted himself to promote the educational scheme started in the West. To further the designs of the Union of American Hebrew Congregations, he made appeals wherever he set foot, and soon twelve thousand dollars were subscribed, mainly through his individual efforts.

Mr. Peixotto took part in the Presidential campaign of 1876, ardently supporting Mr. Hayes. In 1877 he was tendered the appointment of Consul-General at St. Petersburg, Russia, which he declined. President Hayes subsequently nominated him as Consul at Lyons, France, and the Senate confirmed the selection. This position he accepted, and he now fills.

Besides being Honorary President of the Society "Zion" of Roumania, Mr. Peixotto is connected with the *Alliance Israélite Universelle*, the Anglo-Jewish Association, the Union of American Hebrew Congregations, and other influential bodies. His eldest son, George, a student of the Royal

Academy of Dresden, gives extraordinary promise of genius as an artist.

The labors of Benjamin Franklin Peixotto in Roumania have not proved ineffectual. The recent determination of the Congress of European Powers, with regard to religious emancipation, is an evidence of that fact, and it should call forth unfeigned admiration for one who, by indomitable energy and perseverance, accomplished a glorious purpose.

EMILE PEREIRE.

Of eminent Jewish families, that of Pereire commends itself to special notice. In the eighteenth century, Jacob Rodriguez Pereire, (or Pereira), grandfather of the subject of this sketch, established a school for the training of deaf mutes. This system had never before been put into operation, hence to M. Pereire we are indebted for its practical application. All are fully aware of its utility, and the benefits reaped therefrom. But it is of the French banker and politician, Emile Pereire, that a faint portraiture is about to be drawn.

Emile Pereire was born at Bordeaux, France, on December 3d, 1800. When still young he lost his father, but under the guidance of an enlightened mother, both he and his younger brother, Isaac, received a suitable education, and soon learnt to understand how greatly success depends upon one's exertions.

For a number of years, Emile Pereire was an ardent supporter of the principles of Saint-Simon, who believed in the equal distribution of property among all classes, as a preventive of the evils resulting from insurrection and revolution. M. Pereire early began to identify himself with financial affairs, and contributed articles to the *Globe*, and then to the *National*, with which M. Armand Carrel was connected. He conceived the project of attempting a railway to St. Germain, but three years elapsed before he and his brother could bring together the amount requisite for the building of the road. With the consummation of this extensive undertaking their reputation and fortune increased, so that they were able to engage in still more important works. Both Emile and Isaac soon figured among the most prominent of Parisian bankers. They took active part in the construction of the Northern Railway, the Southern Railway, and the Lateral Canal.

The huge financial scheme devised by the Messrs. Pereire is known as the *Crédit Mobilier*. It was set on foot in 1852, with a capital of sixty million francs. Over twelve hundred millions of francs were loaned to the French railways, and the *Crédit Mobilier*, intermixing with other colossal operations, exercised an exceedingly powerful influence upon European industry.

M. Emile Pereire gave his aid to the promotion of literature, science, and the arts. He was instrumental in obtaining a posthumous exhibition of the works of Paul Delaroche, at the *Palais des Beaux Arts*, in 1856. His lofty position in the commercial world made him the recipient of decorations from the French Government, and, as its candidate, he was chosen to the *Corps Legislatif*, in 1863. M. Pereire declined a re-election to that body, in 1869. He died at Paris, France, on January 7th, 1875.

The events of the life of Isaac Pereire, as late as the year 1875, are so much interwoven with those of his brother's, that it is deemed a needless repetition to offer a separate account. Suffice, that both afford striking examples of what can be wrought by diligence, associated with sagacity and broad views.

LUDWIG PHILIPPSON.

The loss of any of the faculties graciously bestowed on man by the Creator is greatly to be deplored. How inexpressibly lamentable to remain with "eyes that roll in vain to find the piercing ray, and find no dawn;" with eyes wont to search the depths of learning, but wherein the "sovereign vital lamp" has been forever quenched. All honor then, and all praise to him who, so afflicted, still bids his energies not relax, and who works on vigorously. Such a one is Ludwig Philippson. He has been assigned a pre-eminent station in the Jewish literature of our time. His valued labors, particularly in the department of Biblical exegesis, give him a fame which extends far beyond the city of his birth, and the country in whose language his thoughts have found expression.

Dr. Ludwig Philippson was born at Dessau, Germany, December 27th, 1811. He frequented a school in his native place, and made noticeable progress. Thence he passed to the Gymnasium at Halle, continuing his studies with unabated earnestness. At Berlin, for four years, philology engrossed the attention of the student. In 1833 his course was completed, and our graduate made his literary bow to the public.

In the fall of 1833, the Jewish Congregation in Magdeburg selected Dr. Philippson as their preacher. This office he filled until 1862, adding to its *préstige* by being titled Rabbi in 1840. The unhappy circumstance of having been deprived of his sight compelled the relinquishment of an honorable position. The Doctor has since lived on a pension at Bonn. But the physical privation did not disable the mind. The scholar determined to maintain his activity, and strained every nerve to follow in the line he had marked out. He has, indeed, fulfilled his intentions.

From 1837, Dr. Philippson's paper, *Die Allgemeine Zeitung des Judenthums*, has appeared regularly. It is very ably edited as an exponent of the principles of Reform Judaism, to which the Doctor became attached. For several years a supplement called *Das Jüdische Volksblatt*, was added. While yet a student, Philippson published, in a German translation, the fragments of the tragic poet, Eze-chielos, and of Philo of Biblos—1830. He has also brought out a biography of Benedict Spinoza, in which he endeavors to defend the character and actions of the Dutch philosopher from the censure of his antagonists. As a contributor to the *Jenaer Literatur Zeitung*, and other publications, our author acquired a wide reputation for classical knowledge, principally in the writings of Aristotle.

Dr. Philippson issued his lectures on the development of the religious idea in society, and later, concerning the results of Universal history—1847–'8. Perhaps his most important work is a German rendition of the Hebrew Scriptures, with illustrations and a commentary, together with notes, and upon

which he labored from 1839–'53. It has been asserted that extreme opinions are occasionally set
forth in this production, and that some of the in-
terpretations are more ingenious than accurate.
Among other writings we may mention "Jewish
Religious Instruction," "World-Moving Questions,"
"Rome and Sepphoris," in two volumes; "Jacob
Tirado," "The Ego," "The Dethroned One," and
several catechisms, school-books, and song and
prayer-books.

The Doctor founded, in 1855, the institute for
advancing Jewish literature, which existed until
1874, and which published an excellent series of the
compositions of Jewish authors, including some of
the above-named emanations of its founder. Other
organizations for the spread of Hebrew learning
have been likewise conceived and established by
him.

Dr. Philippson's success as a preacher was evidenced in the impression which his utterances created, by an eloquence that appealed to the heart.
When incapacitated from discharging ministerial
duties, the indefatigable divine sought another channel to convey the yieldings of his mental investigations to the comfnunity.

In the columns of his journal, the Doctor urged
the calling of the conventions that were severally
held at Brunswick, Frankfort–on–the–Main, and

subsequently at Cassel, Leipsic, and Augsburg. His aim was to promulgate Reform doctrines, and to promote a discussion of ritualistic questions. The High School for the knowledge of Judaism at Berlin, a Reform Seminary, owes its origin mainly to Dr. Philippson.

Whatever ideas persons may prefer touching the Law and precepts, the thanks and respect of multitudes are highly due to him who has braved a serious difficulty, and who, with exceeding endurance, works in obedience to his nature and convictions.

BENJAMIN SAMUEL PHILLIPS.

Respect for the ancestral belief is one of the main features characterizing the Israelites of Great Britain. Wealth or talents have not been allowed to dampen their religious ardor. A pardonable pride it is for our co-religionists of the United Kingdom to point to Sir B. S. Phillips, the second of their number to have become Lord Mayor of London. Great he is among men, but humble before his God; courted by the nobles of the land, but mixing with his fellow-believers in Congregational and charitable objects.

Sir Benjamin Samuel Phillips was born at London, England, on January 4th, 1811. He early engaged in commercial pursuits, displaying, at the same time, warm interest in politics. But, despite a pronounced inclination to make himself felt in matters of importance to every Englishman, no chance was open to carry out that wish. Jews, at that period, were not permitted to take any part in the administration of public affairs, The first Hebrew who held municipal office in Great Britain was Mr. Phineas Levi, and Mr. Phillips the first who served as a Common Councilman of London.

Mr. Phillips was chosen an Alderman of his native city in 1857, and so faithfully did he perform his obligations that the people elected him Sheriff, a post which he filled in 1859–'60. The opponents of Jewish rights soon perceived that a Hebrew could discharge the duties of an office as capably as a Gentile. But prejudice dies hard. Though the bearing of the incumbent of the Sheriffalty brought home to the minds of many the conviction that they had long been in error, yet there remained a large number who could not overcome religious bias. The only way to disarm opposition was to exercise abilities with remarkable tact and discretion.

Mr. Phillips' popularity increased to such a degree, that, on September 29th, 1865, he was made Lord Mayor of London. In deference to his strict conformity to Jewish observances, the outgoing Chief Magistrate postponed the usual festivities, from the 29th of September, which fell on the eve of the Day of Atonement, to the 3d of October,—another clear proof that those who are staunch in their faith, will ever secure the consideration of the intelligent.

During Mr. Phillips' Mayoralty, he had the honor of entertaining the King of Belgium at a grand banquet. The royal appreciation was shown by decorating the Lord Mayor with the Order of Leopold. But Mr. Phillips won a nobler title to admiration, when, in 1866, he devised means to relieve the distress caused by the visitation of the cholera, and the famine in India. These measures added to his well-earned reputation, and when, on December 28th, 1866, Queen Victoria knighted her officer, she expressed what the whole nation felt.

Sir Benjamin, since the close of his term as Lord Mayor, has been Deputy Lieutenant for Middlesex, and a magistrate for the county of Kent.

Not a little of the credit due to this exalted Israelite belonged to his estimable wife, who died on February 1st, 1880. Her courteous demeanor and engaging address, especially as Lady Mayoress, endeared her to the people of London.

SIMCHA PINSKER.

Numerous and interesting investigations have been made into the character of the sect known as Karaites. But each writer or traveller has given his impressions a coloring which reflects his personal preferences. It is therefore not surprising, to read in one instance extravagant praises, and in another a sad description of the habits and intellectual standing of the schismatic members of the Hebrew race, mostly dwelling in the Crimea. A learned Galician studied deeply to arrive at a conscientious conclusion of what is due to those who, in the Ninth century, separated from their fellow-believers,—the adherents of oral traditions. Men whose judgment can be relied on have declared that Simcha Pinsker's contributions to literature are of a value that can scarce be estimated. Some remarks about their author, as well as to what they comprise, may be of interest to the reader.

Simcha Pinsker was born at Tarnopol, in Galicia, Austria, in 1801. In his young days, the seeming religious fervor of the *Hassidim* drew the enthusiastic student to their fold. But the learning our youth had obtained, combined with his natural good sense, could not allow the opponents of enlightenment to rule his discerning mind. It must, however, be admitted that Pinsker's susceptibility to momentary impressions occasionally warped his judgment. Thus, for example, he at one time gave himself up to commercial speculations, which proved ruinous, without heeding his aptitude for an entirely different career. Reduced to straitened circumstances, he was compelled to accept the humble post of Rabbinical Secre-

tary in Odessa. He had, probably, gone to that flourishing city in the hope of retrieving his decayed fortune. He did not find what he wished, but literature
gained through his humble condition.

Education among the Jews of Odessa demanded
a wholesome reform. Simcha Pinsker conceived the
thought of establishing schools for elementary instruction, and communicated it to a cultured friend, Isaac
Horowitz, a native of Brody. This gave the idea
every encouragement, and the two young men conferred with several influential persons, through whose
instrumentality arrangements were made with the
congregation and the government, for practically
carrying out the object. Pinsker, as chief instructor
in the newly-founded school, effectively labored until
1840. In that year he received a pension for the
remainder of his life, and betook himself to Vienna.

Before we proceed, it must be stated that the subject of this sketch had become known beyond the
limits of the institution he established and fostered.
Abraham Firkowitch, an active and erudite Karaite,
unearthed in the Crimea, in 1839, some curious and
unknown manuscripts. Among these was a code
of the later prophets, which, like several fragments
of the Pentateuch, with the prophetical lessons for
the Sabbath, and the Aramaic or Syriac translation,
had a singular punctuation—the vowel-points and
singing-accents deviating in form and position from

such as are mainly in use. Those writings he presented to the Odessa Society for history and antiquities. Devotion to the cause of learning was seen,
when, defying all difficulties, Pinsker found out, by
dint of restless study, the method of deciphering the
newly-discovered system of punctuation, and revealed
it to the delight of scholars. His researches in bibliography, biography, and literary history were in-
exhaustible.

In order to acquaint himself with the contents
of each of the manuscripts brought out by Firkowitch, Pinsker learned the Arabic language—a task
not easily accomplished in a Russian town like Odessa.
But the results of unwearied labors remained hidden
from the world. Pinsker, in his genuine modesty,
believed that what he had acquired was not worth the
attention of literary men. Fortunately Osias H. Schorr,
the eminent editor of *Hè-Chaluz*, knew better.
He applied to the retiring scholar for contributions
to his publication. Pinsker complied, and at first
gave an account of the labors of two Karaites, Mose
Darai and *Radba* (David ben-Abraham), natives of
Fez, who lived during the Middle Ages, and enjoyed
a wide reputation. The articles swelled in size until
they formed a bulky volume, issued afterwards under
the name, *Likkutè Kadmoniyoth*, (Collections from
the Days of Old), and likewise under the title " The
History of Karaism and the Karaite Literature."

. The author describes the periods of the development of the Karaitic doctrines and views; one preceding Anan, the founder of the sect; another of that man's own time; a third of the reformer, Nohawendi; and last, the Karaites proper. According to him, the latest period occasioned the final breach concerning Talmudic traditions. The Karaites, anxious to increase their number, sent messengers to Jewish congregations, to stir up the people to join their ranks. Our author sees the derivation of "Karaite" in the Hebrew *Kara*, (to call), alluding to the summoning of the Jews in various communities to declare themselves in favor of the new sect. Pinsker, moreover, holds that to those schismatics all are indebted for a reliable system of Biblical orthography, grammar, lexicography, and modern Hebrew poetry. They, he contends, wrote on those subjects, even before Saadiah Gaon and Dunash ben-Labrat had brought forth their works.

Important Karaite writings are quoted and dwelt upon, among which are the *Lexicon* by Radba and the *Divan* by Mose Darai; the Ninth century being given as the time when the last-named lived. Gabirol, Moses and Abraham Aben-Ezra, and Jehudah Halevy, are said to have had in Darai a model, from whom they copied tropes and even strophes.

The *Likkuté* met with a reception most flattering to its accomplished author. Pinsker awoke to find himself famous, and deservedly so, for very rich, and rare, and honestly wrought out was the information afforded. His production had not yet been fully published, when Jost and Graetz, the acknowledged representatives of Jewish history, and Dr. Schmiedl, the noted scholar, publicly avowed their indebtedness to him.

In 1863 Pinsker published at Vienna his *Mebó ha-Nikkud*, an explanation of the system of punctuation, according to the Babylonian school. This work critically describes the progress of a branch of Hebrew literature, most essential and still insufficiently cultivated. Pinsker's researches into the origin and development of the vowel-points and singing-accents prove him a born grammarian. In fact, he fondly cherished the idea of issuing a Hebrew grammar—a beautiful *résumé* of his profound investigations. Unfortunately, his health was not equal to his will. He vainly tried to grapple with the destroyer. The great scholar succumbed on the 29th of October, 1864.

Pinsker left a large number of manuscripts, bearing on the writings of ancient authors, alike of the Karaites and the Rabbinists. The publication of these would, undoubtedly, be greeted by all who desire to know what was done in olden times in the realm of exegesis.

ELISABETH RACHEL (FELIX).

The pulpit has had, of late, its fling at the stage. That a change for the better in public representations is necessary, few will doubt. But the views of some are too sweeping. The entire closing of places of amusement as unmitigated evils, is not the proper remedy. It would be like uprooting the tree, on account of the rottenness of one of its branches. For it must be conceded that the theatre, notwithstanding its faults, has a tendency, in many instances, to improve morals. Refined amusement and instruction are often afforded at the same time. Nor are all professional actors and actresses wanting in respectability and honor. In the pursuit of their avocation, they are occasionally compelled to meet with persons of ordinary character. But it does not follow that they must become tainted by the contact. These hints are not intended to forestall an opinion. The prominence of Rachel as a *tragédienne* suggested them.

Elisabeth Rachel (Felix) was born, of humble parentage, at Mumpf, Switzerland, February 28th, 1820. So needy was the family that she, and her sister, Sarah, roamed about the streets of Lyons, France, whither the household had removed, singing to earn a coin.

In 1831 Rachel went to Paris, and, to cultivate her voice, took lessons from an eminent teacher. But her success by no means equalled anticipations. Neither did her *début* on the stage, in 1833, prove a triumph, though her talents had been previously tested by well-known critics, such as Jules Janin, and Mademoiselle Mars.

Undaunted by the first failure, Rachel continued steadfast to her adopted profession, and public admiration soon began to clearly manifest itself. When she appeared, in 1838, as *Camille*, in the tragedy of *Les Horaces*, the enthusiasm became intense. From this time forward, her histrionic powers were warmly applauded and encouraged. In many characters she stood almost without a rival, but her greatest triumphs were achieved in her rendition of *Phèdre*, and of *Adrienne Lecouvreur*—a play expressly written for her. "Her *Phèdre*," observes a writer,—" by common consent her masterpiece—was an apocalypse of human agony, not to be forgotten by any one who ever witnessed it." Rachel's acting, in general, left an impression that probably none of her sex, who preceded or succeeded her, have created.

During the Revolution of 1848, she publicly recited the *Marseillaise Hymn*, and the *furor* it excited has connected her name with the history of that stormy period. Rachel visited different parts of Europe and America, and was tendered everywhere public ovations.

In 1855 her health began to fail, and she sought several places for rest and renewed vigor. But all in vain. Her constitution was completely broken down, and on January 3d, 1858, death relieved her of further suffering, at Cannet, near Toulon, in France.

Providence had lavished mental riches upon that daughter of our race. Had she valued the gifts as a divine trust, and employed them always in a manner that might add to the respect of self and of Israel, she would have been glorious, as she is eminent.

MORRIS JACOB RAPHALL.

It is not uncommon to hear foreigners complain of the difficulties which the English language presents, specially in its orthography, and in the application of particles or terms most in use, when a large variety of a like character exists. Peculiar, therefore, must be the merits of one who, not "to the manner born," can overcome impediments in speaking, and write with fluency and unexceptional purity. Of the foreign Rabbis who have ascended American pulpits, the late Dr. Raphall employed the language in which Shakspeare wove his thoughts, with unsurpassed perfection.

The Rev. Dr. Morris Jacob Raphall was born at Stockholm, Sweden, in September, 1798. When a mere child, his parents sent him to a Jewish college in Copenhagen, which conferred upon the student, as early as his thirteenth year, the degree of *Habér*, or *Socius*. In 1812 he went to England, and studied the language of the country and its literature, with splendid results. Having made a tour through France, Germany, Switzerland, and Italy, Raphall sought a German university as the spot whence to rise higher in knowledge. From 1821 to 1824 he remained at Giessen, and returned to England in 1825, where he was married, and took up his abode.

Dr. Raphall entered public life in 1832. The course of lectures he delivered on Post-Biblical history, at Sussex-hall, in London, and elsewhere through the United Kingdom, was a triumph to the scholar. For he saw the most intelligent among Christians, as well as among Jews, attentive listeners. The publication of the *Hebrew Review and Magazine of Rabbinical Literature*, a weekly periodical devoted to Jewish learning, began in 1834. It was ably edited, but after seventy-eight numbers, full of instructive and interesting articles, had appeared, it was suspended, partly because of the editor's impaired health, and partly for want of proper support. An idea of the value of that magazine may be formed, when it is known that it contained translations of several of Maimonides' works; *Sépher Ikkarim*, or "Book of Creeds," by Rabbi Joseph Albo; and *Yen Lebanon*, which treats of ethics, by the celebrated Rabbi Naphtali Herz Wessely; besides original writings on the "Customs and Observances of the Jews;" biographies, and poems of merit. Dr. Raphall worked on a translation of eighteen treatises of the "Mishna," published jointly with the Rev. David A. De Sola; and a very learned exposition in English of the Book of Genesis, in conjunction with Messrs. De Sola and I. L. Lindenthal.

The Doctor acted for a time as Secretary to the Rev. Dr. Solomon Hirschel, Chief Rabbi of the German Congregations of the British Isles. But in 1841 his labors were asked for at Birmingham, where he was elected Rabbi-Preacher of the Synagogue. His zealous efforts for the promotion of education and beneficence, during eight consecutive years, were not forgotten by the grateful inhabitants, For in 1849, when about to leave for the United States, a purse of one hundred sovereigns was presented to him by the Mayor and corporation of Birmingham, in acknowledgment of the many services he had rendered. The University of Giessen, fully aware of his scholarly abilities, had attached to his name the titles of M. A., and Ph. D.

The learned Doctor received a cordial greeting on arriving at New York, and he was installed as the spiritual guide of the congregation *B'nai Jeshurun*, then worshiping in Greene Street. He remained in that office until his death. During his ministry, the new Synagogue of the congregation in Thirty-fourth Street, was dedicated. Dr. Raphall,—assisted by the Rev. Ansel Leo, the popular Reader, who died in December, 1878,—pronounced one of his discourses, always so eloquent and impressive.

A very short time elapsed ere the subject of our sketch gained a wide-spread reputation throughout America. The acquirements which he eminently possessed, brought his name into connection with all matters of a public character. Many Philadelphians will remember his comely and venerable appearance, at the annual banquets given by the Hebrew Charity Association. Seated by the side of well-known divines and scholars, he electrified his auditors by a display of oratorical powers of the highest order.

In the year 1855 Dr. Raphall offered the world a work in two volumes, entitled " Post-Biblical History of the Jews," from the return to Palestine of the Babylonian captives, to the conquest of Jerusalem by Titus. It is a production that cannot be overrated;

for it at once exhibits the author's profound knowledge of, and his strict conformity to, truth. If Dr. Raphall had not written aught else, this would have been sufficient to immortalize his name. But his indefatigable efforts for Judaism still proceeded unabated. "Devotional Exercises for the Daughters of Israel," compiled and enlarged from several German writers, soon appeared, and it was followed by "The Path to Immortality," etc., etc. Before his demise, the Doctor had made considerable progress in a translation of the Scriptures with annotations.

A long life of usefulness was brought to a close on the 23d of June, 1868. The loss was serious to the House of Israel, and to the cause of learning generally, and dust was consigned to dust, with every demonstration of sorrow by Jews and Gentiles.

SALOMON LOEW RAPOPORT.

A practice which originated in the Middle Ages has continued to our day. Jewish writers are made known to the world by the initials of their Hebrew names. At times, the word thus formed does not represent any idea, but often it is fraught with meaning. That Rapoport should have chosen *Shir* as his *nom de plume*, may be ascribed to the chance that gave him the appellation from which the initials were taken. But who that knows the Sage will deny the fitness of the term? A *Song* was his life, in praise of the ancient teachers of Israel; a melodious chant, with which he would win a people, estranged from their sacred literature, back again to its steady culture.

Salomon Loew Rapóport was born at Lemberg, in Galicia, Austria, on the 1st of June, 1790. Reared in the severe school of Orthodoxy, which, at the time, forbade research, he felt an eager wish to break asunder the fetters that bound the mind. It is related that he stealthily obtained gratuitous instruction in French from a military officer, and that he had made considerable progress, when his mother, hearing of the circumstance, consigned all his books in that language to the flames. This conclusively shows that knowledge was then a terror, rather than a delight. Study must be, by force, confined to the Talmud, and works partaking of its nature. Rapoport was destined to be the leader in the effort to break through such restraints, and root out bigotry and narrow dogmas.

The young man's education was of a two-fold character—the pursuit of theology, and the cultivation of divers branches of secular learning. This training led to earnest reflection as to the course he should follow in the future. Rapoport determined that, while remaining strict and firm to the doctrines and ordinances of traditional Judaism, he would do his utmost to improve the mental status of his fellow-believers. Upheld by that resolve, he enlarged the domain of literature, working with singleness of purpose. None can accuse him of enunciating notions subversive of accepted principles, in any of the numerous writings that emanated from his pen. His criticism had truth for its aim, and not notoriety by the declaration of startling opinions; and if he failed to please all, he must have borne the satisfaction of having clung to deep-set convictions.

Rapoport was first employed as clerk in a public office of his native city; but when still a youth he wrote in Hebrew with the facility of an expert. The columns of the two Hebrew Annuals, *Bikkuré Haittim* and *Kérem Chémed*, were early graced by his contributions, the worth of which elicited the plaudits of the discerning.

The retirement of the venerable Joshua Heshel left a void in the district Rabbinate of Tarnopol. Those who appreciated Rapoport's qualifications urged him to let his name appear among the candidates for the vacant position. The *Hassidim* naturally opposed the choice of a man whose name was synonymous with enlightenment—so abhorrent to their souls. But the fanatical elements were overcome by the liberal and intelligent, thus securing the election of a scholar that any community might have been proud to look up to as its ecclesiastical chief.

The Rabbi devoted his first leisure moments to dive into philosophy and history, and to survey the vast field of Hebrew literature. During the period of half a century, multifarious articles showed the extent of wonderful investigations, unique as they were astonishing.

Exegetical analyses became the sustaining pillars of Rapoport's fame. Various dissertations were published, critically explaining Holy Writ, and advancing profound ideas as to the authenticity of certain books, or portions thereof, contained in the Scriptures. For instance, the expositor conceded that there were psalms of the Maccabean period embodied in the Psalter, and that the sections of Isaiah, from chapter XL to the end, evince a later authorship. Still he would not sanction any addition or suppression of the text, by reason of the abstract theories formed. We may easily perceive that Rapoport noticed peculiarities in the diction of the prophetical writings and the Hagiographa, and perhaps the sentiments expressed therein, which created his impressions, but not finding sufficient ground to establish his conceptions beyond peradventure, and fearing to take too bold a stand against the *Massora*, he wisely abstained from assailing that which time has hallowed.

Following the path of Aaron the High-priest,

"loving peace, and cleaving to peace," the pastor's calm and deliberative addresses to his flock set at rest opposition, and effected a thorough reconciliation between parties embittered towards each other, merely because of personal antagonism. Sincerity, coupled with sterling ability, gained the victory for Salomon Loew Rapoport, and proved his guide in the prosecution of every design. In 1840 he was chosen Chief Rabbi of Prague, receiving the heartiest congratulations of the learned throughout Europe.

A cursory view will now be taken of some of the most noted productions of the honored literator. A perusal of any will disclose the capacities of the author, and his scientific workings of the subject in all its bearings, going into the minutest details, with the penetration and skill of a master. Besides assisting in the preparation of the *Kérem Chémed*, and beautifying it by charming contributions, anonymous, or over his initials, Rapoport brought forth his critico-biographical sketches of *Saadiah Gaon; Rabbi Nathan*, the author of the Talmudical lexicon; *Hai Gaon; Eliezer Kalir; Rabbenu Hananel;* etc. These were published in the *Bikkuré Haittim*, to the edification of many eager readers. A poem entitled *Sheérith Jehudah*, adapted from Racine's "Esther," with a splendid preface, appeared; followed by *Dibrè Shalom Veemet*, a defence of Dr. Zacharias Frankel's *Darché Ha-Mishna;* and *Erech Millin*, a linguistic and archæological encyclopædia, of which only the first volume, (letter *Aleph*) has been issued. This work is in itself a most glowing illustration of the author's erudition. Continuations of it have been found in manuscript. So likewise, fragments of a geographical collection as a sequel to *Anshé Hashem*; a criticism of Dr. Abraham Geiger's *Urschrift*; a commentary on the Book of Job; a series of discourses; an extensive correspondence with contemporary scholars; and a book of genealogies, which embraces important materials for the history of Jewish science in the present century, are among the literary remains of the great Rabbi.

Rapoport's life-mission closed at Prague, in Bohemia, Austria, on the 16th of October, 1867.

Faithful to his trust as a spiritual leader, conscientious and indefatigable as a writer, the Sage of Lemberg will be known and revered while Hebrew literature has a student and the Hebrew language a lover. He has served as a beacon-light to the multitude who have rendered this age illustrious, reviving the palmy days of Spain and Portugal under Moorish dominion.

ISAAC SAMUEL REGGIO.

As years roll on, the amount of learning which constitutes a scholar immeasurably swells in size. Hence few can boast of having grasped all that should be retained on any given subject. Experience has shown this even in Hebrew literature, which is comparatively limited in extent. But Isaac Samuel Reggio brought under his will the accumulated knowledge of contemporaries and predecessors, and he lived to see others reap the rich harvest of his toil.

Isaac Samuel Reggio was born at Gorizia, in the province of Illyria, Italy, on the 5th of August, 1784. His father, Abraham V. Reggio, Rabbi of that city, had acquired renown as a theologian. He early trained his son in Biblical and Talmudical lore. The question being then agitated about the introduction of reforms in the method of instruction, men of great calibre—as Wessely and Mendelssohn—took part in it in favor of the change; others, again, bitterly opposed it. The father of Isaac took side with the chief advocates of the proposed improvements, whom he represented to his son as ideal-masters, and counselled the youth to follow in their footsteps. As young Reggio grew up, he displayed ardent zeal for religion and science, and his extraordinary capacities soon became noticeable.

When Illyria was annexed to the French Empire, Reggio received the appointment of Professor of Belles-Lettres, History and Geography, at the gymnasium of his birth-place. For three years he rendered important services to the institution. On the decease of his father, he held the situation of Rabbi of Gorizia, declining to accept any pecuniary remuneration.

But it was the literary endeavors of Prof. Reggio that made him famous. His various productions are of an inestimable character, and their influence upon literature must be conceded. With vast ability and immense erudition he issued works explanatory of most abstruse subjects, and, therefore, indispensable to Jewish students. Reggio has written his autobiography, in which he frequently alludes to the many trials he underwent, and to the aspersions cast on his name and his writings. It was necessary for the author to be ever watchful, for foes surrounded him on all sides.

Scarcely had the first of Reggio's works, an essay intended as an introduction to his commentary on the Pentateuch, made its appearance, than an anonymous writer publicly attacked it, accusing the author of gross blunders and errors. This evoked a reply from Reggio, in which he proved how wrongly he had been dealt with. In 1812 Reggio gave us one of his most extensive productions—an Italian translation of the Five Books of Moses, with a Hebrew commentary, in five volumes. Fifteen hundred copies were published at his own expense, as he himself narrates. No Jewish library can be termed complete that does not possess it.

The establishment of the Rabbinical College at Padua was greatly due to Reggio's exertions. His Hebrew work, *Ha-Torah ve ha-Philosophia*, on the connection of Revelation with Philosophy, appeared in 1827, and it so remarkably disclosed the true scholar, that Reggio received numerous requests to contribute to different magazines. Many of these demands on his time were complied with, and the learned articles he published won the commendation of the literary world.

It would be impossible to review, or even to name, all the productions of this splendid Hebraist. They have been accorded their merited praise by competent authorities. But allusion to some of them is in order, on account of their weight on Italian-Hebrew literature.

Reggio gave a version in his native language of several difficult portions of the Bible, particularly the Book of Isaiah. This metrical translation has been critically reviewed by Dr. S. I. Mulder, who added a preface in Dutch, evincing the high esteem which he entertained for the author. *Bechinath Ha-Dath* (Investigation of the Law), by Elias del Medigo, with an introduction and explanatory notes was published. Reggio also issued, at intervals, *Iggeroth Yashar*, (his *Literary Correspondence*), of which he relates the following : " I sent the manuscript of the second part to the printing office at Vienna, but the stage-coach which conveyed it from my place of residence (Gorizia) to the metropolis, was overtaken in the night by highwaymen, and, among other articles, this manuscript was also stolen. When this was brought under my notice, I collected as much as possible of the notes I had left, and from these I succeeded in writing another volume, which came from the press at Vienna, in 5596 (1836), as a second part of my above-mentioned *Correspondence*." An introduction to the Book of Esther in 1841, was reviewed by Dr. Jost, in his paper, *The Israelitish Annals*. Reggio wrote for the *Zion*, the *Bikkuré Haittim*, the *Kérem Chémed*, and the *Central Organ*. He also published "A Guide for the Religious Instruction of Jewish Youth," which was translated into English by the late M. H. Picciotto, father of the author of "Sketches of Anglo-Jewish History;" and a lengthy correspondence between himself and the famous Prof. Samuel David Luzzatto, for whom he prepared a genealogical tree of the Luzzatto family.

Of Reggio's other works there are *Bechinath Ha-Cabbala*, on a writing of Leon de Modena; "A View of Astronomy"; an Italian version of the Book of Joshua, with a Hebrew preface; one in the same language, of the Lamentations of Jeremiah, with an Italian preface; another of the Book of Ruth; another of the treatise *Aboth* (Ethics of the Fathers), with an introduction and copious annotations; an Italian translation of the *Correspond-ence about Faith*, between Mendelssohn and Lavater; and another of many Psalms.

Prof. Reggio died on the 29th of August, 1855. His life was spent in the effort to prepare Israelites for the reception of critical views on Biblical and Rabbinical volumes, and what he said was always expressed in a style, at once attractive, and almost unrivalled.

ROBERT REMAK.

Attempts to crush the Jewish mind have never been attended with success. On the contrary, they have contributed to strengthen its powers. In Poland, for example, Hebrews have been levelled with the ground, and yet, in that very same country, and from among the outcasts and the reviled, arose some of the intellects that shaped modern science.

Medicine and physiology have been most ably represented. A notice—for only such can we term it—of an Israelite, who has been extolled by the far-famed Claude Bernard and Ernst Haeckel, will here be offered. He must, indeed, be considered excellent, whom the greatest acknowledged great.

Prof. Robert Remak, M. D., was born at Posen, in the Duchy of Posen, Prussian Poland, on July 30th, 1815. He received rudimentary instruction, and, from

1829 to 1833, attended the Gymnasium, whence he proceeded to the University of Berlin. He took rapid strides in the pursuit of his various studies. Medical work, however, drew forth the fulness of his capacities, and Prof. Reimann, seeing it, foretold the future reserved for the earnest student. Remak graduated in 1838. With a deep consciousness of the importance of the avocation chosen, he followed a special course under John Miller and Schoenlein, till he felt that the knowledge acquired was equal to the demands of the profession. Then he came before the public.

In 1847 Dr. Remak was appointed *Privat Docent.* In 1861 he achieved his crowning triumph by being elected Professor Extraordinary at the University of Berlin. His elevation to that office, through the instrumentality of the immortal Alexander Von Humboldt might well have been a cause for glorification, at a time when Jews were debarred from ascending the ladder of fame.

Both as a practitioner and an author, Prof. Remak is renowned in the department of medicine which treats of the nerves. "His principal merits," observes a writer, "lie in his researches into the more delicate nerve-constructions, and into the development of the vertebrates, and in the introduction of a constant electric current, as a remedy for the diseases of the nerve system." His works include

" Diagnostic and Pathogenic Researches at the Schoen-lein Clinic"—1845 ; " Concerning an Independent Nerve-System of the Skin"—1847 ; " Concerning the development of Vertebrates"—1851–'5 ; "Methodic Electrization of Palsied Muscles"—1851 ; and " Galvano-Therapeutics of Nerve and Muscle Diseases" —1858,—translated into French, in 1860. The Professor also indited valuable articles for journals, and he was, from 1842, a contributor to the *Yearly Reports for Medical Science* (in Physiology).

Robert Remak's extraordinary career closed at Kissingen, in Bavaria, on August 29th, 1865. In him, medicine lost one who had greatly extended its limits.

A fluent writer he was, but likewise an ardent laborer who aimed at the alleviation and the cure of bodily ailments. He would serve to his successors as a light with which they might search still deeper and farther into a science, very intricate, but very essential and noble, when applied with loving care to the human sufferer.

GABRIEL RIESSER.

Progress, in ages gone by is, so to say, microscopic when compared with that brilliantly visible in this era. The state of the intelligent beings that people the earth forms the important question which has occupied many minds. But the solution of the problem constitutes the crown which will adorn the brow of this golden age. Liberty, equality and fraternity are a triad, no longer imaginary, but likely to become a reality in our own day. The law which has declared sentient creatures entitled to freedom of will, and the pursuit of happiness, is finding its application. We see it in the effects of the labors of a Wilberforce, a Lincoln, a Mazzini, and a Garrison. As these intellectual heroes strove with might and main to raise their fellow mortals oppressed by the tyrant's rule, so did Gabriel Riesser gird his loins to hasten to the deliverance of his co-religionists. The sphere of his actions was by no means as wide, nor were the results of his efforts as great. Still, the services he rendered were of a character demanding hearty recognition.

Dr. Gabriel Riesser was born at Hamburg, Germany, in 1806. Having received a careful instruction at home, he subsequently went to the Gymnasium, from which he graduated, and passed to the University of Kiel, and later to that of Heidelberg.

Early in life, Riesser became imbued with the ideas that were soon to make him a prominent actor in the struggle for liberty. He revolted at the injustice done to his fellow-believers, and while yet at college the conviction took deep root within him that a feeling of popular indignation must be aroused; an enthusiasm capable of such deeds as would burst asunder the chains of persecution.

In 1831 Riesser issued a pamphlet with the caption, "The Position of the Professors of the Mosaic Faith in Germany," in which he courageously assails the German Government for its ill-treatment of Israelites, and argues soundly and with exceeding vigor. He compares the intolerance of the time to the fanaticism of the Middle Ages, and calls upon his brethren to join hands, and fight the spirit of darkness. His bold assertions and outspoken denunciations were attended with the issue at which he aimed. Though adversely criticised by some, the opinions enunciated brought over a host of friends to the daring champion.

In the same year, Riesser penned his "Defence of the Civil Equality of the Jews, against the Objections of Dr. J. E. G. Paulus." This work, intended to disprove the sayings of a bigoted theologian, displays a judgment and logical reasoning, to which a dispassionate and calm exposure of the disabilities of the Hebrews lends additional strength. It exercised considerable influence on the author's religious adversaries, and tended, to a certain degree, to abate prejudice.

Dr. Riesser began, in 1832, the publication of *Der Jude* (The Jew), a periodical devoted to the interests of the Jews, and with an eye to their political emancipation. The erudition and zeal with which its editor refuted calumnies against his brethren were not ineffectual. The man who had assumed an arduous, but glorious undertaking, saw his indomitable will, unwearied patience and perseverance, lead step by step to the final goal. *Der Jude* became a medium for the advocacy of staunch principles and equal rights. It frequently contained articles of uncommon merit, contributed by men of learning. Its issue was, however, discontinued in 1834.

Besides the articles inserted in his organ, Dr. Riesser published, in 1835, "Strictures on the Proceedings of the Diet of Baden, of 1833, on the Emancipation of the Jews," wherein he expresses himself freely on the hypocrisy cropping out of the discussions held. There also appeared at different intervals, "Boerne and the Jews," and "Jewish Letters," the last-mentioned notably evincing the author's scholarship. "Apprehensions and Hopes as to the Future of the Jews in Prussia," a political dissertation, which came from the press in 1842, betokens ingenuity and a consummate knowledge of national affairs. Riesser also wrote for different journals and magazines. In all his productions, the true spirit of a Jew is manifested. He would not part with his religion for worldly advantages, and he ever censured those who abandon the faith of their fathers, for a fleeting reputation.

The sacrifices Riesser brought to the altar of his belief are the best proofs of his unimpeached sincerity. He was hindered from practising as an advocate in his own native city; he was refused even an unsalaried position at the University of Heidelberg, for being a Jew. Of course, these checks upon a high-spirited man caused mortification, but they could not shake the firmness of a resolute heart.

Finally, in 1848, Dr. Riesser was elected to the German Parliament. Now did the voice which had long been lifted in vain, resound within the halls of legislation. The tone and fervid eloquence of the speaker made him nobly conspicuous in that representative assemblage. He stood among the foremost, battling for a United Germany, based on the will of the people. His very opponents observed in the honest Israelite, one really attached to his fatherland, and Riesser was honored by being chosen Vice-President of Parliament, and also a member of the delegation sent to Berlin, to offer King William IV. the crown of Germany.

The year 1860 saw Gabriel Riesser a Justice of the Supreme Court, in the city of his birth. Thus were his labors rewarded, and deeply he appreciated the victory. His own words will show how he re garded his elevation to that judicial post: " Not for my own sake, but for the sake of the Jews, do

I rejoice in the distinction I have received; I see in it the recognition of the rights of the Jews."

Dr. Riesser died at Hamburg, Germany, in 1860.

Let the revilers of Jewish patriotism be hushed into silence; let them never again attempt their mendacious onslaughts, lest the ghost of Gabriel Riesser rise in all its majesty, and mark them out as objects of scorn.

ROTHSCHILD.

The origin and progress of a family whose controlling power in the commercial world is everywhere felt, must, of necessity, be of interest. But to trace the exertions of each individual member of a house so incomparably famous, would be too extensive an undertaking. The presentation of some characters preëminently historical, is the object we seek to attain.

————

I.—MEYER ANSELM ROTHSCHILD was born in the *Judenstrass*, at Frankfort-on-the-Main, Germany, in 1743. When but eleven years old, his parents died, and the surviving relatives trained the boy for a teacher. This occupation not suiting his taste, young Rothschild engaged in an humble trading business, and, shortly after, he was employed in a counting-house, at Hanover. In a few years, he became master of a small capital, and, returning to Frankfort, he married, and started in business for himself, as a banker and broker. Industry and integrity soon obtained for him a reputation, and he was authorized to raise a loan to stay off the French republican forces, and save Frankfort from pillage.

In 1801 the Landgrave or Elector of Hesse-Cassel, who had accumulated about a million pounds sterling, by hiring his subjects to fight for England and France, was obliged to flee on account of the approach of Napoleon, who, after the battle of Jena, had declared that ruler's estates forfeited. Before leaving, however, the Elector sent for Rothschild, and offered him the free use of the treasure, without interest, if he would convey it to a place of safety. With the aid of his friends, the prudent banker succeeded in secreting the money, and thus prevented its being seized by the French. His affairs now began to prosper to such a degree, that he was able to contract for a Danish loan of four million dollars.

Rothschild had five sons, and, previous to his death, which occurred in September, 1812, he experienced the pleasure of seeing them all securely established as the monarchs of European finance—Anselm in Frankfort, Solomon in Vienna, Nathan in London, Charles in Naples, and James in Paris.

II.—NATHAN MEYER ROTHSCHILD, third son of

Meyer Anselm, was born at Frankfort-on-the-Main, Germany, on the 16th of September, 1777. He became associated with his father in banking operations, and went to England in 1800, to represent the firm. He first proceeded to Manchester, where he purchased goods for the Continent. Removing to London, he invested large sums of money for the house, and with so much judgment, that the principal multiplied with great rapidity. He was appointed, by the interest of the Landgrave of Hesse-Cassel, agent for the payment of the £12,000,000 sterling, which, by the treaty of Toeplitz, Great Britain stipulated to pay her German allies. A large profit accrued to the house by this transaction.

During the war between England and Spain, which began in 1808, the Rothschilds gave evidence of their immense wealth, by their remittances to the English army. In a period of twelve years, five hundred millions of dollars were raised for different powers, as loans or subsidies, exclusive of various other large sums. It is said that Mr. N. M. Rothschild knew the result of the battle of Waterloo several hours before the English Government, thereby gaining £200,000.

The wonderful tact displayed by the Rothschilds in the management of their resources, is none the less remarkable. They never took a bad loan in hand, and hardly any good loans fell into the hands of others. In addition to the co-operation of the five brothers, important agencies exist in many other cities, both of the Old and the New World. Were it not for the extraordinary means which the Rothschilds possess, reverses which entailed serious losses, might have proved fatal. But extreme watchfulness served as a safeguard to future success.

On the death of the father, Mr. Nathan Meyer Rothschild was considered head of the firm, and, as such, was always consulted by his brothers, on matters pertaining to the welfare of the house. He introduced the business of negotiating foreign loans in England, and an act of denization was passed in his favor in 1821. Though created a Baron of the Austrian Empire, Mr. Rothschild never adopted the title, preferring the renown he had achieved as a financier.

The Baron had special claims to public attention as a philanthropist. He donated large sums alike to Jewish and Christian institutions, and his moral and pecuniary aid was ever lent to the promotion of good objects. As a member of the Board of Deputies of British Jews, Mr. Rothschild gave the weight of his influence to further the designs of that organization.

While at Frankfort, to witness the marriage of his son, Lionel, to Charlotte, daughter of the Baron Charles Rothschild, an illness overtook him, and he expired on the 28th of July, 1836. His remains were brought to England, and interred, with great solemnity, in the cemetery of the Great (German) Synagogue. Many thousands of pounds were left by Mr. Rothschild, to be distributed to the poor by his widow. His brother Anselm, who died childless, in 1856, left a fortune valued at from 40,000,000 to 50,000,000 florins.　　：

III.—LIONEL NATHAN DE ROTHSCHILD, son of Baron Nathan Meyer, was born at London, England, November 22d, 1808. He received an education at Göttingen, and his father early initiated him into the business of the firm. Applying himself to the task, he materially assisted the house in extending its colossal enterprises.

The earnestness Mr. Rothschild evinced in Jewish matters, and his labors to induce the removal of the political disabilities affecting Israelites, redounded greatly to his credit. The British Government recognized his hereditary title of Baron, in 1838, and, in 1847, he was chosen by the Liberals to the House of Commons. Declining to be sworn "On the true faith of a Christian," he was not allowed to take his seat. The contrast between the will of Parliament and that of the people was proven by Baron Rothschild's re-election for the city of London, in the years 1849, 1852, and 1857.

Many bills were introduced for the recognition of Jewish rights, which, though they usually passed the House of Commons, were invariably rejected by the Upper House. In 1858, on motion of Mr. Duncombe, Baron Rothschild was placed on a committee to hold a conference with the House of Lords, which virtually ended in the declaration of Jewish emancipation. The Commons sent up another bill, and a general belief prevailed that, if it were, like the rest, thrown out by the Lords, Jewish members would be admitted by resolution of their own House, instead of by act of Parliament. The Lords gave way, but their groundless fears impelled them to take measures against the admission of Israelites into the Upper Chamber. Baron Rothschild assumed his seat, amid cheers, on the 26th of July, 1858, and he was successively returned to Parliament until the general election of 1874. He died June 3d, 1879.

IV.—ANTHONY DE ROTHSCHILD, son of Baron Nathan Meyer, was born at London, England, in 1801. He entered the great banking house established by his father, and, in later years, became one of the principal members of the firm. His business talents were shown by the sharp discernment, excellent management, and sagacity which he exercised in conducting its affairs.

This large-hearted Hebrew was distinguished both
for charity and uniform kindness. He expended vast
sums to ameliorate the condition of the poor of
Palestine, and also contributed to numerous institutions, irrespective of the assistance given to private
individuals. Countenancing and supporting everything of a Jewish nature, he assumed a prominent
part in the English community.

Education among his co-religionists claimed the
attention of the Baronet. As President of the Jewish
schools in Spitalfields, he exerted himself to foster
knowledge, and his personal influence proved as
beneficial as the dispensing of his means.

Sir Anthony was created a Baronet of Great
Britain in 1864; but the honor did not lessen the active interest he took in the prosperity of his brethren,
and the whole English nation. When, on January
4th, 1876, his earthly career terminated, none could
say ill of the man. His record remained clear and
untarnished to the end.

At present our fellow-believers in Great Britain are
subject to few, if any, disqualifications. As representatives of the Bench and of the Bar, as members
of legislative bodies, and as occupants of other civic
stations, they have insured public confidence. But
the Rothschild family has not lost caste by reason
of the immunities and preferments shared by many

of its own denomination. It still holds the power which opulence and liberality secure, and, though the intermarriage of some with non-Israelites must be deprecated, the main portion of this renowned household makes itself felt for good, in whatever conduces to the perpetuation and elevation of the belief of the ancient race.

MICHAEL SACHS.

In the second volume of the Hebrew poems of Prof. S. D. Luzzatto, there is a rhythmical composition dedicated to a revered Israelite. The writer tells of a heart from which persuasive eloquence would flow, and of a mind that would confound unbelievers by its divinely-supported learning. He apostrophizes the man whose virtues had inspired his poetic genius. It was Michael Sachs,—just then elevated to a position for which his exact scholarship eminently fitted him,—whom Prof. Luzzatto extolled. Praise was never more deservedly bestowed.

Dr. Michael Sachs was born at Gross-Glogau, Prussia, on the 3d of September, 1808. The extraordinary abilities he evinced at an early age determined his father to educate him for one of the learned professions. Accordingly, he was sent to the University of Berlin, where his mild disposition, combined with great natural powers, gained the good will of both preceptors and classmates. Science and oratory divided his attention, and both were designed as aids in his study of Jewish theology.

Sachs' career as a writer began with a translation of the Bible into German, undertaken in conjunction with others. In 1837 his knowledge of the art of public speaking was put to the test in the famous city of Prague. For seven years, his eloquence and winning manners made him the object of the deep-felt regard and affection of the entire community.

Dr. Sachs became a warm personal friend of the great Rapoport, who admired his colleague's ardent devotion to Jewish learning. In 1844 Sachs responded to a call from the Berlin congregation. The invitation extended by a Hebrew community so influential was flattering, and Sachs wended his steps where Providence destined that he should remain during the rest of his too short existence. About the time he removed to the capital of Prussia, changes in the Jewish worship had been making there considerable headway. His effective labors were directed to stay the progress of what he considered mischievous, and he succeeded in checking the members of his own flock from adopting the new system. The talents of the noted Hebrew were too brilliant to remain unnoticed by the German Government, and he was appointed a member of the Council of Education.

The publication of works of surpassing worth gave evidence of. Dr. Sachs' signal ability. "The Religious Poetry of the Jews in Spain" appeared in 1845, exhibiting a very intimate acquaintance with a literature which undoubtedly occupies a vast and important place in the world of letters. Then followed a magnificent translation of the Prayers, in ten volumes, published in 1855, and of which many thousand copies were sold. There came also, in succession, "Voices from the Jordan and the Euphrates;" a series of contributions on Jewish Antiquities; and other writings of sterling value.

Dr. Sachs won the greatest renown, however, as a preacher. He was considered, without exception, the most finished pulpit orator of the day among Israelites. Crowds would breathlessly listen to his extemporaneous outbursts of eloquence. It is to be regretted that, because his sermons were delivered impromptu, a collection thereof cannot be made, and preserved to posterity. One of his last efforts was an address on "Moses, the Champion of God," wherein he paid a glowing tribute to the character of Sir Moses Montefiore.

Dr. Sachs died on the 31st of January, 1864. The profound sorrow his loss occasioned testified to the esteem in which the gentleman and scholar was held by men who can adequately appreciate learning joined to high principles. It will not be claiming too much, to say that Michael Sachs was one of the brightest luminaries in the Jewish horizon in our century.

DAVID SALOMONS.

When King John compelled Jews to part with their gold to fill his exhausted coffers; when he pulled their teeth to frighten them into a quick delivery of their substance, he did not dream that their posterity would sit among the highest functionaries in the very metropolis of his dominions. But this is a wonderful century, and Israelites have every cause to thank Providence who has wrought great ends through human means. It is quite appropriate to direct a thought to a bold defender of right; to the Englishman whose determined, yet dignified, deportment became the instrument to erase the vestiges of antiquated and proscriptive laws.

Sir David Salomons, Bart., M.P., a son of Levy Salomons, Esq., was born at London, England, in 1797. He early engaged in commercial pursuits. On reaching manhood he manifested much interest in Jewish affairs, and, as his fellow-believers were deprived of their rights as citizens, he soon employed his zeal in advocating their cause. In connection with Sir Moses Montefiore, the Rothschilds, the Goldsmids, and several noble-minded Christians, he finally obtained for his brethren their immunities and privileges as Englishmen.

Mr. Salomons attracted notice in the year 1835, on being elected Sheriff of London and Middlesex, and, in the same year, Alderman of Aldgate Ward. He became a candidate for Parliament from Shoreham, in 1837, but was defeated. The same happened in 1841 and 1847, when put forward for the constituencies of Maidstone and Greenwich, respectively. Still Mr. Salomons was chosen High Sheriff of Kent in 1839–'40, Alderman of Portsmouth in 1844, and of Cordwainers' in 1847. What militated against his election to several stations was his refusal to subscribe to the required declaration, "On the true faith of a Christian." Curiously enough, he could be called to the Bar at the Middle Temple in 1849, and also act as Magistrate and Deputy-Lieutenant for Kent, Sussex, and Middlesex; but the Hebrew who was permitted to assist in administering the laws was denied participation in the formation of them.

Severe were the struggles in both houses of Parliament. The friends of freedom fought bravely. Noted personages, as Lord Macaulay, Lord John Russell, Lord George Bentinck, Mr. O'Connell, Mr. Grote the historian, Mr. Disraeli, Mr. Gladstone, and several dignitaries of the Church, tried to kill the hydra of prejudice. In 1847 Baron Lionel de Rothschild, supported by the Liberal party, gained an election to the

House of Commons; however, he could not take his seat, by reason of the oath, "On the true faith of a Christian."

But the unsuccessful result of this election did not deter Mr. Salomons from offering himself to represent Greenwich, in 1851, though he had thrice previously been frustrated in his attempts. He was returned to Parliament, and, entering the House of Commons, insisted on being sworn on the Old Testament, and omitting the objectionable words. He maintained that he was lawfully there, and he had the boldness not only to take his seat, but to speak and vote three times on the very question of his right to remain in the House. His conduct was loudly denounced by the Speaker, and some of the members, but others sustained his course. Mr. Salomons was compelled to withdraw. The penalty incurred for his action was £500, and the affair led to prolonged legal proceedings before the Court of Exchequer.

In 1855–'6 Mr. Salomons served as Lord Mayor of London. He was the first of the two Hebrews (the other being Sir Benjamin S. Phillips) who graced that exalted position. Of Sir David, *The Times* said: " At last we have, for the first time, a Lord Mayor who can speak the Queen's English with propriety,"

The obnoxious oath, which had called forth the antagonism of David Salomons, was repealed in 1858, and Baron Rothschild assumed his seat in Parliament. He who had grappled with the evil, and crushed it, was again chosen to the House of Commons, from Greenwich, in 1859, and he continued to fiulfil important trusts, always maintaining and defending the honor of his fellow-believers. On July 18th, 1873, this venerable son of Jacob was gathered to his fathers.

Sir David wrote several essays on Religious Disabilities, Persecution of the Jews in the East, Currency, Corn Laws, Oaths, etc. He was, at one time, a Trustee of the London and Westminster Bank.

The sterling qualities conspicuous in the character of this English Jew, raised him so loftily, that it would be superfluous on our part to attempt a panegyric.

JOSEPH SALVADOR.

Religious discussions conducted with calm and impartial judgment must be productive of good. Points presenting difficulties are put to a crucial analysis. Thus the verities they contain come up resplendent, while the fiction sinks low. The doctrines which guide the ancient people have nothing to fear from the searching trial. But it cannot be denied that debates of a dogmatic nature have frequently occasioned a vast amount of evil. Passions were conjured up which obscured the serene regions of the intellect.

All should feel glad that, in this age of enlightenment, and in liberal France, polemical productions
will command attention and respect. The works
of Joseph Salvador do not exactly belong to that
category. But as they have elicited adverse strictures, and again writings vindicating former assertions, they may be classified with literary labors
purporting to ventilate accepted ideas in religion, and
to serve the cause of truth.

Joseph Salvador was born at Montpellier, France,
in 1796. His ancestors, whom the ruthless arm of
the Inquisition aimed to strike dead, fled from Spain
in the fifteenth century, and found safety in France.
Their illustrious descendant showed a precocious understanding, and an eager desire for knowledge in the
days of his boyhood. He early displayed a preference
for science and philosophy, nor did he part with them
when pursuing other studies. The youth attended a
medical school, from which he graduated in 1816, as
Doctor of Medicine, choosing for his thesis, "The Application of Philosophy to Pathology." He did not,
however, steadily follow up the medical profession,
but responded to the promptings of his nature, by devoting his time to literature.

M. Salvador betook himself to Paris, and did
not delay carrying out his cherished plans. He pur-
posed treating of the Jewish people, their origin and
history. He endeavored to signalize the undertaking

by system and thoroughness, so that it might offer accurate information, and suggest thoughts never before entertained by the readers of the Mosaic volumes.

M. Salvador, looking from his own standpoint, has surely succeeded in giving the Pentateuch a foremost station. In the sphere of philosophical criticism he differs from the German school, whose theories, transplanted into France, are greatly in vogue. He is original in many instances, and applies scientific knowledge to matters dwelt upon. He sees the omnipresence of God in the affairs of nations, and clearly in the history of the Hebrews. Not that he recognizes an immediate communion of the mind of Moses with the Spirit that governs the universe ; but, ascribing to the leader of the tribes the whole credit for the sublime legislation which bears his name, Salvador, nevertheless, admits the invisible direction of the Supreme Being in whatever did and will civilize the world.

The following works have emanated from M. Salvador : "The Law of Moses, or the Religious and Political System of the Hebrews," in 1822, which may be termed a prelude to the "History of the Institutions of Moses and of the Hebrew People," in two volumes—1828. The latter book has passed through several editions. Much comment was occasioned by its appearance, and the author's elucidations, concerning the administration of justice, as enforced in the case of the man of Nazareth, provoked a controversial writing from the widely-known jurist, Jean Jacques Dupin, entitled, " Jesus before Caiphas and Pilate." Salvador maintained his ground, and in his famous production, " Jesus and his Doctrine," in two volumes, 1838, he shows with immense erudition whence the son of Mary derived his knowledge, and why he could not receive the homage of the Jews. Important facts relative to the founder of Christianity are there disclosed. " History of the Roman Domination in Judea, and of the Destruction of Jerusalem,'' in three volumes, was published in 1847; and " Paris, Rome, Jerusalem ; or, The Religious Question in the Nineteenth Century," in two volumes, in 1860, and which is the latest and ripest of Salvador's works.

The author had watched, with the eye of a profound philosopher, the events that followed each other since 1848. In a series of letters he describes the impressions created, the hopes and aspirations of his soul. Therein is given a comprehensive summary of all upon which he had reflected. He recognizes in the revolution of 1789 the beginning of an era that cannot be terminated until religion permeates politics, and both form an indissoluble alliance.

M. Salvador died at Paris, France, in 1873.

FLAMINIO SERVI.

A journal in the interest of Judaism is a thing of recent date in Italy. The first appeared in 1853, at Vercelli, a city of Piedmont. *L'Educatore Israelita*, a monthly magazine, was edited by Joseph Levi, who, while bringing to the task all the versatile knowledge requisite, secured a valuable co-laborer in Ezra Pontremoli. But in 1874 death removed him who had made his organ a vehicle to popular instruction, and to the exaltation of Israel. The keynote which that zealous worker struck, met with a response during his lifetime. At Trieste, the eastern end of the Italian peninsula, A. Curiel began *Il Corriere Israelitico*, a monthly, which still adds to its high merits, by keeping its readers constantly informed of the doings of the *Alliance Israélite Universelle*. A third publication, that of Rabbi G. E. Levi, called *Mosé, Antologia Israelitica*, inscribed to Sir Moses Montefiore, and issued at Corfu, Greece, in the Italian language, is specially devoted to Jewish science. But *L'Educatore Israelita* did not die with its founder. Rabbi F. Servi, of Casale, assumed the management of the periodical, and it lives to-day under the name of *Il Vessillo Israelitico*. Its learned editor is the subject of this sketch.

Flaminio Servi, Chief Rabbi of Casale, was born

at Pitigliano, in Tuscan Italy, December 21st, 1841.
He studied under Moses Sorani, now Chief Rabbi of
Cento, and David J. Maroni, at present Chief Rabbi
of Florence. But he derived most of his knowledge
from his own father, who, though a layman, successfully cultivated theology. Parental precept and example, together with lessons on Holy Writ and
Talmud, instilled principles which developed an un-
shaken attachment to historical Judaism. Gifted with
great aptness and a retentive memory, feeling an inborn
fondness for literature, the lad did not incline towards
his father's vocation.

When only eight years old, Servi's unfitness for
commerce, and his qualifications for the pursuit of
learning could have been foretold. For he would,
when even so young, try his hand at versification,
and, as he grew, the most trivial event elicited poetical
effusions. When eleven he translated the Book of
Proverbs, and completed a version of the Psalter, left
unfinished by an elder brother who had died very
early in life. The youth soon became a contributor
to Jewish journals, and some of his numerous articles
met with so much favor that they were reproduced
in other languages.

When twenty years of age, Servi was deemed
worthy of the title of *Habér*, and only two years
afterwards of that of *Rabbi*. He was therefore
chosen assistant to the Jewish ecclesiastical chief of

Pitigliano. Subsequently, being made a *Morénu*, he ministered respectively at Monticelli and Mondovi; and he has officiated since 1872 at Casale.

But Rabbi Servi is best known as editor of *Il Vessillo Israelitico*. This magazine has a large circulation, and its pages are gráced by the contributions of noted men in Italy. Prof. Salvatore De Benedetti, whose work on Jehudah Halevy would alone suffice to give him celebrity; Moses Soave, a truly great scholar, whom Steinschneider does not disdain to consult; Rabbis Bachi, Luria, and Jaré, and other excellent writers help to maintain the literary standard of this periodical while, at the same time, a choice collection of domestic and foreign news is regularly presented.

Of Rabbi Servi's productions, the principal is *Gli Israeliti D'Europa* (The Israelites of Europe)—1871, containing valuable accounts of what has been done by our co-religionists for the cause of civilization, from 1789, when France gave them freedom, to 1870, when the unification of Italy was effected. The narrative of historical events in which men of our race played a conspicuous part, the copious statistics of population and of institutions, and the large number of notices of the lives and writings of illustrious Hebrews, won for the author the prize of one thousand francs, offered by the Committee for the Diffusion of Good Works among Italian Israelites. One thousand

copies came from the press. The Rabbi has also published sermons, short poems written in his boyhood,
and "Jewish Tales," and he is said to have in manuscript a translation of the best part of the Mishna,
with explanatory notes, a treatise on Rhetoric, etc.,
etc.

In reward for his services, Rabbi Servi was created a *Chevalier of the Crown of Italy*, in 1877, when
he received a flattering letter from the Minister of
Public Instruction.

The Rabbi–Chevalier is yet young in years, and
by keeping in the course he has evidently determined
upon—that of fearless honesty and independence—
he will, in the end, realize his most ardent hopes,
and add to the distinguished reputation already
achieved.

MORITZ STEINSCHNEIDER.

Students whose noble self-denial incites them to
endure hardships, while intent upon rising to distinction, have, at times, ignobly denied those left
below the light which might serve as a guide.
Literary misers are they, valueless to society. We
turn from such, to cast a look upon one who has
cheerfully shed around the radiance of his ency-
clopedic learning. Moritz Steinschneider, gifted with

powers that few possess, commanding an erudition acquired by endless exertions, does not repel multitudes who seek his teachings. He gives abundantly of his own. He is no less a "lover of language" than a lover of men. His philology and his philanthropy react upon each other.

Dr. Moritz Steinschneider was born at Prossnitz, in Moravia, Austria, on the 30th of March, 1816. His father, Jacob Steinschneider, a Talmudist, also well versed in secular knowledge, imparted to him instruction, while, at the same time, the boy attended school. Young Moritz attained a broader view of practical affairs than was usually afforded, by visiting the work-shops of various tradesmen. In his thirteenth year he became the pupil of the celebrated Rabbi Nahum Trebitsch, whom he followed to Nicolsburg in 1832.

Having thus obtained a liberal education, Steinschneider gave private lessons in the French and Italian languages. He at length went to Prague, where he remained until 1836, and devoted himself to philosophy, philology, æsthetics, and other branches, receiving diplomas from several authorities. During the period of his residence at Prague, he formed the acquaintance of a number of eminent scholars, among whom were the late Dr. Abraham Benisch, afterwards editor of the *Jewish Chronicle*, and the Rev. Albert Löwy, now a Jewish Minister in London.

In 1836 Steinschneider proceeded to Vienna, and pursued different studies, but in 1839, by the advice of the *savant*, Leopold Dukes, he initiated himself into the literature, history, and bibliography of the East.   He was anxious to join the Oriental Academy, but the prejudice of the day against his race debarred him from realizing his desire.   He could not even secure the list of Hebrew books in the Imperial Library.   Not discouraged, he attended the lectures at the Polytechnic Institute, and, to gain an insight into the learning of the Orient, he took up Kärle's course in Arabic, Syriac, and Hebrew, and in Biblical exegesis.

With the aim of adopting the Rabbinical profession, Steinschneider turned to theology.   But, for political reasons, the Austrian Government prohibited his stay at Vienna, nor could the intercession of the famous preacher, Isaac Noah Mannheimer, who enjoyed popularity among all classes, procure a revocation of the unjust mandate.   Having applied for a passport, so as to reach Berlin, he immediately left Vienna.   On arriving at Leipzig, news came of the refusal to grant him said passport; hence he was now in a serious predicament, unable to go on, or return.   Compelled to remain at Leipzig, he continued Arabic under Fleischer, and undertook the translation of the Koran into Hebrew, while interesting himself in divers matters.   He contributed to Pierer's *Universal Encyclopædia*.

In 1839 Steinschneider was permitted to go to Berlin, and, after several brief sojourns in other cities, he settled at the capital, where he passed the so-called Rector examination, and became a Prussian citizen. His position as reporter of the *National Zeitung* at the sessions of the National Assembly, and likewise his correspondence published in the *Prague Zeitung*, edited by Prof. Hasner, brought him into prominence during the crisis of 1848. The same year he received a commission to prepare a catalogue of the Hebrew books in the Bodleian Library. In order to accomplish this task—one that required a learning as accurate as profound—he made his abode at Oxford for a decade. There he took part in etymological conferences with Prof. Max Müller.

In 1859 the University of Leipzig honored Steinschneider with the degree of Ph. D., and he was elected Professor of the Jewish Seminary of *Veitel-Heine-Ephraim*, at Berlin. He also superintends the *Töchterschule* of the Berlin Israelitish community. He has been obliged to decline numerous advantageous offers, either on account of his principles, or by reason of his many duties.

Dr. Steinschneider's literary endeavors are almost beyond reckoning. The intellectual height he has risen to, renders his views on all subjects of vital importance. Though, perhaps, not as deep a thinker

as Leopold Zunz, nor as terse and polished a writer as
Michael Sachs, the Doctor is distinguished for a
scholarship, the extent of which is sufficient to
create amazement. The "Catalogue of Hebrew
Books in the Bodleian Library," embodying the
results of his researches at Oxford, is a monument of erudition. A production on the Hebrew
manuscripts in the Bodleian Library has also been
issued; moreover, "Foreign Philological Elements
in the Modern Hebrew;" "Bibliographical Manual
of the Literature of the Hebrew Language;" "Jewish Literature from the Eighth to the Eighteenth
Century," with an introduction on Talmud and
Midrash, translated into English by Spottiswoode; on
the ritual of Saadiah Gaon; "Manna;" *Reschith
Hallimmud*, a manual of the Hebrew language, compiled in accordance with a new system; "Lives of
Arabian Mathematicians, drawn from the inedited
work of Bernardino Baldi, with notes;" and "History of the Arabic School of Medicine."

In addition to many other works, in Hebrew,
Latin, German, French, and Italian, the Doctor has
furnished articles, specially on Mathematics, Astronomy and Medicine, for *Der Orient* of Dr. Fürst, and
has contributed to nearly every magazine in the
sacred tongue; also to the *Scrapeum*, and to the
Journal of the German Oriental Society.

Moritz Steinschneider still continues at his post.

His natural activity forbids him rest. New publications, professional functions, and an extensive correspondence, engage every hour of the man who has, indeed, consecrated his life to the service of Israel and the world at large.

HEYMANN STEINTHAL.

Throughout the many stages of history, whether in the enjoyment of ease, or in the distress of oppression, the Hebrew people presented one peculiar feature—a love of knowledge. To this may be ascribed that elasticity which prevented their being crushed under the heavy burden of despotism, and their marvellous preservation. Mental culture became the most formidable of their defenders.

A short space will be devoted to exhibiting the course pursued by an individual whose opinion, on questions that none but lofty minds can attempt to solve, is of exceeding interest to the votaries of modern science.

Prof. Dr. Heymann Steinthal was born at Gröbzig, in Anhalt, Germany, May 16th, 1823. Qualified by a sagaciously directed education in his boyhood, for the reception of instruction of a high order, he went to Berlin, where he assiduously cultivated philosophy, comparative philology, and mythology. In the first-named branch of science, Hegel's theories exercised, for a time, an exceeding influence on the mind of the student. But he soon threw off the yoke, and chose as his standard, the teachings of William Von Humboldt, brother of the world-renowned Alexander Von Humboldt.

Steinthal became lecturer at Berlin, and continued in that capacity until 1852. He afterwards repaired to Paris, and took up the language and literature of the Chinese. Returning to Berlin, in 1863, he was elected Professor Extraordinary at the University—a graceful tribute to his industry and immense acquirements.

Together with his brother-in-law, Prof Dr. Moritz Lazarus, Steinthal began to edit the *Journal of National Psychology and Philology*. In *National Psychology* a new theme was given to scholars to work upon ; viz: the consideration of the development and manifestations of the spirit of a people, in contradistinction to the psychologic features of an individual. To this day the publication referred to, holds sway respecting matters connected with its object.

Only a few of Steinthal's works can be named, it being beyond our present province to review the topics the Professor discusses with great depth. Suffice that their author is confessedly regarded as an authority. "Classification of Languages," a production of rare excellence, appeared in 1850; "The Origin of Language," with respect to late theories on all sciences, in 1851; "The Development of Writing," in 1852; "Grammar, Logic, Psychology," their principles, and relations to each other, in 1855; "History of Philology among the Greeks," in 1863; and "Synopsis of the Science of Language," in 1871. Besides a large number of other writings, Prof. Steinthal has contributed, to different periodicals, articles, clear and expressive in style, and conveying profound ideas. The disputes which the Professor has had with Whitney and other scholars, have also tended to heighten his reputation.

As a Jew, it is said Professor Steinthal does not take a prominent part in religious affairs, albeit he adheres firmly to the cardinal points of his faith, and shows an attachment to some of the ceremonial tenets, the observance of which distinguishes his fellow-believers from the rest of mankind.

JUDAH TOURO.

Philadelphia possesses a building known as the Hebrew Education Society's School, where children are taught the language of the Scriptures. In the main room is to be seen a tablet on which is recounted the good done that institution by a benevolent co-religionist. But this same sight meets the eye in nearly every chief city of the Union. Who was he that Americans of the olden faith delight to honor? Did he surpass his contemporaries in knowledge, or did he make his power felt in the Federal government? These questions which naturally suggest themselves, are answered by the simple mention of one word,—Philanthropy. The exercise of that virtue in its full sense, has given Judah Touro eternity in the memory of his fellow-citizens of all creeds.

Judah Touro was born at Newport, Rhode Island, on June 16th, 1775. His father, the Rev. Isaac Touro, had emigrated from Holland. At that time a highly respected congregation of Portuguese Jews flourished at Newport. The Rev. Mr. Touro was chosen, in 1762, *Hazan*, or Minister, of those Americans.

Judah did not remain in his native city, but removed to Boston, and engaged in business with his maternal uncle, Moses Hays, in whose employ he sailed to the Mediterranean in 1798, as supercargo of a vessel. During the voyage, the officer distinguished himself by a successful engagement with a French privateer. In 1802 Touro definitely settled at New Orleans, and became a merchant of commanding wealth, acquired through industry and thriftiness. Pending the war with Great Britain, he, obeying his patriotic impulses, enlisted as a volunteer in the American army under General Jackson, at New Orleans. On January 1st, 1815, he received wounds of so severe a nature that his body was left almost lifeless on the battle-field. Had it not been for the bravery and unremitting attention of a Christian, Rezin Davis Shepherd, he might not have recovered. Mr. Touro had a memory on which the record of favors was chiseled as on marble. He did not forget the humane services of his non-Israelite friend. So intense was the affection cherished for his deliverer, that on his death he bequeathed to him the residue of his property, amounting to an immense sum.

But Mr. Touro's liberality to him who saved his life when exposed to imminent danger, did not cover the entire range of his benevolence. Considering how vast this was, he may be styled the Montefiore of America. Institutions of all kinds owe the generous man a debt of gratitude, for endowments which enable them to alleviate misery, or to foster education. Families and individuals constantly felt the effects of his inherent kindness. An admirable trait evinced, was the unsectarian distribution of charity, while the donor ever continued a strict adherent to the principles of his faith. The Congregation, *Nefutzote Jehudah*, (Dispersed of Judah), of New Orleans, and other Synagogues and churches, recognize Touro as their founder and supporter. It would be an impossibility to enumerate all the acts of munificent beneficence performed by Judah Touro. But it is not inappropriate to say—when Jews are declared incapable of any sentiment above racial clannishness—that the Jew Touro donated ten thousand dollars towards the erection of the Bunker-Hill Monument, intended to commemorate the second battle fought for American freedom. Cities besides New Orleans, have reason to connect his name with the sentence of the Scriptures, " The memory of the righteous is a blessing."

The private character of Mr. Touro was untainted. Simplicity, unostentation, and courtesy,—qualities always reflected in the deeds of a true philanthropist,—found a bright exponent in the subject of our sketch.

Mr. Touro's eventful life terminated on January 18th, 1854, in the city of New. Orleans. His remains were brought to Newport, followed by a long cortege of eminent co-religionists and Christians. They were permanently interred in the Jewish cemetery, so touchingly described by the poet Longfellow, and for the preservation of which the honored dead had made ample provision.

As Judah Touro regarded his opulence as a trust from above, and employed it to strengthen the foundations of society, by encouraging religion and morality, he was, in very deed, a faithful servant of his Maker.

EMANUEL VENEZIANI.

There is a man—a native of Munich—who can lay an undisputed claim to the exalted title of bene-factor. Baron de Hirsch acquired his vast wealth through railroad operations. How does he apply it? Let thousands of unfortunates of the human race tell! During the late Turco-Russian war he signalized him-self by deeds which will ever shine brighter than all the decorations conferred on him by royalty. Yet, it is to his renowned almoner, Chevalier Veneziani, that this sketch is devoted, acting, as we do, on the Tal-mudical axiom, that "he who is the instrument in doing good, is even greater than he who supplies the means."

Emanuel Veneziani was born at Leghorn, Italy, in July, 1826. The child of parents in the humblest condition of life, he had often to depend upon the kindness of friends to satisfy hunger. When still young he was seized with an alarming disease, from which, however, he soon recovered through the tender care of a family that loved him.

Veneziani attended the Jewish free schools, and his talents developed fast. A key to the leading sen-timents of the youth's heart was the following inci-dent: Several pupils were competing for a prize, he among the number. Veneziani won it, but he insisted on sharing it with three of his classmates who had nearly come up to his standard. This generosity pleased the directors of the seminary, and the action of the Jewish lad of Leghorn was mentioned with due praise in a magazine published at Florence.

Veneziani pursued his studies with success, under different preceptors, and commenced very early to impart privately what he had learned at public institutions. But in 1846, an Italian family,—whose head, Dr. M. Allatini, has since become famous from his connection with the *Alliance Israélite Universelle*,—determined to settle at Salonica, and to engage the Leghorn young man as tutor. It was at that city that he made the acquaintance of the Camondos, the opulent bankers. His knowledge, discernment, and high character, secured for him the position of private secretary of that celebrated Turkish firm. He settled at Constantinople in 1854, and utilized the influence which his office lent him in founding savings-banks, and charity associations. Considering Masonry a powerful element of liberalization, he instituted numerous lodges of that Order. He, moreover, established hospitals, and homes for the destitute, and took active part in everything that might promote the general welfare. The heroism he displayed in staking his own life, during a disastrous fire, to save many from being burnt to death, made his name famous throughout Italy.

The labors of Veneziani were not forgotten by his native country. The King of Italy, Victor Emanuel II., having heard of the brave conduct of one of his subjects, sent him a double decoration with expressions of royal approval. The Chevalier found special favor with the Government of Turkey, and on more than one occasion he pleaded successfully in behalf of his unhappy fellow-believers, and obtained for them privileges before denied.

But Veneziani's ceaseless activity has best been shown in the promotion of the grand object aimed at by the *Alliance*. For he created branches of that organization, formed committees, established schools, animated teachers, encouraged pupils, and, enjoying the implicit confidence of Baron de Hirsch, distributed large sums to aid the cause of humanity, freedom, and enlightenment. Millions of francs were expended through the almoner of the noble philanthropist to bring the homeless under shelter, to cover the shivering limbs of the aged and infirm, and of children fleeing from the bereaving sword, to afford food to the body and the mind.

The good work still goes on; Veneziani planning noble acts and De Hirsch practically approving of them by wonderful munificence. May the world see both so engaged long after the next century shall have dawned.

GUSTAV WEIL.

The investigation of the soil upon which language was born, has given rise to the science of modern philology. The philosophic mind casts off the chains of Western thought, and turns to seek for the hidden treasures of the Orient. So earnest has been the spirit manifested, so important the discoveries made, that nothing short of personal observations in Asia and Africa will satisfy many inquirers. Among this class, Gustav Weil stands preëminent.

Prof. Gustav Weil was born at Sultzbach, in Baden, Germany, April 24th, 1808. The Talmud gave him food for thought. He discovered in his nature an aptitude for philology and history, and to follow up the study of those two elements of human learning, he went to Paris. After long application, he set out for the East, in order to grow familiar with the languages and customs of the nations of that portion of the globe. Of the cities he visited, Cairo became his residence for five years, and there he acted, not simply in the capacity of student, but also of tutor and interpreter. He arrived home in 1836, having mastered the Arabic, Persian, and Turkish languages.

Weil was in every manner eminently fitted for a high station. Therefore, the very same year of

his return to Germany, his abilities were rewarded
by his appointment as Assistant Librarian at Heidelberg. He discharged the duties of this office with efficiency and zeal, bringing his vast theoretical and practical knowledge to bear upon the exercise of his
important, though arduous, functions. In 1845 he
was elevated to the chair of Oriental Languages
in the University of Heidelberg, a position to which
many may aspire, but few can attain.

The numerous literary productions of Prof.
Weil teem with erudition, and exhibit ripe judgment.
Public opinion has stamped them with the seal
of authority. The poetry of the Arabs, the Koran,
the Biblical legends of the Mussulmen, and other
topics of a kindred nature, are critically discussed
by the Professor. There appeared, moreover, a
German translation of "The Arabian Nights," in
four volumes,—1837-'41 ; "Life of Mohammed,"
—1843, a work which met with an extremely
favorable reception, by reason of its unparalleled
comprehensiveness; "History of the Caliphs," in
five volumes, embracing a wide sphere,—1846-'62;
"History of the Mussulmen Peoples, from Mohammed to Sultan Selim,"—1866; and a biography of Levi Ben-Gerson, the celebrated philosopher,
—1869.

Gustav Weil may now rest on his laurels,
and feel contented that his exertions, like those

of his illustrious compeers in the realms of Eastern thought, have compassed the object which inspired the worker with unflagging energy and untiring perseverance.

NAPHTALI HARTWIG WESSELY.

Could the man who gave new life and spirit to Judaism in Europe, appear here by right of chronology; could he, whose intellectual might drew Hebrews out of obscurity and isolation, have a place in this work as a contemporary, his name would embellish and ornament our series. But Moses Mendelssohn, the philosopher, the sage, and the author, did not live to see the age in which we live. Wessely, the admirer and faithful co-laborer of the Socrates of Dessau, though not strictly of our own days, crossed the threshold of this century. This fact will justify the presentation of his character, so that his services may be depicted, and his memory venerated.

Naphtali Hartwig (or, as he is sometimes called, Herz) Wessely was born at Hamburg, Germany, in 1725. He was a descendant of a Polish family, almost annihilated by the Cossacks in 1648, and of whose members only one, named Joseph, effected an escape from the slaughter. This refugee wandered through several European countries,—a prey to misery. At last he settled at Amsterdam, Holland, where liberty flourished. One of his sons, Moses, established himself at Wesel, where he assumed the name of Wessely or Wesel, from the city in which he resided. Moses soon acquired a large fortune, as a contractor for supplies to different governments. His second son, Berend, the father of Hartwig, also came into the possession of considerable means, and these he liberally used to educate his child, whom he had destined for a Rabbi.

Eagerness for learning fastened the mind of young Wessely to his books. First, he received some instruction from his mother; then, at the age of five years, he was sent to the Academy of his native place, where teaching was confined simply to Talmudical lore. Wessely himself narrates that during full four years he continued this study, without knowing aught of the Scriptures. Fortunately, in his tenth year, the youth became acquainted with an individual who imparted the rudiments of grammar, and the knowledge of that essential branch enabled the pupil to read the Bible with ease in its original tongue, and to apply himself profitably to other Hebrew works. With the aid of a chart, which his father showed him, Wessely, in three days, obtained an insight into geography. At thirteen, he proceeded to Amsterdam, to complete his studies. Notwithstanding the attention he was obliged to

give to theology, he still found spare moments to
devote to the German, French, Danish, and Dutch
languages, and to mathematics, physics, history, geography, and the sciences. The zeal with which he
labored, coupled with quickness of comprehension,
promised a brilliant future.

Wessely, on reaching manhood, had the un-
happiness of seeing all his father's wealth suddenly
swept away. That melancholy event compelled the
scholar to enter as clerk in the commercial
house of Benjamin Feitel, at Amsterdam. The vocation was uncongenial, but this did not dampen
his ardor for literary pursuits, and in the hours
of the night he worked at what served to establish
his reputation. At the same time he gained
much favor with his employer, and, through the
influence of the brother of the latter, he was, in
1774, placed at the head of the house in Berlin,
Prussia. While constantly engaged in business,
in order to obtain a livelihood, he never abandoned his cherished purpose,—to elevate Judaism
by his literary efforts.

The works of Wessely are so numerous that
it is impossible to mention them all, or in the
order they came out; but slight allusions will be
made to the origin of some, and others will be
merely named. Before proceeding further, however,
it must be stated, that the failure of the house

of Feitel, in 1779, put an end to Wessely's career as a merchant, and reduced him pecuniarily to such a strait that, to relieve him, a class for Scriptural tuition was formed by young Israelites. They appointed him Professor, with a salary sufficient for the maintenance of his family. This acted as a greater stimulus to his endeavors in the field of Hebrew literature.

Wessely's first production, *Sépher Gan Naool*, and *Lebanon*, in two volumes, appeared in 1764 and 1765. It treats principally of Hebrew synonyms, and evinces great Biblical and Rabbinical knowledge. In 1774 was published *Yen Lebanon*, a comment on "The Ethics of the Fathers," which attracted much notice, and of which an English rendition was made for the *Hebrew Review*, by Dr. M. J. Raphall. "The (Apochryphal) Book of Wisdom," by Solomon, he translated into Hebrew, adding an exposition, styled, *Ruah Hen*. In 1785 he issued *Sépher Hammidoth*, on morals. Commentaries on the Pentateuch, and on other sacred writings were brought to light at different times. But the most celebrated of all Wessely's works, is an epic poem, in eighteen cantos, *Shiré Tifèreth*. It treats of the birth and mission of Moses, as far as the delivery of the Decalogue. That emanation of genius has been rendered into several European languages, thus widening and enhancing the fame of the author.

The elegance of diction, as well as the beauty of expression and depth of sentiment pervading it, tend to make the poem both instructive and charming to the lover of Hebrew verse. Three years were spent in its preparation. Wessely also wrote about the Jews of Cochin-China, several vindications of Rabbinical traditions, and many other works, including contributions to Hebrew journals, both in prose and in poetry.

But Wessely will always hold a place in the hearts of true Hebrews, for reasons higher than those which endeared him as a sweet writer of the sacred language. He was a healthful reformer. Indeed, he is second only to Mendelssohn in the history of modern Judaism, as far as it regards the creation of a new system of education. In 1782 he addressed his *Dibrè Shalom Vèemeth* (Words of Peace and Truth) to the Hebrews of Austria, in which the liberal spirit of Joseph II., whom he compared to Cyrus, is extolled. He spoke of the lack of knowledge prevailing among Jews, in everything unconnected with the mere disputations of Talmud, and some casuistical works. Attributing it to the very defective manner in which the young were trained, he advised a complete reform. No sooner had this letter of Wessely's become known, than he encountered a storm of abuse. The writer was publicly denounced as an opponent of religious instruction, as a seducer trying to wean away the young in Israel from the Law and traditions, and, blackened as such, some dared to hurl an anathema at him. But the Rabbis of Italy came to his rescue, and conclusively proved that Wessely was acting in perfect accord with the directions of the ancient Rabbis, and with the plan always followed in Italy. The educational movement gained ground, despite the sturdy opposition, and the Jews of Europe are to-day much indebted for their intellectual improvement to the manifold services of Naphtali Hartwig Wessely.

The 3d of March, 1805, closed the career of one who prepared the way for Rapoport, Zunz, and all that host of brilliant scholars who have rendered the nineteenth century a golden era; whose achievements will be sung by generations yet unborn.

ISAAC MAYER WISE.

In casting a glance at the career of one who figures very conspicuously among American Rabbis, it may not be inappropriate to advert to the progress of Reform in this country. For the divine about to be spoken of, has been closely identified with that movement. All are, doubtless, aware that changes in the Jewish ritual in America were effected gradually.

The first minister in the United States who advocated innovations was the Rev. Gustavus Posznanski, of the Congregation *Beth Elohim*, of Charleston, South Carolina. Over thirty-five years ago he introduced an Organ into the Synagogue. This act met with strenuous opposition, and finally caused a division in that body. But, supported by a large number of his flock, the Pastor succeeded in maintaining his stand. Several alterations in the form of worship, which gave it a novel appearance, were adopted. Still, Mr. Posznanski proceeded cautiously, not venturing too far. He may have feared that radical measures would jeopardize the permanence of the Jewish Church. At all events, others stepped boldly forth, took rapid strides, and, to judge from the present outlook, they have reached a point which a near future will tell whether it is to be deemed a pinnacle or a precipice. But to the main subject.

The Rev. Dr. Isaac Mayer Wise was born at Steingrub, in Bohemia, Austria, on the 3d of April, 1819. Until his eighteenth year he studied little besides Talmud. After a course of secular instruction at Prague, to which was added a grammatical understanding of the language of Holy Writ, he entered the University of Vienna, graduating in 1843. In the same year he was appointed Rabbi in Radnitz, Bohemia, where he remained till 1846. At that stage of his life Dr. Wise resolved to come to the United

States. He arrived in New York, and up to 1850, ministered to the *Beth-El* Congregation of Albany, and from that year to 1854 to the *Anshé Emeth*, of the same city.

During that period the Doctor evinced considerable interest in Jewish matters. He contributed to *The Occident and American Jewish Advocate*, of the Rev. Isaac Leeser, and editorially assisted Robert Lyon, Esq., in the management of *The Asmonean*. But what has made, Dr. Wise's name a household word among the Jewish public in this land, is his bold defence of the Reform system. He has preached, written, and travelled in behalf of the ideas espoused. His marked individuality, strong opinions, and forcible expressions, led the *B'nai Jeshurun* Congregation, of Cincinnati, Ohio, to secure his services as its leader, in 1854. The popularity which the Rabbi enjoys was lately made apparent at the celebration of the twenty-fifth anniversary of his installation.

Dr. Wise declined the offer of a more remunerative station in the East, so that he might retain the influence he commands in the West. For, notwithstanding the decided antagonism he has encountered in the views which he restlessly advances, his power has widely extended. Gentiles, not less than Hebrews, know the Cincinnati Rabbi by his literary labors.

In July, 1854, Dr. Wise brought forth a journal which became the principal instrument of his strength.

It appears weekly, under the name of *The American Israelite*. A German supplement called *Die Deborah*, has also been regularly issued since July, 1855. In the many cities which the Doctor has visited, and in the numerous Synagogues he has been called upon to consecrate, he has urged with much earnestness. the adoption of his formulary of prayers, entitled *Minhag America*.

The comprehensive plan devised and set on foot in the West about seven years ago, and known as. The Union of American Hebrew Congregations, which includes a large number of Jewish congregations, from the borders of the Atlantic to the Pacific, owes its origin to the unremitting exertions of Dr. Wise. That organization has established The Hebrew Union College, at Cincinnati, for the education of future Rabbis, and a preparatory school in New York City. Since the opening of the Seminary proper, the Doctor has been President of the Faculty, and he still continues his unflagging efforts to promote the cause.

Despite advancing age, the Rabbi fulfils his ministerial functions with unabated vigor, and ·occupies. the editorial chair with no indications of faintness.. For he speaks from it in sentences, which, if not always carefully chosen, show extreme eagerness to repel attacks and to defeat the opposite camp.

Dr. Wise has found time to indite a number of literary works. " History of the Israelitish Nation," in which the author presents facts in accordance with his own preconceived notions, came out in 1854. It has been followed by "Essence of Judaism," and "Judaism, its Doctrines and Duties,"—religious catechisms. Other productions of his pen are: "The Martyrdom of Jesus of Nazareth," in which he aims to prove that the Jews had no hand whatever in the Crucifixion; "The Cosmic God," treating of fundamental philosophy, and exhibiting depth of thought and a vast acquaintance with the schools of modern science; "Three Lectures on Jesus, the Apostles, and Paul;" "The Wandering Jew," a lecture on that fabulous being, intended to dispel prevailing errors; and "History of the Hebrews' Second Commonwealth," which has just come from the press.

The reader has thus been given a brief narrative of the doings of a man whose name will ever be prominently connected with the history of American Judaism. The industry and indomitable zeal with which Dr. Wise prosecutes his various designs will secure his popularity, and, if the project of training future Rabbis in the West succeeds, he will have drawn towards himself a still larger number of staunch followers.

SIMON WOLF.

Of all countries, free America has ever shown a generous recognition of human worth. An individual may be of humble extraction; he may have been early compelled to drudge for a livelihood. But let him watch over his character, and utilize his talents, and he may feel certain of reaping here a commensurate reward. A man who brought neither high lineage nor wealth to bear on the attaining of a creditable position, but who owes the name acquired solely to his own exertions, is the Israelite, Simon Wolf. He may rightly be styled "a self-made man," employing his inherent capacities in the direction which leads to personal and social advantage.

Simon Wolf was born in Rhenish Bavaria, Germany, on October 28th, 1836. When not twelve years of age he emigrated to the United States, and was employed by his uncle in Ulrichville, Ohio, first, as office-boy, and later as cashier in the business house of that relative. The occupations of the day left no opening for the lad to improve his mind, but he devoted the night to hard study, and this was the key to his success in after years. In 1855 his uncle retired from the business in the aforenamed locality, and Mr. Wolf undertook it. But in 1857 he succumbed, with many others, to the financial crisis, then prevailing throughout the country. Giving up commercial pursuits, he adopted the legal profession, being admitted to the Bar in Ohio, on July 20th, 1861, where he obtained a lucrative practice.

In June, 1862, Mr. Wolf removed to Washington, his present home, and became the senior member of the law-firm of Wolf & Hart. As such, he soon gained a wide reputation. His lively interest in politics was specially evinced during the late rebellion. Ardent in his support of the Northern cause, loud in his expressions of faith in Republican institutions, he became well-known to those in power. Enjoying the friendship of President Grant, he was appointed Recorder of Deeds of the District of Columbia, a responsible post, which he filled with honor for nine years. On his vacating that office, Mr. Wolf returned to the practice of the law, and his advice is sought for by a large number of clients, even beyond the city of his residence.

It becomes us now to refer to Mr. Wolf's services to Judaism. Aside from his endeavors during the war, to induce the retraction of General Grant's hasty and unjust "Order No. 11," directed against the Jews, he urged the United States Government to interpose in behalf of the down-trodden Jews of Russia and Roumania. His representations carried with them great weight, in securing the appointment of Mr. Peixotto, as Consul at Bucharest, and in retaining him there, as a restraint upon the persecutors of our race.

Mr. Wolf's multifarious labors in associations with which he is, or has been, connected, are clear evidences of his earnestness. He was prominent in the Board of Delegates of American Israelites; he presided over the deliberations of the annual Council of the Union of American Hebrew Congregations, held in Washington, in July 1876; he was Chairman of the Yellow Fever Relief Committee, during the plague in the Southern States, in the summer of 1878; he is an important member of the Independent Order of *B'nai B'rith*, and acted as presiding officer of the Chicago convention of 1874, and of that of Philadelphia, in January, 1879. Mr. Wolf has been President of the Supreme Lodge of the Order of *Késher Shel Barzel*. Our co-religionist is the chosen chief of the *Schiller Bund*, a literary society of the Capital. For eight years he has been President of the Washington *Schuetzen Verein*, and of the Orphan Asylum, of District Grand Lodge, Ne. 5.

As an orator, Mr. Wolf is very impressive and effective. Of his lectures, " The Influence of the Jews on the Progress of the World," " Roger Williams," and " The Stage and Actors," are the most notable. But he has spoken on various other topics, exhibiting in every instance a right understanding of current events.

Of Mr. Wolf's attachment to his fellow-believers, let his own words speak: "I have had but one ambition in my life, and that has been to ennoble and elevate my people, and to that end I have not spared time, influence or means, and I shall not cease to labor in the same direction, desiring no other epitaph than the one, ' He was a Jew, and was proud of it.' "

We could add nothing to this noble sentiment, save the wish that our Jewish youth, adopting it as their own, may exemplify it in their lives.

HENRY DE WORMS.

Courage, self-reliance and endurance are indispensable aids in the pursuit of every undertaking. By the exercise of these qualities, obstacles will be overcome, and success will crown one's efforts. A fellow-believer who has endeared himself to thousands by his moral bravery, is the illustrious Baron de Worms. The spirit of a Crémieux dwells within him, for whenever oppression aims a blow at his brethren he manifests a burning wish to come to the rescue, and chastise iniquity. His voice, his means, and his influence are free-will offerings on the altar of humanity.

Baron Henry de Worms was born at London, England, in 1840. His father had been created

Baron of the Austrian Empire, and to that hereditary title the son succeeded. The education afforded him at King's College of his native city was thorough ough, and he obtained the highest academical degrees, being elected a *Fellow* of that institution in 1863. For a decade he served as Captain of the King's College Company of the Queen's Westminster Rifle Volunteers, hence the skill for which he is distinguished as a marksman.

Baron de Worms was called to the Bar, at the Inner Temple, in 1863, and he practised for some time on the Home Circuit. The death of an elder brother induced him, however, to abandon the legal profession, and, in 1865, he entered as a partner in the firm of Messrs. G. & A. Worms, of Austin Friars.

The Baron is a Magistrate and Deputy-Lieutenant for Middlesex. His proclivities, which are with the Conservative wing, led him to become a candidate for Parliament, from Deal, at the general election in. 1868. Though not chosen; he did not sink into inactivity. He works on with a will, and so clearly pronounced is his political creed that not long since he received a request, signed by nearly seven thousand electors of the City of London, to stand for that constituency in the coming contest. Yielding to the wishes of the Government, he withdrew in the interest of the party, in order to obviate the necessity of the candidacy of four Conservatives. But lately

he acceded to the solicitations of an influential
deputation from the Royal Borough of Greenwich
to be the second Conservative candidate, in conjunction with Mr. Boord, the present member.
His popularity has been the means of securing his
election with an increased majority.

But the feature in the character of Baron de
Worms whereon Jews delight to gaze, is that which
discloses his loyalty to Judaism.   Immovable in his
purpose to vindicate the title of his brethren to equal
justice, he challenged civilization to explain the conduct of Bratiano, Cogalniceano, and men of their ilk
in Roumania.   The Baron acted as first Vice-
President of the International Convention of. Israelites, held at Paris, in 1878, where his mettle was put
to the test.   To speak of his abhorrence of
compromises, of his resolve to see the clause
of the Treaty of Berlin, affecting civil and religious
liberty, literally fulfilled, would be to say what is
familiarly known.   Some may not, however, be aware
of his genuine enthusiasm, of his keen discernment,
and of the admirable tact displayed on that occasion.

Indeed, Baron de Worms is indefatigable in what-
ever may promote the welfare of his co-religionists.
He is President of the Anglo-Jewish Association,—
a model organization; and President of the Borough
Jewish Schools; also a Warden of the Central United
Synagogue, of London.

The Baron is the author of many valuable literary productions. Among them are " The Earth and its Mechanism," and " The Austro-Hungarian Empire, and England's Policy in the East." The last, published in 1877, passed through six editions.

As will have been noticed, Baron de Worms is but forty years of age. The great name he has built for himself, when only in the prime of life, is the pledge of a grand and glorious future. Baron Henry de Worms will most assuredly continue to rise, by his advocacy of wise and beneficial measures, and his efforts will be attended with the blessings of the entire House of Israel.

LEOPOLD ZUNZ.

The sovereignty of the Jewish world of letters, in the nineteenth century, can be accorded to no one of the noble minds that aspire to the title of ruler. Too many are the rival claims to that position. Let us rest contented with the rich fruits we can gather from different sources, and bow reverentially to the glorious laborers. Yet, taking all in all, who greater than Leopold Zunz? Surely, if he be not the crowned monarch of Hebrew lore, he is a mighty prince, to whom generations yet unborn will pay obeisance. As an interpreter of Synagogue poetry, deep in pathos and grand in diction, he is unexcelled. As a critic, Solomon L. Rapoport may divide honors with him. But as a general scholar, few can call themselves his peers, and scarcely any his superior. We might seek to find an epithet suiting his abilities, and fail in our endeavors. Let us call him a Titan, whose intellect towers heavenward.

Dr. Leopold Zunz was born at Detmold, in the principality of Lippe, Germany, on the 10th of August, 1794. Preliminary instruction preceded his studies under such men as Wolf, DeWette, and Boekh, at Berlin. The young pupil followed up his course with great diligence, and early did the flower bloom.

From 1820 to 1822 Zunz officiated as preacher of the Jewish Congregation at Berlin. He was one of the editors of the *Spener'sche Zeitung* from 1824 to 1832, and principal of the new Jewish communal school from 1825 to 1829. In 1835 he accepted a ministerial call from Prague, and from 1839 to 1850 he directed the normal seminary at Berlin. In 1845 he became a member of a commission appointed by the government for devising measures to improve the educational and political status of Hebrews in Prussia.

It is our main desire to refer to Dr. Zunz's literary productions—for it is to these that he owes his laurels. And let the pertinent remarks of the Rev. A.

Löwy be quoted: "Dr. Zunz has laid a solid foundation for the proper study of the history of Jewish literature, and by his numerous writings he enables his readers to appreciate the intimate connection between the political vicissitudes, the intellectual and emotional cravings, and the literary productions of the Jews. He leads the student through the mazes and intricacies of a widely scattered literature, with unsurpassed perseverance, with unswerving directness of purpose, with the accuracy of a powerful intuition; and he uses an elegance of diction which may be termed classical, and whereby he invests even didactic and abstruse matter with the attractions of poetry."

The Doctor's first important work, "Something about Rabbinical Literature," appeared in 1818. A pamphlet of fifty pages which, though bearing a title by no means high-sounding, was fraught with learning and sagacious counsel. The author administers a sharp rebuke to scholars who attempt to belittle the Jews, by drawing comparisons between Hebrew and contemporary literature, without knowing aught of the former, and he urges all to divest themselves of prejudice and personal antipathies.

In 1832 Dr. Zunz issued his "Liturgical Lessons of the Jews, Historically Investigated," to which he made valuable additions in 1845, 1855, 1859, 1864, and 1867. In this work, the connection of the Bible with tradition, the development of the different Chaldean versions of Holy Writ, the nature of the study of the Scriptures, the divisions of ancient Jewish learning, and other points are severally treated. A production of so wide a scope, and so vastly important in each department, could not but have become the text-book in many an institution throughout Europe.

The pen consecrated to literature did not refuse its office to avenge wrongs. The Doctor labored zealously for the emancipation of his German co-religionists; and often he entered an energetic protest against actions of the Government. "History and Literature," another of his emanations, comprises a number of essays, of which, however, only the first volume has come forth—1845. It is of special interest to students, embodying an account of events of different Jewish communities at different periods. A full index to this excellent work is the labor of Dr. David Cassel.

What may probably be considered Dr. Zunz's masterpiece is the "Synagogue Poetry during the Middle Ages," published in 1855. The magnitude of this work forbids our offering more than a simple notice of its contents. It is divided into five sections. The first traces the origin and adaptation of the Divine Service, or the relation of the Prophets to the Psalmists; the second graphically depicts the sorrows and sufferings of the Jews in the various countries of their dispersion; the third portrays the nature of poetical compositions, notably of Spanish authors, as read on the Day of Atonement; the fourth gives a glowing picture of the poets themselves, including those of Greece, Italy, Provence, France, and Spain, and, later, Germany, and presents specimens of their sweet outpourings; the fifth is a chronology of the misfortunes of the Jews during the two centuries succeeding the Middle Ages. The far-reaching and diversified information afforded by copious notes and appendices, render this volume, independent of the main subject, a mine of learning. We are, besides, carried away by the choicest and most touching language. Tears must flow at the harrowing description of tortures and merciless persecutions of men and women whose crime was a steadfast devotion to principle. We cannot refrain from quoting the first few lines of this treatise; soul-stirring words, so true, and so nobly told : " If there be an ascending scale of sufferings, Israel reached its highest degree. If the duration of afflictions, and the patience with which they are borne, confer nobility upon man, the Jews may vie with the aristocracy of any country. If a literature which owns a few classical tragedies is deemed rich, what place should be assigned to a tragedy which extends over fifteen centuries, and which has been composed and enacted by the heroes themselves?"

A second part of the Synagogue Poetry, called "The Rites of the Synagogue Service, historically elucidated," was issued in 1859. In this writing, the gradual accretion and modification of the forms of prayer in use are dwelt upon, and the ideas set forth are both useful and instructive. A third part is the "History of Synagogue Poetry," which made its appearance in 1865, and concludes the series referred to. This last reviews the various compositions heretofore mentioned, and other poetical effusions from the close of the Talmud to a modern epoch. A supplement was added in 1867.

To speak now of what mental efforts such a work must have entailed, would be an act of supererogation. All must have learnt that a Zunz alone could have brought it to completion. Yet that veritable Titan modestly remarks that he has solely given some faint outlines, and he trusts that "the future workers in this precious material will bear with him who labored merely in dressing crude ore." But, despite such humility, authorities have agreed that many of Dr. Zunz's translations will compete with those of Goethe, Rückert, and other renowned masters.

The fertile mind of Dr. Zunz has produced more than what can be enumerated in a brief sketch. But we may name "The Days of the Calendar; a

Commemoration of the Departed," wherein the author cites dates of the deaths of Jewish celebrities, and also of Christians who proved of advantage to the cause of Judaism. This has been rendered into English by the Rev. Dr. B. Pick. *'Ir ha-Tsédek*, or " The City of Righteousness," was issued in Hebrew in 1874, and the first volume of the Doctor's " Collected Writings" came from the press in 1875.

Giants have arisen since Leopold Zunz began to benefit Israel by unceasing toil. Can any, among the earliest or latest, say to him, " Thy light is obscured"? No! It still shines with brilliancy! May it long continue to emit its radiance. May it arouse a spirit of reverence for those truths, of which the man of Detmold became a mighty champion.

THE END.